ECHOES OF THE PARIAH STATE

Tale of a Junta

Boniface Ossai

This book is dedicated in loving memory of my brother Felix Ossai. Felix will be deeply missed by the whole family.

This book wouldn't have been a success without the effort of my wife Nkem, who worked tirelessly to ensure the success of this book, not to forget my children Ikechukwu and Ifeanyichukwu.

Finally, a big thanks to my friend Mark Campbell for his immense contribution towards the success of this book.

CHAPTER
ONE

Sheikh Shafee was whisked away, blindfolded in a helicopter by some government security agents to a secret governments' black site. The helicopter hovered in the air for a while, and then landed, and in a twinkle of an eye, the Sheikh was again hurtled into a dark room that allows just a tiny ray of light peering through a pin hole to create a false sense of hope.

Moments later, the blind fold was taken off, and the Sheikh didn't hesitate to ask where he was, and what it is he was doing in such a dark room that gives him nothing but heebie-jeebies that makes his skin crawl. Sadly, all the Sheikh could hear was "shut up, your pen can't save you this time," from some growling security agents of government. This Sheikh has had better days, but this isn't one of those days because he's incredibly isolated and outmatched. He looked around the room and was suddenly overwhelmed by his voicelessness and now constrained by his inability to use his pen to galvanise support for his views on governance. Sheikh Shafee is scrupulous for reporting nothing but the truth, and it's now glaringly obvious that living in peace in the Republic of Kitan means fostering the cult of President Ambo Hussein, which this Sheikh finds difficult to stomach.

"Err..., what do you mean my pen can't save me?" asked Sheikh Shafee.

The security agents whose hearts are lacking mercy, shunned and reminded him that the toxicity of his journalistic mischief brought him here and made it clear to the Sheikh that things have unfortunately gone south for him. This renowned Sheikh that's known for his journalistic impact in the lives of the people of the Republic of Kitan has suddenly found himself in a bind.

Sheikh Shafee thought he still had everything under control as he continued to hold his ground as he insists the security agents should consider it absolutely comical if they think they can manage the reverberations from his disappearance. The Security Agents laughed and suddenly their laughter turned into hysteria. "Does this place look like a place where your voice will be heard?" asked a security agent.

It now dawned on the Sheikh that his room for manoeuvre is quite limited, and he suddenly asked the merciless crooks who whisked him away. "This is a black site, isn't it? Where those who disappear find themselves and did General Ambo Hussein order this?" he asked.

"Stop bombarding me with your deluge of questions," said the security agent.

While the conversation persisted, a second helicopter arrived and the President, General Ambo Hussein alighted. His face beamed with smiles as his feet touched down. His smile was more like that of a cat that has a mouse in its mouth, and after all, this journalist has been a nagging concern to this brute of a President.

Sheikh Shafee saw the President walked in. "Mr President, did you order this?" asked the Sheikh.

"Yes, of course! You were calling for a protest to disrupt my silver jubilee anniversary," said President Ambo.

Sheikh Shafee mistook the President's cheeky grin for gesture of goodwill and underestimated the odiousness of the situation. He continued to insist he thinks a protest against the President is the right thing to do as a journalist, and their country needs a change.

This President who is evil personified looked on as the Sheikh became chatty, and he then suggested to the Sheikh that he'd no choice but to take the journalist out of circulation.

"That doesn't change the fact that your people need better governance," said the Sheikh.

President Ambo reminded the Sheikh that he's in a bind and now at his mercy because his awkward attempt at pulling cynical stunts across the pond has arguably backfired.

Sheikh Shafee remained stubborn and insists his stunts didn't backfire because the President seized him against his will, and then asked if this is how he addresses the concerns of his citizens. The President poured his heart out as he reminded the sheikh about why he remained gobsmacked by the Sheikh's stupidity. "What riles me the most is your refusal to accept my hand of friendship and yet refused to remain tight-lipped about my offer," said President Ambo.

Sheikh Shafee then looked away, before muttering under his breath and said he can't trade his conscience for the President's blood money. After all, it's blindingly obvious that he's forcing the offer down his throat.

President Ambo laughed at this Sheikh that insists on piety, because his hush money didn't bring the Sheikh to parley with the President. As far as President Ambo is concerned, it's time to give this journalist his comeuppance, but firstly, he'd to take the Sheikh down memory lane to remind him of his generous hand of goodwill. "I offered you comfort, you chose distress. I offered you an olive branch-peace, you chose war. I also offered you life, an opportunity to live-my friend, but you chose death," said President Ambo.

Surviving on political crumbs falling off the President's table in exchange for unalloyed loyalty won't do the trick either for this Sheikh who's keen to see good governance in the Republic of Kitan.

Sheikh Shafee looked on as the incensed president poured out his heart, yet he made it clear to the President that his rhetoric emphasizes a junta's philosophy. The Sheikh went on to remind the President that the name 'Shafee' means "intercessor," and that his destiny is to intercede for the people and not betray them.

President Ambo's patience has grown so thin, and his interest in continuing this chat with the Sheikh has suddenly waned. He then chuckled and said since the sheikh has rejected his offer of a gesture of goodwill, he has equally chosen not to be philosophical anymore with the Sheikh. This time he's ditching civility and decided to act.

"I'm inundated by your quest to hold onto power," said the Sheikh. President Ambo smiled with an apology and said his love for power overwhelms him, and cockroaches like the sheikh won't make him look like a stinking corpse before his people. Each time the President gets this mad, death is what follows in its wake, and it doesn't matter if the person that turned him into a nutcase is journalist. The presidents' action goes with the territory, just that this Sheikh didn't see this coming. Sheikh Shafee who has always been the go-to-journalist as far as the politics of the land is concerned, looked on, as the President suddenly brought out his service pistol and pointed it at the Sheikh.

"What's it Mr. President? Shooting me into submission isn't the way out," said the Sheikh.

President Ambo shook his head to apprise the Sheikh that he isn't cowering but taking action because the Sheikh has suddenly become menacing and dangerous to his government. It's arguably obvious that his appetite for power is ravishing, and his grip on power overwhelms him.

Sheikh Shafee was shocked to see how this drama suddenly precipitated from a conversation to something ghastly. He quickly pleaded with the President not to do this, and after all, they could work out a transition of power to better their nation.

"Goodbye journalist." He fired three shots at him. "Good riddance!" exclaimed Mr President.

"My blood is on you," the Sheikh muttered, then slumped before breathing his last.

President Ambo then turned to his security agents and ordered them bury the journalist's body somewhere secret. For what it's worth, the killing of this Sheikh was well orchestrated, and not a decision taken at the drop of a hat. Yet, this secret killing won't stop the citizens of the Republic of Kitan pointing fingers of suspicion at their President over the Sheikh's disappearance.

General Ambo Hussein, a man who has ruled the Republic of Kitan, one of the Arab nations in the Middle East with an iron fist was celebrating his twenty-five years in power as a military President. He's married to his wife Aisha and has four children in the following order; Malik, Aasim, Umar and Nawal their only daughter. Malik studied in Egypt, Umar Studied in Qatar, Aasim studied in Europe while Nawal is studying in Turkey. Aasim and Nawal chose secular nations for their study, which explains why Aasim and Nawal see things differently from Malik and Umar.

A week after the silencing of Sheikh Shafee, the President's Silver Jubilee celebrations is here, and a day to the celebration the President and his family members were all seated in his living room when his Cousin, Sheikh Ali, came to see him.

"Ambo, I suppose you're going to inspect the venue for tomorrow's occasion," said Sheikh Ali.

"Ali, must I be involved in everything?" asked the President.

Sheikh Ali advised that he'd just come from the venue, and it's all set, yet urged the President to inspect the venue one last time. After dawdling on the matter, General Ambo Hussein decided he'll pay the venue a visit one last time.

Sheikh Ali then turned to the President's wife, Aisha, to inquire how she's preparing for her big day. Interestingly, Aisha was all smiles as she replied and said that's what her and her children are talking about.

Sheikh Ali finished with Aisha and asked the President's heir apparent, Malik, about his planned party to know if it's still going ahead tonight.

"Uncle, the party is still on, and I'll be coming to your place later," said Malik.

"Your party has nothing to do with me, Malik. It's for youths, so why're you coming to see me?" asked Sheikh Ali.

"No uncle, it's about the program for tomorrow's occasion," replied Malik.

"Ok then, you're welcome," said Sheikh Ali.

Not long after his brisk visit Sheikh Ali bid the President goodbye and made his way through the door. General Ambo wanted the Sheikh to stay a bit longer, and asked Ali where he's hurrying off to, after all, he just came in twenty minutes ago.

Sheikh Ali turned around and said he has some business to attend to at the mosque, and he then continued through the door and left the President and his family.

The President and his family continued their conversation after Sheikh Ali left. Aisha became chatty as she asked Umar who came in from Qatar for his dad's Silver Jubilee, what time he returned the day before. "Mum, I came in last night," he said. Aisha left Umar and turned to Malik who had issues with his wife lately and inquired if he's bringing her along.

General Ambo interjected and asked Umar when he's completing his bachelor's degree in information technology. Funnily, Umar is just two months away from getting this done and dusted, and everything will be over with his degree.

The General has other plans up his sleeve, he urged Umar to give him some time because he intends to make him the Director of the Kitan Broadcasting Corporation. Sadly, the person currently holding this office is Sheikh Abdul, the President's uncle, who is also Sheik Ali's dad.

Aasim who understands his dad's mischief and the workings of his dad's heart quickly interjected and asked what will happen to Sheikh Abdul who's currently holding that position.

General Ambo smiled, displaying a cheeky grin, and he then looked away and muttered under his breath, before saying his uncle would be gone when he is ready. Aasim turned to his dad and protested, and reminded his dad that Sheikh Abdul is family, and shouldn't be treated shabbily.

This warm ambience has suddenly turned sour as Malik picked on Aasim for sticking up for Sheikh Abdul. "Your moronic version of a family saddens," said Malik.

"Hmm Malik, never mind, it's your pathetic mind that's speaking I guess," said Aasim.

"What do you care? Dad should throw the sheikh out and replace him with Umar. After all, the interest of our immediate family should come first," insists Malik.

The simmering beef between these two brothers would quickly come to the fore with the slightest disagreement. Aasim protested as he confronted his brother with the question of why he thinks their dad should just continue to hurt people because of his children.

Malik urged Aasim to save himself the headache and insisted the President's family is the first family of Kitan. He then stressed that the first family is entitled to take first before others and that's how he himself will rule when he becomes President.

Aasim stood up and used his finger as gesture then urged Malik to look around to see the trouble in the Middle East, he then asked Malik what makes him think the people of Kitan will be foolish enough to allow him sit on the throne.

General Ambo became incensed at Aasim's negativity and went ballistic at Aasim. He then yelled at Aasim with his usual audacious tone. "Stop, Aasim, are you wishing your brother ill luck?" yelled President Ambo. The temperature of the room has suddenly become heated, and the scene isn't something out of the blue but a regular occurrence each time the family is seated together. Aisha decided to wriggle herself out of this drama as she stood up from her seat and beckoned on Nawal to come with her to her room so she could help her out with something. Aasim and Malik continued at each other's throat despite their dad's prejudices towards Aasim's denigration of his brother.

"Malik is naive to think the Presidency's seat is for us till eternity," insists Aasim.

General Ambo Hussein cautioned Aasim, reminding him that his western education is beginning to affect the dreams of his family.

As Nawal stood to follow her mum, she turned to her dad to remind him Aasim is right, stressing that Aasim's views on issues is a blessing to the family except they decide not to attach value to it.

"Let's go, Nawal, your dad doesn't take good advice when he gets it," said Aisha.

By the evening of the same day, Aasim and his security details were driving through town and suddenly stopped their convoy of cars by the roadside to check out the reason for the noise coming from beneath his car. While he bent to see what was wrong with his car, a little boy from the neighbourhood tried negotiating through the security guards to get to Aasim.

The little boy was quite excited as he approached and speaking, even as he attempts to walk past Aasim's bodyguards. "Hey, I used to see you on the television," said the little boy.

Bodyguard 1: Hey stop, where are you going? Stop, stop.

"That's Aasim, I know him, I know him, he's a footballer," said the little boy, while still wanting to make his way through to Aasim.

A second Bodyguard grabbed the little boy. "Stop, I say stop," said the bodyguard.

Aasim interjected and asked the bodyguard to let the boy be. "No, leave him, let him through, let the boy come to me," said Aasim.

The brave and excited little boy thanked Aasim for letting him through. "You're Aasim, aren't you?" he asked.

Aasim turned to this shirtless street boy and became more engaging, he then shook hands with the little boy. "How did you know my name? I don't think we've met before," asked Aasim.

Bodyguard 1: Let the boy be, I don't think this is safe.

"Why do you think this isn't safe?" asked Aasim.

Bodyguard 1: What if the boy has a bomb strapped on him?

"Why the puffery? The boy has no shirt on, and I don't think he has a bomb strapped on him," replied Aasim. He then turned to the boy again and continued with a formal introduction.

The little boy said to Aasim, he used to watch him play football on the television and reckoned. "You're a good footballer," said the little boy.

"Hmm, it means you watch football a lot, eh?" asked Aasim.

"Yes, of course, I like football and I want to be a good footballer like you," said the little boy.

"Don't worry, if you put your mind to it, you'll be a great footballer," said Aasim.

The little boy assured Aasim, and told him not to worry, and promised he'll work hard to be like him. Aasim then asked the little boy what his name is.

"Kabir, my name is Kabir," said the little boy.

"Do you know the meaning of your name?" asked Aasim.

"Yes, 'the great,' said the little boy.

Aasim smiled the moment Kabir mentioned what his name meant. "It means you're going to be a great man," said Aasim.

The little boy little then stretched his hand and points to one of the cars in the convoy. "Hmm yes, is that your car?" he asked.

"Yeah, it's mine," said Aasim.

"It's a nice car, and maybe if I start playing football like you do, I'll get a car like yours," said the little boy.

Aasim then held the boy's hand and asked if he would like to ride with him. The boy didn't hesitate to grab the offer of a ride with Aasim. For this shirtless street boy, seeing the President's son on television is one thing, riding in his car with him, is a big ask. "Yes, of course, I like to," said the little boy. The bodyguards cringed at Aasim, and considered this to be a carelessness that's characteristic of Aasim, and feared if they didn't voice their concern, the President might be on their case, sooner than later.

Bodyguard 1: I don't think this is safe, what if the boy is used as a pawn to get at you?

"Then so be it," said Aasim.

Bodyguard 2: As the son of Mr. President, warming up to poverty-stricken kids doesn't befit you.

Aasim hates his bodyguard's description of the little boy as someone chasing a rainbow. "I suggest you get off your high horse and try a little kindness," said Aasim.

Serendipitously, this is just a lucky street boy, without any unhealthy interest in the content of Aasim's pocket. Providence is on his side today, and even when he asked for nothing, he surely will get plenty for crossing path with Aasim.

The little boy proudly entered the car, even though he had no shirt on. Aasim drove the little boy around, but their first point of call was a supermarket. "Where are we going?" asked the little boy.

Aasim pointed to a supermarket. "We're going in there to get you some clothes," said Aasim.

The boy's face was wreathed in smiles. After all, this boy is now walking into places he only sees on television. "Oh..., thank you," said the little boy.

As they walked into the supermarket, Aasim asked the little boy to pick whatever item of clothing he wants from the hangers.

The boy pointed to a shirt, and said he likes that shirt, and he then turned to Aasim and asked how many shirts he should take. "One, or two?" he asked.

"Take as much as you can, don't worry I'll pick for you," said Aasim.

Aasim bought lots of clothes for Kabir, as well as a football, and a pair of jerseys. He made Kabir dress into something more decent and drove him around town, taking him to posh places meant for the selected few. They dined together, laughed together, and he finally drove the boy home.

"Aasim, thank you so much, may the Almighty Allah reward you," said the little boy.

"I'm honoured to have you with me today, and I guess you enjoyed yourself?" asked Aasim.

The little boy became tearful. Funnily, when he woke up that day, he wouldn't have believed he'll be a guest to such a high-profile person. "Yes of course, thank you for the football and the jerseys, I like them," said the little boy. Aasim played his role as the adult in the room, by thanking Kabir for choosing to be his guest.

"I've to go now, Kabir, it's getting late," he said. Aasim bent down and gave Kabir a handshake, as they bid each other goodbye. The little boy was quite thankful for the gesture, if this is a dream, the dream shouldn't end, but sadly it's real life, and as Aasim turns to leave Kabir asked Aasim if he'll come to see him again.

"Maybe, maybe not, but we'll see again if fate make us cross path," replied Aasim. After the emotional goodbye, Aasim and his bodyguards returned to their cars and left.

The day of General Ambo Hussein's Silver Jubilee celebration is here. It's 8.am, Malik spotted Aasim driving out and questioned where he's headed.

In his usual fashion, Aasim is heading to the football field to train and Malik think his brother must be mad, to be heading to the football pitch on the day of his dad's Silver Jubilee celebration. At least, this shouldn't happen, not today of all days.

"To do what, Aasim?" asked Malik.

"To train of course, or what else should I be doing on the field?" asked Aasim.

Malik reminded his brother, about what day it is, and made him aware the event is just two hours away. "You we're meant to be at the venue of the Silver Jubilee, and dad will be giving his speech," said Malik.

"Oh sorry, I'd forgotten," said Aasim.

Malik insists they've got a function to attend by 10.am and now that he knows, he then asked Aasim, if he's still going ahead. Aasim turned on the ignition of his car and said he has already made up his mind to go out, but he'll back on time. He then turned to Umar and asked him to please tell their dad he'll be a bit late.

This is equally a big day for Malik to show off to the Arab world, he's the heir apparent because occasions like this help to give credibility to his future. He was stunned to see his brother going ahead with his plan for the day, after being reminded of what day and time it was. "Just be damn sure, dad will spit the dummy when he hears of your aloofness," said Malik.

"Enough of the buzzing, Malik, you've got a function to attend, make the best of it as the son of Mr. President, and there isn't any need to look droopy," said Malik.

Malik looked on even as he accused Aasim of using Umar as his spokesperson.

"Whatever!" said Aasim.

Malik was like a man chasing a rainbow after he laboriously failed to restrain Aasim who seemed determined to go ahead with his plans for the day. At this point, Malik had no choice but to resort to banter.

Your intransigence concerning your association with the beggarly is insulting to our family, I heard about you and the little boy," said Malik.

"Err..., is that your chilling rebuke for showing an innocent little boy a weensy favour?" asked Aasim.

Malik isn't still letting this go as he reminded Aasim that the dereliction of his privileged status and making a mockery of his silver spoon makes him a clown.

"Silver spoon you said? Considering all human as equals is something close to the bone, I don't care about your flouncing around," said Aasim.

"Remember, this might come back to bite you," said Malik.

Aasim then proceeded with his business for the day, and left Malik sulking over this spilt milk.

The same morning of the Silver Jubilee, Sadeq Qadri was being admitted to the Bin Alyardiz Memorial Hospital in Tunisia where he lives. Rukiyat, Sadeq's wife, was quite upfront with the doctor as he approached and asked what the problem was because they've been waiting, and no one is saying anything to them.

"We've been looking at your husband's scan result," said Dr. Mahmud.

"What about it?" asked Rukiyat.

Doctor Mahmud subtly told Rukiyat her husband needs to go for surgery immediately because his lungs are collapsing, and delay could be fatal. The news of her husband's lungs failing gave Rukiyat quite a scare, and she then asked the doctor if the state of her husband's lungs is the reason, he's always feeling dizzy and tired. Yet proceeded to ask the doctor how soon he intends to commence surgery.

"Possibly, later today, provided the minimum deposit payment is made to commence, the surgery can be done immediately," said Dr. Mahmud.

"Doctor, how bad is it?" she asked.

Doctor Mahmud looked at Rukiyat and said if the situation wasn't that bad, he wouldn't be suggesting surgery immediately. Sadeq then spoke to his wife in a faint voice and asked Rukiyat to go with the doctor and get the bill. Rukiyat then left with the doctor but ended up in the office of the medical director.

Moments later, Rukiyat finished with the doctor, and returned to her husband and was looking quite saddened. She tearfully said told Sadeq the hospital wants them to deposit ten thousand United States dollars to commence surgery.

"Err…, that's a lot of money!" exclaimed Sadeq.

Rukiyat wasn't quite impressed that the bill was given in a foreign currency as opposed to the Tunisian local currency.

Sadeq reminded his wife that this hospital mostly attends to foreigners, yet he asked his wife to know how much they have left in the account.

"We've an equivalent of about six thousand United States dollars and that won't be enough," said Rukiyat.

"Meaning, we'll need to source the funds fast," said Sadeq.

Rukiyat steered the conversation away into Sadeq's past as she urged him to seek help from quite an unlikely source. Sadeq hesitated because opening this can of worms might send worms swarming all over the place, and sadly, retuning these worms back to the can might be costly. "Why don't you call your mum and tell her about it?" she asked. Sadeq looked away and muttered, then said he doesn't have a mum.

"Stop holding onto the past, you need her now, more than ever," she retorted.

Sadeq admonished his wife and said this isn't about what he said or didn't say, and as far as his mum is concerned, he doesn't exist, and to him she doesn't exist either because she's still running from him.

"How much efforts have you invested in trying to rekindle your relationship with her?" asked Rukiyat.

Sadeq didn't hesitate to remind Rukiyat that all efforts towards rekindling a relationship with his mum have been futile, burdensome, laborious and useless. Sadeq insists that crossing the tumultuous sea of loneliness to the shore of uncertainty just to curry his mum's favour isn't worth it.

"Then what do we do?" asked Rukiyat.

Sadeq felt it's more appropriate to reach out to his dad as opposed to his mum, he then asked Rukiyat to call his dad to see if he's able to help out.

Rukiyat obliged and quickly reached for Sadeq's phone and then dialled Asif Qadri's number.

"When it starts ringing give me the phone," said Sadeq.

It didn't take long Rukiyat passed the phone to Sadeq and asked him to speak to his dad because the phone is ringing.

Asif Qadri picked. "Sadeq, how're you?" he asked.

"Dad, I'm ok, but not too fine," said Sadeq.

"What's wrong with you?" asked Asif Qadri.

Sadeq had to mildly inform his dad he has just been admitted to the hospital and needed some money for surgery.

"What, when did all these happen that you never bothered to tell me?" asked Asif Qadri.

Sadeq continued his line as best as he could to save his dad from any unnecessary panic, and said he's just been informed his lungs are bad and he needed to go for surgery today.

Asif Qadri suddenly became quite distressed, shaky and apprehensive rather, after he learnt his son's lungs were failing. "If you're talking about your lungs then this is serious, how much did they need?" asked Asif Qadri. This isn't the kind of news this man expects to hear from his only child, whom he single-handedly raised after General Ambo Hussein snatched his wife from him. Sadeq was quite in pain yet managed to speak to his dad as he told him they needed ten thousand United States dollars as initial deposit before they commence surgery.

"I've just deposited most of my money into my customer's account, this information didn't get to me on time, and where do I get ten thousand United States Dollars?" asked Asif Qadri. Sadeq can palpably feel his dad's fear, and efforts to assuage the old man of his fears didn't yield much result. He then told his dad he already has six thousand, and all he needed is four thousand dollars.

"All I've at the moment is an equivalent of two thousand United States dollars, I'll run around to look for the rest and send to you," said Asif Qadri.

Sadeq tried to play the adult in the room as he played down his desperation, as well as mange his wife's despair. He calmly asked his dad to send the two thousand dollars first, while he looks around to raise the rest money elsewhere.

"Ok, I'll do that, but is there anybody with you there?" asked Asif Qadri.

"Yes dad, my wife is with me," said Sadeq.

Asif Qadri felt his son should come first, particularly now that he's sick. He then suggested travelling down from the Republic of Kitan to Tunisia to spend some time with Sadeq.

Sadeq interjected and said travelling down all the way from the Republic of Kitan just to be with him won't be necessary if his dad's business will suffer.

"What profit will be enough to compensate for the wellbeing of my only child, I'll be in Tunisia tomorrow," he insists. After the conversation with his dad, Sadeq still needed two thousand United States Dollars to make up for the surgery.

Rukiyat realised her husband has unexpectedly being boxed to the corner, she the urged Sadeq to give his mum a call for the balance of the money.

Interestingly, Rukiyat is known for her penchant for answers, and each time she thinks of her mother in-law, the only thought at fore of her heart is the answers her husband deserves. This time she's turning to her for quite a different purpose other than that which she dearly seeks.

"Sadeq turned away and insists he can't because she hasn't been there for him at all. Sadeq is now a grown man, and has no idea of what a mum's warm embrace feels like. Yet Rukiyat is ready to lay down her sword to get her husband the help he needed.

"Your health matters to me, if anything happens to you now, I'll be the one at lose," said Rukiyat. Despite shrugging off the idea of speaking to his mum, Sadeq couldn't have it his way because Rukiyat impressed on him until he'd to succumb.

"Ok, I'll give her a call, so my dad wouldn't be running around looking for money," said Sadeq. He felt bad making this phone call because his hunch tells him there's no way he will come out smelling like a rose after making this phone call.

That same morning in the Republic of Kitan, General Ambo Hussein and his family members were preparing and getting ready to leave to the venue of the Silver Jubilee celebration.

"Ambo, have you your speech?" asked Aisha.

General Ambo Hussein cynically asked his wife what speech she's talking about. Today is this family's big day, and the citizens' wants to hear what their leader has to say, and Aisha asked to be sure the speech is well prepared. The President's daughter, Nawal, was helping to dress her mum.

General Ambo Hussein was quite dismissive and said he doesn't need a speech to talk to his people, and even if the speech wasn't well delivered who dares criticise his speech. "I'm a lion, and this is my territory," he said.

"Why do you think too little of your people? There isn't any crime embellishing your speech to make it more acceptable," said Aisha.

General Ambo takes delight in lionising himself, and said he understands that some conceited politicians are edging to take his job even when they have a paucity of administrative knowledge. Aisha continued to press on her husband and advised that if he isn't perturbed about the people of Kitan what about the international community.

"Leave the international community to me, they're only after my oil, and don't worry I know what to say, Aisha," he then kissed her on the forehead, just as their first son Malik walked in.

Malik jocularly told his mum if she's dressed like this for the Silver Jubilee, how then will she dress for the Golden Jubilee? Aisha smiled and turned to Malik and then asked if this is his way of telling his mum she's looking good.

"If so, then yes," said Malik.

Nawal interjected and said their mum is trying to steal the show of the day's occasion.

Aisha reminded Malik that the talk of a Golden Jubilee that's twenty-five years away is a tall order. She believes her and her husband will be old then, and most likely it'll be Malik in power then, so how will she celebrate the Golden Jubilee as the first lady of Kitan?

Malik concurred with his mum's assertions, and after all, a bird in the hand is worth more. Aisha was quite in a chatty mood this morning as she turned to Nawal and urged her not to worry because her time will come, and there isn't any need for a mother-daughter competition.

Malik then walked to his dad and asked if he's ready.

"Yes Malik, I hope your brothers are ready?" asked the President.

"Yes, except for Aasim," said Malik. "Where's he?" asked President Ambo.

"He went to the football field to train," said Malik.

General Ambo Hussein has always found Aasim insufferable, and this time he growled and asked Malik if Aasim knew what day it is. Malik quickly threw Aasim under the bus, and said he warned Aasim not to go ahead, yet reminded his dad that it's common knowledge that Aasim likes doing things is own way. Umar, the president's third son walked into the conversation.

Aisha interjected in response to Malik's vague description of his brother as one doing his own thing and reminded him Aasim lives in a different world. Funnily, while she was still talking her phone rang and it was Sadeq her first son born to Asif Qadri that's calling from Tunisia.

Aisha sensed it was Sadeq that's calling and quickly rushed to the bathroom to maintain the callers' anonymity, she then picked the call. "I told you not to call me, except I call you," said Aisha.

"Give me one reason why I shouldn't call you, then I'll stop, and we'll speak to each other no more," insists Sadeq.

Discretion means a lot to Aisha as she reminded Sadeq that today is her husband's Silver Jubilee celebration as president. Sadly, Sadeq's frustration is that this phone call is just another little walk in the park.

"Do you rather I stay away? And sadly, you never had the decency to tell me about your celebration," said Sadeq.

"Stop talking like this, Sadeq. You know my husband never wants to set his eyes on you," Aisha retorted.

Sadeq is a man with too many pains, and sadly, Aisha possessed certain anecdotal qualities that leave the relationship between this mother and her son constantly in a frozen state.

Sadeq thinks his mum's silver jubilee isn't much of a celebration, as he asked his mum if she isn't equally celebrating the day she left him and ran off with Ambo Hussein.

"If you don't have something better to say then I've to go," said Aisha.

"For your information I'm being admitted to the hospital for an emergency surgery," Sadeq muttered.

Aisha became quite worried over the mention of surgery and asked Sadeq if he's ok before proceeding to ask to know what the problem was.

He then informed her he's calling from the hospital bed, and just as he was about telling her what the crux of the matter about his stay in the hospital was.

Aisha sensed her husband was approaching and quickly told Sadeq she has to go, and she then ended the conversation abruptly.

General Ambo knocks the door to the bathroom where Aisha hid to pick her call. "Aisha, we're waiting for you, and we're ready to go?" he said.

"What about Aasim?" asked Umar.

"Sorry, we can't wait for your brother. Though, his churlish qualities have turned him into the black sheep in this family," said the President.

Just as Aisha turned to leave, she stopped as she realised Nawal was rummaging through her make-up box. "Nawal, what are you doing with my make up? We're leaving," said Aisha.

Nawal pleaded with her dad and promised to join them downstairs because she wants to change her makeup.

"What happened to your make up, and why this mother-daughter competition?" asked President Ambo.

It didn't take long, Nawal joined them downstairs where they were already waiting, and they all left. They were all gorgeously dressed, and after all, he indulges his family with good stuff, and good things of life, as the entire resource of this oil rich nation is in his care.

While at the hospital in Tunisia where Sadeq was admitted, Rukiyat was stunned by Aisha's insistence that Sadeq mustn't call her except she reaches out to him.

"Why's she sounding like that?" asked Rukiyat.

"I told you, but your insistence made me make the call, at least you now have a glimpse of what my relationship with my mum looks like," said Sadeq.

Rukiyat still have some faith in Aisha, she urged Sadeq not to take things to heart, and maybe his mum will call back.

She thinks Sadeq is giving too much verbiage to the strained relationship with his mum. Sadeq on his part asked Rukiyat if she rather, he continue chasing the rainbow, after all she heard his mum telling him and insisting he should never call her unless she calls him.

"When last did you speak with your mum?" asked Rukiyat.

"Hmm, that would be five years ago, and sadly, I was the one who called but the response was the same. Don't call me unless I call you," said Sadeq.

"Does she know you now have a wife?" she asked.

Sadeq said he doesn't think so, and his mum doesn't even know he's a Mechanical Engineer either, and after all, she's in love.

"What do we do now?" asked Rukiyat.

Instead of hoping for help to suddenly show-up from an unlikely source, Sadeq asked Rukiyat not to look any further, as he intends to seek help from his place of work.

The Silver Jubilee celebration has begun and it's time for the President's speech.

Citizens of Kitan, allies, investors and friends present, I must say today is a very good day for me, my family and for you the citizens of the Republic of Kitan. The fact that you've entrusted the Republic of Kitan in my care for the past twenty-five years is an attestation of my good leadership.

As you all know, this country pulled itself by the bootstrap when I took over power, I've brought development into our nation by creating an enabling environment that'll encourage investors to take interest in our resources. At the moment the speed rail from Abidkitan our nation's commercial hub to Ansarouh our nation's capital has already taken off. The ultra modern hospital in Shambihya is one of the best in the world, and our scholarship scheme, among many other improvements are some of the benefits our citizens have enjoyed in the last twenty-five years.

I announce to you citizens of the Republic of Kitan that from today, this country is now a democratic nation and I'll lead the transition to democracy. Therefore, I'll no longer be addressed as General Ambo Hussein, and rather I shall be addressed as President Ambo Hussein.

I want to thank those of you who have supported me in the last twenty-five years since my ascension to office, and to also ask you to continue supporting me as I hold this office for the next twenty five years.

Funnily, Aasim made it to the Silver Jubilee event but not until after his dad's speech. Later that day, President Ambo went to Aasim's flat to check him out, but started by asking Aasim if he listened to his Presidential speech.

"Yes dad, I heard your speech," said Aasim.

"Did you hear what I said about you?" asked President Ambo.

Aasim looked lost, he rubbed his head with his hand in sign of guilt and asked his dad if he said anything about him. The President was quite infuriated, he already finds Aasim insufferable, but it just got worst this time.

"You mean you never cared to listen to what I've to say to the people of Kitan, and the world in general?" asked President Ambo.

Aasim realised this conversation could escalate into a raging fire and quickly precipitate into something he can't wriggle out of unscathed. Aasim then muttered under his breath and said he listened to the speech, just that...,. Aasim then scratched his head again and looked away in guilt, but President Ambo interjected this time as he got all riled-up and asked. "Just that what, Aasim? Is your playing football all I could get from sending you to a military school in Europe to study intelligence and logistics?" he asked.

"Dad, football is my thing, that's where my passion lies," replied Aasim.

"Just shut up, Malik studied in Egypt, your brother Umar is studying in Qatar, can't you see they keyed into the vision of this family?" asked President Ambo.

Aasim muttered again and said he and his brothers aren't the same, and they see things differently based on their orientation.

President Ambo then turned to Aasim and said if he must know the content of his speech, then he has to sit down and listen. He made it clear that he has announced to the world that Aasim will be the head of the nation's military intelligence, so he could put the knowledge acquired from Europe to use.

"Dad, sorry to disappoint you, I'm already in talks with a football club in England, I might be moving to England next week for trials," said Aasim. The President's face suddenly became pale like a poisoned dog.

"What! You studied military strategy and you're good at it, why not be useful to your dad for once in your life," said President Ambo. Aasim sensed he's heading on a collision course with his dad and could feel his dad's anger simmering. He then looked away and promised to join his dad after his football career. "Where in England is this football club?" asked President Ambo.

"It's in Manchester," said Aasim.

The President was almost going ballistic on Aasim, but he did a good job to can his simmering anger and asked Aasim if he prefers running around in the pitch like a headless chicken to the amusement of spectators in the name of football as opposed to being treated like a royal.

"Dad don't worry, I'll see what I can do about it since you've already mentioned it in your speech," said Aasim.

"You've more military might, and also the military physique than your brothers. Why not use it to assist your father instead of playing football?" asked President Ambo.

Aasim didn't think his physique is for military purposes and protested that his physique is from nature and not for military purposes. Yet promised his dad he'll think about the offer since the announcement has gone out.

The President growled in his usual fashion and told Aasim he doesn't want him thinking about it, he should rather get on with it and work for his father.

"Ok, I'll start the day after tomorrow," said Aasim.

"Good, I'll make arrangements for you immediately," said President Ambo, before returning to his flat.

Two weeks later, all arrangements are in place for Aasim to resume his work at the Defence Headquarters.

Aasim had to first walk into the office of the chief of Army staff to report for duty.

"Good morning Brigadier," said Aasim.

"Morning Aasim, you're welcome to the defence headquarters," said Brigadier Sale Mai.

"Thank you, sir," said Aasim.

"I must confess, this uniform fit's you so perfectly," said Brigadier Sale Mai.

Aasim smiled. "Really?" asked Aasim.

"You're a true soldier, though an officer. But your physique leaves me in no doubt to think you're born to be a military officer," said Brigadier Sale Mai.

Aasim isn't one giving into corrupt flattery, he then asked the Brigadier if he's just echoing his dad's usual comments, or this is coming from the Brigadier himself. The Brigadier continued speaking in his quite distinctive voice that will leave the common man in the street quite unnerving, particularly with that accent that can't be chopped off with an axe.

"I've always wondered why you look so much different from your brothers; you look very physical and huge compared to them," said Brigadier Sale Mai.

Aasim smiled and said his brothers took after their dad in size while he took after his mum in size. The Brigadier continued his physical appraisal of Aasim's physique. "I also learnt you're very fast on your feet," said Brigadier Sale Mai.

"That's a quality I acquired as a footballer," replied Aasim.

Brigadier Sale Mai smiled before denoting that Aasim's jiujutsu's skill and his being fast on his feet combined with his imposing stature makes Aasim a one-man army. Aasim laughed in response to the flattery. "Brigadier, you're over stating my capabilities and I'm certain you didn't take a course to become a sensationalist," said Aasim. The Brigadier continued his line and said he doesn't think there's anyone as huge as Aasim in the entire military. "But I've seen a couple," Aasim said, and smiled.

"That explains it all," said Brigadier Sale Mai.

Aasim tried to steer the conversation away from his physique, and said his size has nothing to do with his job, unless the Brigadier thinks otherwise.

Brigadier Sale Mai then dispensed of all pleasantries and then formally welcomed Aasim into the military. "You're next to me, as far as the military is concerned, and you're also a Brigadier by rank even though I'm your superior.

"Thank you, Brigadier," said Aasim.

Brigadier Sale Mai then reached for the phone and then dialled. "Colonel, I want you in my office," said Brigadier Sale Mai.

Minutes later, Colonel Salihu walked in. "Good morning sir," said Colonel Salihu.

"Morning Colonel, and how was your night?" asked Brigadier Sale Mai.

"Fine sir," said Colonel Salihu.

Brigadier Sale Mai then asked the Colonel to show Brigadier Aasim Hussein to his office and show him around.

Aasim turns to the Colonel. "Hello Colonel," said Aasim.

"Morning sir," said Colonel Salihu.

Aasim realised the Colonel wasn't himself the moment he set his eyes on him, and the as they left the Brigadier's office, Aasim had to ask the Colonel why he seem to be under some kind of tension.

"Nothing Brigadier, I'm fine sir," said Colonel Salihu.

Aasim had to assuage this Colonel of whatever concern his presence may have caused. He then turned to the Colonel and reminds him of the obvious. "But you're usually relaxed each time you chat with me before now, do you think I'm here to spy on you or what? I'm only here to do my job," said Aasim.

"I'm sorry, Aasim, just that I was surprised to see you in military uniform, though you look so much of an officer," said Colonel Salihu.

"And you felt intimidated?" asked Aasim.

"Sort of," said Colonel Salihu.

"Then, don't be," said Aasim.

Minutes later, the Colonel showed Aasim to a newly decorated office. "This is your office, Sir," said the Colonel.

Aasim looked around then reminded the Colonel he said earlier that he wasn't expecting to see him in military uniform, how come he knew this office is his.

Colonel Salihu had to clarify his insinuations and said the Chief of Army Staff requested they get the office ready that a Brigadier will be occupying it, but he never knew it would be him.

"Which other Brigadier did you've in mind then?" asked Aasim.

"Brigadier Bachakar, though he's in the barracks in Shambihya, and there are other Brigadiers around the country," said Col. Salihu.

"Thank you, Colonel, you can forget about showing me around for now, we'll do that later. Let me settle down with these intelligence files on my desk," said Aasim.

The next day the President dialled the Chief of Army Staff inquire of how Aasim is settling into his new role.

"Hello Brigadier, how's Aasim doing?" asked President Ambo.

"Aasim is doing well, he's actually taking his job seriously and I must confess that he's quite a remarkable young man," said Brigadier Sale Mai.

The President was quite delighted with the report concerning Aasim, he then urged the Chief of Army Staff to please pass all intelligence documents and information to Aasim so he could help restructure the intelligence unit.

"Ok Mr. President, I'll do just that," said Brigadier Sale Mai.

President Ambo then became a bit friendly and said that boy knows a lot, but he has been shying away from helping his dad. "From what I've seen, he seems more dedicated this time," said Brigadier Sale Mai.

It didn't take long before President Ambo steered the conversation into something he considered needling. He asked Brigadier Sale Mai if he has been seeing the protesters at the central square.

"Mr. President, I've seen them, and they've been there for some days now. Actually, I don't know why the police haven't cleared the square yet," said Brigadier Sale Mai.

Nothing infuriates the President like an opposition to his government in whatever shape or form, and everyone with different view is classed as a dissent. Sadly, the President has this knack for instant justice, call it extra-judicial or whatever, and if he silences opposition then justice is done. He hounds every dissent until he breaks their resolve to speak up against their oppressor.

President Ambo became quite spiky as accused the Chief of Army Staff of dawdling and always waiting for the police to clear protesters. Brigadier Sale Mai was mum over the sharp rebuke from the President, and he then tried to express his concerns over using the military to clear minor protest. It has always been the case that such operation results in national outcry because of the casualties that results each time the military goes for an assignment of this nature.

"Leave the worrying about who gets injured or not to me, Ansarouh is our nation's capital, and I don't want some group of rascals constituting a nuisance in the name of free speech," said Mr. President.

"Ok sir, we'll act immediately," said Brigadier Sale Mai.

"Good, I want that square cleared by the time I pass through there, but use proportionate force," President Ambo retorted and drops the phone.

Immediately the conversation ended, Brigadier Sale Mai dialled Captain Ahmed. "Captain, I want you in my office now," he said. "Yes sir," said Captain Ahmed. Moments later, the captain reported to Brigadier Sale Mai. "Yes Captain, are you aware of those protesters at the central square?" asked the Brigadier. Captain Ahmed asked if the Brigadier is referring to those groups of people protesting for free speech.

Yes, I want them out of that square immediately, you're to clear the square," said Brigadier Sale Mai.

"Yes sir," said Captain Ahmed.

Interestingly, it didn't take long before Captain Ahmed and his men arrived the Central Square and funnily, there were no protesters.

Captain Ahmed then dialled Brigadier Sale Mai to inform him, there are no protesters. "Brigadier, the protesters have dispersed," said Captain Ahmed.

"What do you mean they've dispersed?" asked Brigadier Sale Mai.

Captain Ahmed calmly said the square is empty, and it's either they didn't come out today or that they've left the square. The Brigadier then insists that this is a Presidential order, and this group of protesters must stop congregating at the square.

"What do I do next, sir?" asked Captain Ahmed.

Brigadier Sale Mai felt the need to act proactively to avoid being in the president's crosshairs. He then ordered the captain to go to their houses and arrest those leading these protests, and hoping that this move will stop people from coming out to protest.

"Yes sir," said Captain.

The captain then proceeded to arrest them in their homes.

The next Morning, while Tammim, Suliyat, Ramon and Taj were in the military cells within the barracks, Aasim walked past front of the cell. Suliyat, with pair of eyes as sharp as those of an eagle spotted Aasim as he walked past the cell. "Tammim, Tammim get up," she then pointed to Aasim. "Isn't that your friend?" she asked.

"Which of my friends?" asked Tammim.

"Aasim, Ambo Hussein's son," said Suliyat.

Tammim quickly stood up and looked through the bars of the cell, and funnily he could only see Aasim from behind. He then muttered and said Aasim isn't in the military, but that physique looks like him. It's quite obvious that those who know Aasim can easily identify him even from behind because of his uniquely imposing physic. "That's Aasim, are you guys friends?" asked Taj.

"Yeah, he makes friends with all the guys, and he's friendly to everyone," said Tammim.

Suliyat couldn't help but urged Tammim to make the move of getting Aasim to help them out of the cell because the place stinks, she asked him to shout out Aasim name as a way of attracting his attention.

Tammim continued dawdling as he considers what he could do to attract Aasim's attention.

"I don't think that's a good idea. Moreover, he's a bit far away and I don't think he'll hear us except we start screaming like barbarians," said Tammim.

Suliyat couldn't accommodate any further dawdling from Tammim and decided to take the bull by the horn because she doesn't mind what it takes to get Aasim's attention. She began screaming. "Aasim, Aasim, help us," said Suliyat.

Aasim heard his name and turned to see where the call was coming from. He then walked to the military cell by the security post and asked Tammim of what brought them to the cell. Tammim didn't hesitate to inform Aasim, the military just came to their houses to arrest them.

"Over what?" asked Aasim.

Tammim looked away after all he's protesting against Aasim's dad, and said they were arrested for protesting for free speech in the past, and not that they even met them protesting.

"Is that it?" asked Aasim.

"Yes, that's it," said Tammim.

Aasim then turned to the Corporal and asked about who led these arrests.

"Captain Ahmed led the arrests, sir," said Corporal.

Aasim walked straight into Captain Ahmed's office. "Captain," said Aasim.

"Good morning, sir," said Captain Ahmed.

"Morning Captain, why did you arrest those people in cell A?" asked Aasim.

Captain Ahmed jocularly said those guys are advocating for free speech and the order for their arrest is from Mr. President. Aasim then said he just learnt they were arrested in their houses. Captain Ahmed had to explain to Aasim that when they got to the square there wasn't anyone there, so they decided to go to their homes to pick them.

Aasim insists the arrest was quite ridiculous and said to the captain that his order was to clear the square, he got to the square and there wasn't anyone protesting, and asked why he proceeded to their houses to arrest them.

Captain Ahmed continued to justify the logic behind the arrest and insists the move will prevent the protesters from coming out another day to protest for free speech. Aasim berated the move and said this is nonsense. He then stretched his hand towards the captain and requested for the keys to the cell.

"But sir, I suggest you speak with the Chief of Army Staff about this," said Captain Ahmed.

"I order you to give me the keys now, and I'll speak with him later," said Aasim.

"Ok sir," said Captain Ahmed. He then handed the keys to Aasim.

Aasim collected the keys from the captain, and walked to the cell, and he then opened it and freed the protesters. "You can go," said Aasim.

"Thank you, sir," said Suliyat.

"Thank you, Aasim," said Tammim.

"You guys should stay out of trouble," said Aasim.

"Thank you, man," said Taj.

As they walk away Suliyat turned to Tammim and said her persistence paid off. Captain Ahmed realised Aasim's action has just set him in the Brigadier's crosshairs, and minutes later. "Hello sir, Brigadier Aasim has just freed the protesters," said Captain Ahmed.

Brigadier Sale Mai was quite flummoxed with Aasim's decision and stood up in anger as he queried why Aasim would do a thing like that. He then asked Captain Ahmed if he made it clear to Aasim that the order was from the President.

"Of course I did, but he insisted I give him the keys," said Captain Ahmed.

Brigadier Sale Mai ordered the captain to be on standby because he may have to re-arrest these protesters, at least to save himself from the wrath of the President. "Aasim said he'll speak with you about it," said Captain Ahmed. The Brigadier insists he's carrying out the President's wishes and whatever Aasim has to say wouldn't matter.

"What do I do next, should I go after them?" asked Captain Ahmed.

Brigadier Sale Mai had to manage being in the middle of this father and son. He then urged the captain to wait until Aasim comes to him with his reasons. Though, I might get the President involved to avoid further conflicts of this nature," said Brigadier Sale Mai.

An hour later, Aasim walked into the office of the Chief of Army Staff. "You sent for me, sir," said Aasim.

"Yes, Aasim, what's the meaning of that?" asked Brigadier Sale Mai.

"I don't get you, sir. Are you suggesting I wrongfully released the free speech advocates?" asked Aasim.

"Yes, of course, and why would you do a thing like that?" asked Brigadier Sale Mai.

Aasim went ahead to suggest he felt the arrest wasn't justified that was why he released them. Brigadier Sale Mai stood up and spoke on top of his voice, insisting it was a Presidential order, and then told Aasim he has no right to flout such order at his own discretion. Aasim continued to justify his action as he said there wasn't a specific order to arrest the protester, and rather the order was to clear the central square, and not to go into their houses and pick them even when they weren't protesting.

"You aren't in position to ascertain what arrest was justified or not, that's the prerogative of Mr. President," said Brigadier Sale Mai.

Aasim berated the arrests and urged the Chief of Army Staff to use his office to advise his dad aright, and said the world is seeing this nation as one whose citizens are being oppressed.

"I don't know what you're talking about, Aasim, and for your information, we're re-arresting those protesters you just released," said Brigadier Sale Mai.

Aasim had to hit the nail on the head and asked Brigadier Sale Mai why he would do a thing like that and said he won't be part of a military that's known for impunity.

"Aasim, I want you to know we aren't operating outside the law, there's a law that bans protests of every form," insists Brigadier Sale Mai.

Aasim continued holding his ground, as he insisted that these laws that ban protests are skewed against the citizens to keep them repressed.

"You should stop denigrating the President, Aasim, even if he's your dad," said Brigadier Sale Mai.

"The hatred the people have towards my dad is the ripple effects from your actions," said Aasim.

Brigadier Sale Mai realised he's on a collision course with Aasim and suggested it's better to bring the President into this ensuing kerfuffle because working with Aasim is already becoming tenuous.

"That won't be a bad idea," said Aasim.

On the other hand, Malik was driving around town and suddenly reached for his phone, he then puts a phone call across to Police Commissioner, Azeem Aden.

"Mr. Commissioner, what's your role as a commissioner?" asked Malik.

The one phone call Commissioner Azeem dreads is a phone call from Malik, because he finds Malik quite insufferable and if he'd the choice, he wouldn't touch Malik with a ten-foot barge pole. He didn't hesitate to express his exception to Malik's choice of words and asked Malik why he's speaking to him in such a rude manner. He reminded Malik his dad doesn't get this raw and feisty with him.

"I can address you in whatever manner I see fit, you're lucky my dad is formal with you," said Malik.

"I'm going to speak to your dad about this, you're getting on my nerves," said Commissioner Azeem.

Malik then yelled and asked the Commissioner if he's willing to take Presidential orders or not.

Commissioner Azeem shook his head at Malik's spiky utterances; he then muttered under his breath and asked Malik what orders he's speaking about. Yet, he insists he'd rather take instructions from the president than this deluge of insults he gets from Malik.

"Can you go the whole hog with me, Mr. Commissioner? I'm willing to face off with you, if you've bones to pick with me," said Malik.

Commissioner Azeem toned down his voice and reminded Malik he isn't out for any disputation with him and told Malik he's all ears if Malik have any message from Mr. President.

"Glad to hear you're backing down because you can't stand my heat," boasts Malik.

"What's it Mr. President wants me to do?" asked Commissioner Azeem.

Malik then advised the Commissioner that there's a gathering of Christians close to the market, and said he thought that churches aren't allowed to operate in the Republic of Kitan.

"I don't understand what you mean, but from my understanding the President has relaxed that law long ago," said Commissioner Azeem.

Malik insists that the Republic of Kitan is a Muslim nation, and every form of Christian gathering or proselytising is highly prohibited. This is a thorny subject that requires some discretion, Commissioner Azeem then reminded Malik that the President is aware of their gathering and wasn't bothered about it. Interestingly, Malik insists he doesn't think his dad is aware of the gathering of those infidels, he then insisted he wants them cleared.

"Your dad and I were together two weeks ago, while driving around he saw their banner, read it and laughed, and then went his way," said Commissioner Azeem.

"I'm doing something about it now, and your order is to send your men to clear these gatherings, but make sure your men break their legs, so they don't gather again," said Malik.

Commissioner Azeem was flummoxed and calmly advised Malik that he understands his simmering anger, but his idea of absolutism should only exist in his imagination. Malik laughed as he read out the riot act to the Commissioner. "The only reason to consider this a figment of my imagination is if you think of me as an exterminator," said Malik.

The Commissioner insists he doesn't think the President would like this because of the hysteria and paranoia that would follow. Malik quickly resorted to threats, to at least give this dawdling Commissioner of Police a little push. He then told the Commissioner if he can't do this simple task then he should expect his removal from office.

This isn't just a veiled threat, this is a direct threat, and the Commissioner needed to make a decision. "I don't go about my job unprofessionally, and I don't think Mr. President will like me hurting innocent people," said Commissioner Azeem.

"Trust me, I know how to build up stories that will make my dad relieve you of your position shamefully," said Malik.

"Why're you doing this?" said Commissioner Azeem.

"Because I hate to see infidels gathering in the Republic of Kitan, and I'll love to hear their outcry, so make sure you break their bones," said Malik.

Commissioner Azeem paused for a long while. "Ok, consider it done. Though, I hate to play a role in persecuting people for their faith," said Commissioner Azeem.

Later that evening, Malik wants to go clubbing, he then walked downstairs to Colonel Abdallah, the head of the presidential guards and said he's going clubbing, and he needed four of his guards.

"Which of the clubs?" asked Colonel Abdallah.

Malik got pissed with the Colonel's questions and quickly asked what sort of stupid question he just asked. "Do I have to tell you which club I'm going to?" asked Malik.

Colonel Abdallah quickly apologised to Malik and said he's sorry, he thought knowing what club Malik is attending will help him determine who should go with him.

Sadly, Malik didn't bulge, at least to make the job easier for this Colonel. "Just give me four of your soldiers, I wouldn't say much," said Malik.

"Ok sir, I'll get them to join you in a minute," said Colonel Abdallah. He then released four of his men to join Malik and Umar to the club.

Malik was seated in the car waiting for his brother to join him, but his patience grew thing after a fairly long wait. He then picked his phone and dialled Umar and asked if he's yet ready because they're about to leave for the club.

"I'm on my way downstairs," said Umar.

It didn't take long after Umar joined him they left for club. While in the club, Usman who's a citizen of Kitan but based in the United States came home on holiday in the company of his American friends. Sadly, Usman mistakenly stepped on Malik's shoe.

"Hey sorry, my bad," said Usman.

Malik flew up in anger and asked Usman what he just did, he was on Usman's face, and he went quite up-close, as he asked Usman to his face if he's blind. Flying off the handle at the slightest opportunity is Malik's character flaw, after all, he's the son of Mr. President.

"I'm sorry, that's my bad," said Usman.

"And you're walking out on me?" asked Malik.

Karl, who's one of the guests that came with Usman from the United Sates interjected in an attempt to lay this sleeping dog to rest. "He said he's sorry, what else do you want him to do?" asked Karl. Unfortunately, Karl didn't only lay the sleeping dog to rest, and rather he spooked the dog, by making this agitated dog turn aggressive. Karl's involvement only exacerbated the whole kerfuffle, as Malik turned to Karl and put him in his place.

"Shut your stinking mouth, and I'll throw you out of this club this minute if you don't shut your mouth," said Malik.

Karl was taken aback by Malik's authoritativeness, he quickly turned to Usman and asked who Malik is, and what is it that makes him so swollen headed. Malik then turned to the Sergeant and ordered him to throw Karl out of this club right away.

As soon as the Sergeant proceeded to carry out the order, Usman rushed and stood in-between the soldier and Karl, and said Karl is his guest. "I'll clean your shoe, and I hope that'll do," said Usman.

"Ok, I'm waiting," said Malik who stood with his arms crossed.

Usman quickly dipped his hand into his pocket and brought out his handkerchief to clean Malik's shoe, "I'm sorry for stepping on you in error," he said.

Malik looked at Usman, and gave him a cheeky grin, then said he doesn't think the handkerchief will do the trick, rather he wants Usman to use that, as he pointed to Usman's white T-Shirt.

"Use what, I don't get you?" asked Usman.

"Don't make me repeat myself, I want you to use your shirt," said Malik.

"No, that won't be, and that'll never happen," Usman retorted.

Karl looked on as Malik flexed his muscle, and the thought that came to Karl's head was that this is the first time he's up-close to such a sulking and woken character. "What's wrong with this dude? Hey, your action stinks to high heaven," Karl retorted.

"Then, I'll make that happen," said Malik. He then ordered the Sergeant to remove Usman's shirt forcefully, and he should tear the shirt from Usman's body if possible. A scuffle ensued as the Sergeant attempt to pull Usman's T-shirt from his body.

"Wow, what's going on? Stop this," said Karl who stepped in front of Usman as he attempts to stop the Sergeant.

"Hey, leave my front," said the Sergeant. The sergeant then pushed Karl, who staggered haphazardly until he clung to his seat for support.

"Hey! You don't have to push him like that, and don't touch me, don't touch me," said Usman. Sadly, within a minute the Sergeant tore the shirt from Usman's body.

Umar was somewhere else in the dancing floor, and saw the scuffle from a distance, he then rushed to that direction. "What's going on, Malik. I've been waiting for you over there?" asked Umar.

"He stepped on my shoe," he replied. Malik then ordered the Sergeant. "Give the rag he called shirt to him, and let him clean my shoe with it," Malik ordered.

Umar quickly turned to Usman and asked if he's blind and rebuked him for stepping on his brother's shoe.

Karl turned to Umar and pointed it out to him that Usman has unreservedly apologised to Malik already, and said Usman even offered to clean his brother's shoe with his handkerchief, but Malik prefers to tear his shirt.

"You just tore my shirt into a rag, I've heard a lot of things about you, and you're exactly what they say you're," said Usman.

"At least you'll have a taste of me," said Malik.

Usman looked on and was quite disappointed with Malik's treatment of him and his guests. "I've met your brother Aasim, he isn't like this," said Usman.

"Malik, it's ok," said Umar.

"No, it isn't, he must bend down and clean my shoes," said Malik.

Umar then grabbed the torn shirt and cleaned Malik's shoe, and said he hoped this will solve the problem.

Malik wasn't particularly pleased with his brother's intervention he then turned the heat on his brother for letting Usman off the hook. "Who asked you to do that?" he asked.

"We came to the club to have fun, let's do just that and go home," insists Umar.

"Know your place Umar, and don't butt into my business next time," Malik retorted. Umar had no need picking bones with his big brother, yet he'd to remind Malik things mustn't get gritty around the club whenever he's around.

"Usman, let's go, this isn't fun anymore, let him have the club," said Karl. Usman quickly put himself together and left the club shirtless in the company of his friends.

Malik hadn't forgiven Umar yet, he went on sulking after Usman has left. He reminded Umar that the gritty ambience isn't an invitation for his interference. "Going clubbing with you shouldn't bring disrespect," said Malik.

"The guys have left the club, let's put this behind us," said Umar.

Malik suddenly became furious the moment he realised Usman has left. He then accused Umar of helping Usman and his friends escape. After flouncing around for a while, he sulked and walked into the dancing floor.

By morning of the next day Aasim walked into his parents' living room with a scarf in his hand. "Mum, I just saw this, and I think it belongs to you," he said.

"I've been looking for this headscarf, where did you find it?" asked Aisha.

"I found it in my flat, and I think Nawal left it there," said Aasim.

Aisha then lamented and said Nawal is making her lose most of her things. She went on to say she has even tried buying another one but the design is no longer in the market.

Malik interjected from his sedentary position. "Why can't you order the textile company to make it for you, if you so much love the design as you just said?" he said.

Aasim felt disconcerted and took exception with Malik's choice of word. "Why's it that all you do is ordering people? I heard about your brawl in the club last night" said Aasim.

"Umar saved that guy, and I'd wanted to give him a piece of my action," said Malik.

"If not that your dad is the President, will you be able to stand and challenge people? You man of small stature," asked Aasim. Malik insists he doesn't mind, and after all, he'll rule this nation one day with an iron fist just as their dad is doing. He joked that their dad is a man of small stature just like him, yet he's a strong leader. Aasim shook his head in pity at his brother's overwhelming quest for power and asked Malik to stop trying laboriously to remind everyone he's the heir apparent. Malik continued his boasts, and reminded Aasim, their dad's astuteness, strength and agility are the features that kept him in power, and these are features he shares with his dad.

"Just as you ordered Commissioner Azeem to break the legs of innocent Christians?" said Aasim.

"They're infidels, aren't they?" asked Malik.

Aisha had an earful of what Malik has been up to lately, she then turned to Malik, and asked if he did actually order the Police Commissioner to beat up innocent people.

"I can't encourage nor tolerate the gathering of infidels," said Malik.

Aasim interjected and asked Malik to stop deceiving himself, insisting the free and slush money at Malik's disposal makes him delusional.

"Continue making friends with everybody in town, one thing I look forward to is an opportunity of making a mincemeat out of your best friends," said Malik.

"I find myself lost, each time I try to fathom why you choose to be so menacing and dangerous," said Aasim.

Malik seemed to have had enough of Aasim's rebuke, he then turned to walk away, yet he urged Aasim to stop punishing every-one's ears advocating for the nobodies in this country. Aasim's dual personality isn't in conflict, he has a broad shoulder that made him able to navigate between the two worlds of the rich bureaucrat in the Republic of Kitan, and the poorest of the poor in the land.

Aasim was quite incensed with Malik's degrading treatment of the poor and beggarly. He then decided to banter Malik by calling him a miserable man living under the illusion that his path is already laid out for him. "I understand you can't take the banter, the bashing and the ribbing that comes with socializing, that's why you lash out at every opportunity," said Aasim. Malik walked back to Aasim and continued winding him up with words.

"I haven't got time to socialize with some filthy natives," Malik muttered. "Your naivety astounds me," replied Aasim.

"Never mind, your camaraderie with these so-called natives will earn you what? Nothing, but a stab in the back," said Malik.

"You little man! You're just an empty vessel susceptible to making the greatest noise," said Aasim.

Malik walks up to Aasim and looked right into his eye. "Ah, little man you said?" asked Malik.

"Yeah, that's you, chirping away like a cricket," said Aasim.

"Small stature? Yes, but enormous ego," said Malik. Funnily, these brothers find each other insufferable, while Aasim despised Malik for his heartless deeds, Malik in turn hate his brother for his association with the poor. As Malik stepped away from Aasim's face and turned to leave. "Your ideals aren't really savoury, especially for a man your size," said Aasim.

"I know you're huge like mum, but that doesn't make you a man with a stronger will than me," said Malik.

President Ambo already has an earful as he listens to the rants between this pair from his bedroom. He then walked into the conversation. "Enough of this nonsense, Aasim, stop worrying about the people, worry about your family," said Mr. President.

"No dad, your son's actions and inaction are increasing the hatred against this family," said Aasim.

Malik interjected and said Usman is among the citizens of the Republic of Kitan saying awful things about the country abroad.

"Usman isn't one of them, he's proud to be a citizen of Kitan, that's why he always brings his friends here whenever he's on holiday, but all he got is humiliation before his guests," said Aasim. "I don't care what you think," said Malik.

"Aasim, stop using vile words against your brother, you shouldn't vilify your brother for instilling discipline on an irate citizen who goes about stepping on people," said President Ambo.

Aisha realised her husband have failed to play the role of the adult in the room by taking side with Malik and this could rock the boat, she had to get involved to put the conversation back to perspective. She then turned to the President and urged him to stop excusing the vituperations and exuberance of his son. Interestingly, President Ambo's schism precipitated by greed that would not allow any criticism of his son, meant he's a dad who's supposed to be a good role model but has remained his son's reliable enabler.

President Ambo continued to berate Aasim despite Aisha's caution. "Must Aasim pick holes in all his brother's actions?" asked President Ambo.

"Dad, Malik's actions are making people hate you the more, he should learn to be nice to people," said Aasim.

Aisha seemed not to be having her husband look away from their son's excesses. She then turned to President Ambo and asked if that's all he has to say. "I expect you to curb your son's excesses," said Aisha.

Malik expected the same backing from his mum, just as his dad. He finds it frustrating to hear his mum say and act otherwise. He then turned to his mum and asked why she's always taking side with Aasim.

"At your age, I expect you to be wiser, but you seem to grow more foolish by the day, I'm only trying to help you snap out of your foolishness," said Aisha.

Malik was stunned by his mum's remark, and he didn't hesitate to inquire from her to know how he has been foolish.

"You must learn to maintain a less boisterous profile, if you want the people to accept you as your dad's successor," said Aisha.

Malik insists he doesn't think his profile has anything to do with this, he then said his dad understands Aasim more, and he's only trying to contain him.

Aisha isn't buying any of Malik's tale because she considers them a fib. "Your brother is disillusioned, while you're still struggling with delusion," said Aisha.

While the conversation persisted, Brigadier Sale Mai walked into their conversation. "Good morning, Mr. President," he said. Normally the Chief of Army Staff isn't supposed to walk in on the President and his family but the president asked him to come over.

"Brigadier, what can I do for you?" asked Mr. President.

"Sorry Mr. President, I just want to have a moment with you, sir," said Brigadier Sale Mai.

President Ambo then asked Brigadier Sale Mai to follow him to his office. He stood up from his seat and they walked into his office. "Ok, tell me about it," said Mr. President.

Brigadier sale Mai calmly told the president he has come to talk about Aasim.

"Aasim, what about him?" asked Mr. President.

"He released the protesters we arrested because he thinks their arrest wasn't justified," said Brigadier Sale Mai.

"Did you tell him the order was from me?" asked President Ambo.

"Yes Mr. President, but he wouldn't have any of it," said Brigadier Sale Mai.

President Ambo became quite incensed, and his face suddenly became pale, he immediately asked Brigadier Sale Mai to go and get Aasim.

Brigadier Sale Mai walked back into the President's living room, and told Aasim, his dad wants to see him in his office.

Minutes later, Aasim walked into his dad's office. "You want to see me?" asked Aasim.

President Ambo went on to ask Aasim why he released the protesters, even when he was informed the order for their arrest was a presidential order. Aasim insists the order was to clear the square and not to arrest them from their houses.

President Ambo felt slighted by his son, he then angrily said he wanted those free speech advocates arrested and disciplined, and instructed Aasim not to go anywhere near them this time.

Aasim was quite disappointed by his dad's decision to re-arrest these protesters. He then reminded his dad that the world sees his government as brutal, and he's only trying to change that perception by ensuring that only those who deserve punishment are punished.

"I expect you to work with me, and not to interfere in my affairs," said President Ambo.

"How then can I be of help, if I can't interfere in your affairs?" asked Aasim.

President Ambo's anger is beginning to boil from within, and it's now glaringly obvious that this anger could boil over because he can't have his son rubbing shoulder with him. He then ordered Aasim to stop this incessant intrusion into how he runs the country.

"Why then did you bring me into the military, if not to add my knowledge?" asked Aasim.

"Stop questioning me, Aasim," yelled President Ambo.

"Why don't you give me another role in your government outside the military, why do you insist it must be the military?" asked Aasim.

President Ambo had to voice his concern over Aasim and said if he assigns him to a different ministry, Aasim could be taken over by his laxity and allow the people to speak against his government.

"Then, what makes you think I'll act differently in the military?" asked Aasim.

"Because in the military you're to take orders, and that's why I insist you take orders," said Mr. President.

Aasim realised his dad is bent on keeping him on a tight leash and he's obviously on a collision course with his dad. He quickly brought out a piece of paper and scribbled a few lines. "Dad, that's my resignation," said Aasim.

"What do you mean, and are you out of your senses?" asked President Ambo.

Sadly, the President is a hot head, who has obviously found his match in Aasim, and the hope is that cool heads will prevail. Aasim on his part made it clear in no uncertain terms that he can't be part of a brutal regime, and if he can't make things right, then he won't make them worst.

President Ambo withdrew his hand from the resignation letter, and insists he isn't accepting Aasim's resignation.

Aasim needed to walk away from his dad as soon as possible, he had no choice but to leave the letter on his dad's table and urged him to file it away whenever he's ready to do so.

"Your offer of employment is still available, and I still want you to work for me," insists Mr. President. Aasim walked out of his dad's office and left them to do their thing, after all, dealing with his dad isn't just a walk in the park.

"Mr. President, should I go ahead with the re-arrest?" asked Brigadier Sale Mai.

"No, let them off the hook this time because Aasim is right but I won't admit that before his face," said President Ambo.

Days later, Aasim overheard noise of fracas coming from Malik's flat as he drives by, he stopped his car and rushed in, only to realise Malik and his wife were in a heated fight.

"Hey Malik stop, stop, you've to stop doing this, and what are you doing with the gun?" asked Aasim.

"Don't ask me what I'm doing with a gun, what else do people use guns for if not to kill? I can do what I want with my wife," said Malik.

"Do you want to kill your wife? A gun isn't something to play with," said Aasim.

Malik insists he knows too well what a gun can do, and he isn't holding the gun for a show. Aasim tried to constrain his brother, but Malik was quite feisty and insist he wants to break his wife's legs with the gun.

"You seem to be out of control Malik, what's the problem with you?" asked Aasim.

Malik's unrestrained appetite for a quarrel got the best of him as he suddenly turned against Aasim and reminded him he has warned him never to come into his flat whenever he's instilling discipline in his wife.

"I'm your wife and not your slave, and you'll do nothing to me, you imbecile of a man," said Arfa.

Aasim continued trying to hold Malik down. "Stop Malik, stop, your wife is already bleeding, and I think she needs medical attention," said Aasim.

Malik still had the gun and continued saying he doesn't care if his wife is bleeding, and if she dies today, he'll gladly marry another one tomorrow.

"Why's your home like this! What a nuptial fiasco?" asked Aasim.

"I don't want you qualifying my marriage with your sordid adjectives," said Malik. Aasim wasn't particularly keen to involve himself in his brother's drama but qualifying his marriage is an escalation Malik will never acquiesce. After all, Malik considers his brother morally sick over his choice for a non-Arab woman.

"You can't kill me, you can't kill me, you witless evil man!" exclaimed Arfa.

"I'll have to kill you if I can't curtail your curling tongue," said Malik.

Aasim had no choice but to restrain Malik as he reminds Malik, he has always told him beating up his wife is wrong.

Funnily, while Aasim held Malik down, Arfa had the opportunity to run outside the flat. "You've given Arfa the space to escape my wrath," said Malik.

He then turned to Aasim in the fullness of his anger and struck Aasim with the butt of the gun. "Stop interfering in my business with my wife, maybe you should be the one to bear the brunt for letting my wife escape," said Malik, as he struck Aasim a second time with the butt of the gun.

Aasim became quite furious as his head bleeds. "Why did you hit me with your gun?" asked Aasim. Malik continued flouncing around, and it didn't take time before Aasim disarmed Malik and angrily carried him on his shoulder and took him upstairs, he then locked him up in his bedroom. Stay there till you realise what you've done.

"Aasim, I order you to open this door right now, you're interfering in my affair," said Malik.

"Did you realise you just hit me with the butt of your gun?" asked Aasim.

"I don't care about that, maybe I'll have to shoot you the next time," said Malik.

"Then you've to remain locked up, until you learn some manners," said Malik.

By evening of the same day, Malik had to call one of the guards on the phone who came to his rescue. Funnily, immediately he gained his freedom, he realised he needed to pay Arfa's parents a visit, he then walks to Colonel Abdallah. "Colonel, come with me," said Malik.

"Malik, should I come with you alone or with some guards?" asked Colonel Abdallah.

"Did you just call me by name? The next time you call me by name, I'll take that your gun and shoot you with it," said Malik.

Colonel Abdallah apologised to Malik and addressed Malik as Mr. Prime Minister, he then asked if he should come along with some guards. Malik has succeeded in bullying the presidential guards into referring to him as the Prime Minister.

Yes, come with two guards, they have an assignment to carry out. "Please give me a minute to do that," said Colonel Abdallah. The Colonel called out two of the guards under him and returned to Malik. "Let's go, Mr. Prime Minister," he said. Forty-five minutes later, they arrived at Arfa's parents' residence, Malik then turned to the Colonel. "Go in there and drag Arfa out," said Malik.

Colonel Abdallah knocks the door and Arfa's dad came out, he then asked him of Arfa's whereabouts.

"My in-law, is anything the matter? Arfa isn't here," said Arfa's dad.

Malik was quite furious and managing the showy display of his power whenever he wraths his anger is his key character flaw.

"Don't in-law me, bring my wife out, do you think you can shield her from me?" asked Malik.

Arfa's dad reminded Malik he's quite aware Arfa is his wife, but she isn't in his house, he was quite surprise as to what the problem might be. He then asked if anything is the matter because he has no reason to shield his daughter from Malik. Arfa's mum heard the noise coming from her balcony and came out. She immediately walked towards Malik to greet him. "My in-law, how're you, is anything the matter?" she asked.

Malik pushed Arfa's mum to the ground and warned her to stay away from him because he didn't come to exchange pleasantries while she hides his wife away from him.

"Arfa isn't here, please, is my daughter ok?" asked Arfa's mum.

"Don't ask me that," said Malik. He then turned to Colonel Abdallah and instructed him to send his men inside the house to drag his wife out from whatever closet she's hiding.

The guards went inside and searched but couldn't find Arfa, they came and reported to Malik that Arfa isn't in the house.

Arfa's dad was quite in shock over Malik's action, he looked at Malik and reminded him he already told him she isn't here, and assured Malik he can't keep his wife away from him. Malik felt insulted that his wife was able to escape his wrath before he finished with her. He then ordered Colonel Abdallah to bundle Arfa's parents up and throw them in the prison cell until they disclose the whereabouts of his wife.

"My son please don't do this, I'm not feeling too well, give us time to look for her," said Arfa's mum.

"Abdallah, take these lunatics out of my sight," said Malik. He then turned to Arfa's dad and reminded him the privileges they enjoy today are from him, and he'll strip them of those privileges.

"My in-law, please wait, please," pleads Arfa's mum.

"Stop calling me that, go with your gormless husband," insists Malik.

Sadly, if you can't stand the heat then stay away from the kitchen, and if you don't want this kind of treatment stay away from people who can suddenly treat you as if they own the air you breathe. All pleas for mercy by this elderly couple fell on deaf ears, as Malik insists on teaching them a lesson.

A day after the arrests of Arfa's parents, Aasim walks into his dad living room while his brothers were already seated.

"What's the meaning of that Aasim?" asked President Ambo.

"What's it, dad? Maybe I should return to my flat, it's obvious you're always holding a grudge against me," Aasim protested. President Ambo was quick with his harsh rebuke of Aasim. "Interfering when your brother is instilling order into his wife and taking sides against your brother is a step too far," said President Ambo.

Aasim reminded his dad that Malik had a gun with him, moreover Arfa was already bleeding from the injury Malik inflicted on her, and worst of all, Malik wanted to shoot her legs.

"But that doesn't excuse your action of carrying your elder brother on your shoulder like a baby, and locked him up," insists President Ambo.

"Did he tell you he hurt me with the butt of his gun?" asked Aasim.

The president reminded Aasim in no uncertain terms that whatever Malik did to him shouldn't warrant his carrying the next President of the Republic of Kitan on his shoulder like a baby.

"Meaning, you're unaffected by the ill treatment your son meted out on his wife," asked Aasim.

"It doesn't matter what Malik has done, the lady in question isn't your sister, so why're you perturbed?" asked President Ambo.

Aisha couldn't stomach what she just heard her husband said about his son's ineptitude, she then intervened. "Aasim, allow your dad to wallow in his delusion, unfortunately that's the only virtue he could pass to his eldest son," said Aisha.

"Mum, why're you always against me, should I watch my wife disrespect me?" asked Malik.

Aisha turned to Malik and asked, if his dad hadn't been the President, if he would have the guts to shoot his wife and break her legs. Malik remained illusory and urged his mum to stay out of his family affair.

Aasim had to further fuel his mum' anger and reminded his mum that information reaching him was that those Christians Malik ordered Commissioner Azeem to beat up, placed a curse on Malik and even on their dad because they think the President sanctioned their torture.

Malik shrugged off the news and muttered under his breath saying what would the curse from infidels do to a man like him. After all, they are only expressing their miserableness.

"Ahh, a group of Christians placed a curse on you, and you consider it as nothing?" asked Aisha.

Malik insists, these curses are meaningless because they lack potency, and after all, they're coming from infidels.

Aisha turned to Malik, a second time and took him down memory lane. "A group of Islamic Ulamas placed a curse on you the other time for being rude to them. How did your dad respond? He killed one of them, chopped off the hands of another, and cut off the ear of another and fed it to his dog," said Aisha.

"But it's just you and I that knew dad was behind the death of the Ulama," said Malik.

"Do you think the people have no knowledge of this? It's just because they lack the guts to tell your dad he's responsible," said Aisha.

Malik insists he doesn't think his dad's actions are a public knowledge because these things were done secretly. Aisha slapped down Malik's rhetoric as she reminded him that even though the president operates by stealth, people can still sense his handwork, and asked if he has forgotten that close doors no longer close the world out. She was quite pained by her son's stupidity and rebuked him in a manner that wiped the filthy smirk off his face.

President Ambo couldn't bear to hear Aisha dishing out platitudes on her son. "Enough Aisha, I've told you repeatedly that I don't want a weakling for a son," said President Ambo.

"They cursed Malik and you, dad! Don't take the cry of these innocent Christians for granted," said Aasim.

President Ambo then asked what the curse was, but Malik laughed instead, after all, he'd his dad by side. He then described Aasim as an angel who wants to make angels out of them all.

"They prayed for a revolution that will bring an end to dad's leadership, and that you Malik will not ascend into that Presidential office," said Aasim.

President Ambo suddenly stood up in anger and said this group of Christians have bitten more than they can chew. He's not having a group of religious infidels placing curses on him and his son, and he then said he wants these Christians picked up from their houses, so he could teach them some lessons.

Funnily, Aasim subtly informed his raging dad that these Christians have left the country after that persecution from Malik, they now live in Egypt.

"Maybe I'll renew my ban on the gatherings of infidels," said President Ambo.

"Ambo, a curse of this nature was placed on your son, and you take it as nothing?" asked Aisha.

She then turned to Malik and reminded him he's already on the garden path, and his dad is leading him into an untimely ghastly end. Nawal walks in while the conversation was still on, and informed her mum, that Arfa just called to inform her of what Malik did. Aisha responded saying she have just scolded him for battering his wife.

"That's not it, Arfa's parents were locked up in a cell, on Malik's instruction," said Nawal.

Aisha turned to the President. "Ambo, did you hear Nawal, and are you aware of this?" she asked.

"I've no knowledge of this but if Malik did, he must have a genuine reason for doing so," said Mr. President.

Aisha turned to Malik and asked how he dared to lock up his in-laws after inflicting injuries on their daughter, but Malik remained unperturbed and said all he wanted from them is the whereabouts of his wife. Nawal had to break the ice and said Arfa told her Malik injured her, and she's somewhere private treating her wounds.

Aisha quickly reached for the phone and dialled Colonel Abdallah, instructing him she wants Arfa's parents released immediately.

Malik interjected immediately. "No mum, you can't just release them without full knowledge of my wife's whereabouts," he insists.

Aisha went ahead anyway, and immediately she finished speaking with the Colonel, she then turned to Malik. "Colonel Abdallah just referred to you as the Prime Minister, did you order him to refer to you as that?" asked Aisha.

"Mum what are you driving at? I'm the next man to dad, so I deserve that title," insists Malik.

President Ambo was irked by Aisha's excessive scrutiny of Malik's actions. He quickly rebuked Aisha and admonished her for getting too involved in this matter. He insists, Malik should be allowed the latitude to sort things out himself.

"No, I can't sit on my hands and watch my son continue in this slippery path, this is a gross abuse of power," Aisha insists.

President Ambo had to find a way to address Aisha's concerns, at least to take her heat out of the mix, he then turned to Malik. "You're the Minister of Finance and not the Prime Minister, don't attract unnecessary attention to yourself," said President Ambo.

"Mum, allow me to handle my business with my wife," said Malik.

Aisha got back on the on phone to Colonel Abdallah and instructed him not to attempt to return Arfa's parents back to that cell.

Three days later, Malik walked into his dad's office and requested he strip Arfa's parents of all the privileges they enjoy as a result of their association with the President's family. President Ambo stopped what he's doing and asked Malik if Arfa still refusing to return home to him. Malik shook his head in affirmation, and said news reaching him now is that she's presently in Dubai.

"How come! I don't think Arfa can be this stupid to step on the tail of a rattle snake," said President Ambo.

Malik proceeded to inform his dad that he'd just called the airport and it was confirmed she boarded the flight to Dubai.

"Does Arfa and her parents think they can toy with my family in this manner?" asked President Ambo.

"I've had enough of her discourtesy," said Malik.

President Ambo felt Arfa's parents' were taking him for a ride and Arfa has bitten off more than she can chew this time. He then asked Malik to leave the matter to him because he would need to question her parents further.

"I told mum to allow me deal with this matter in my own way, but she ordered Abdallah to set them free," said Malik.

"I won't take insults from Arfa, get her parents, I want them brought before me," said President Ambo.

Hours later, the Presidential guards marched Arfa's parents before the President. President Ambo looked around and asked. "Where's Arfa? I want to see her now," he said.

"My inlaw, that won't be possible, Arfa isn't in the Republic of Kitan as we speak," said Arfa's dad.

"Why won't that be possible? I said I want her to explain herself to me," asked President Ambo. Arfa's dad confessed to President Ambo that she called him from Dubai this morning, and he'd no idea she was travelling.

"Hmm, ooh, you're encouraging your daughter to run away from her husband, do you think you can humiliate my family?" asked President Ambo.

"My inlaw, Arfa said your son wanted to shoot her with a gun, and if not for Aasim Arfa would've been dead," said Arfa's mum.

President Ambo quickly came to his son's defence, insisting the allegation isn't true, and if Malik had wanted Arfa dead she would've been dead long ago.

Arfa's dad continued to plead with the President as he said they'd no knowledge she was travelling to Dubai, and they only learnt she's outside the country in the morning of that day.

"Meaning, you've been in contact with your daughter, and you want to take us for fools?" asked President Ambo.

"No, Mr. President we've tried talking Arfa into returning home, but she refused," said Arfa's dad.

President Ambo looked this couple straight in the eyes and said he'd to strip them of some of the privileges they enjoy from him. Arfa's mum interjected, she then turned to Malik to help.

"My in-law, please give us a little more time to address this matter," she pleads.

Sadly, Malik isn't a likely source to turn to for help, as he now insists he's no longer interested in taking Arfa back.

"Please don't do this," said Arfa's dad.

President Ambo changed his demand of having Arfa return to his son, and said he'll get another woman for his son since he's no longer interested in Arfa. Malik insists he's no longer interested in their daughter. He then put a phone call across to have their bank account frozen and ordered them to vacate the President's properties and return to their old life.

A week later, Aasim travelled to Germany to see his fiancée, a German. President Ambo walked into the living room, he then turned to Nawal. "Where's your brother?" he asked.

"Dad, which of my brothers?" replied Nawal.

President Ambo rhetorically reminded Nawal that Malik and Umar are sitting right beside her, so she should know it's Aasim he's talking about.

"Why should it be me you're asking? There are four of us here, including mum," said Nawal.

Malik interjected and reminded Nawal that their dad directed the questions to her because she and Aasim are but two peas in a pod, that's why their dad believes she should know where he is. "Then, you're right, he left for Germany last night," said Nawal.

This isn't the kind of response President Ambo wants to hear, Nawal's response actually spooked him, he then growled, and said Aasim has no right to leave the house without informing him. Aisha quickly came to Aasim's defence and subtly reminded the President that he and Aasim don't see eye to eye on a lot of issues, and maybe this is his way of avoiding another altercation.

"I told him to work with me instead of going to play football in England," said President Ambo.

Nawal knew her dad doesn't forget and doesn't forgive, she quickly told him Aasim travelled to Germany to see his fiancée, and not to England, and maybe the thought of continuing to work with his dad is still in his mind.

"But dad told him to bring his fiancée here, so he wouldn't be travelling here and there," said Malik.

"Most of his Aasim properties are in Germany, so why ask him to stop travelling to Germany?" asked Nawal.

"He'll meet me here when he comes back," said President Ambo.

Nawal just couldn't get her head around why her dad insists it must be Aasim that should be his eyes in the military. She then asked her dad why he isn't offering Malik the job of the head of intelligence in the military.

"He's the minister for finance and he's understudying me at the same time, because he'll be President one day," said President Ambo.

"Ok, but Aasim has a better idea of how a true leader should govern his people, and if only you'll give him a free hand, he'll help your government prosper," said Nawal.

Weeks after President Ambo Hussein's announcement, declaring the political process open for all. The leader of the Democratic Alliance Party Sheikh Suleiman Zurumi and his deputy Engineer Habu Kanti, who are fierce critics of General Ambo Hussein visited the electoral commission's office to pick the form for the Presidential election. Suleiman Zurumi is based in Abidkitan the second largest city in the Republic of Kitan and he's a man loved by many in Kitan. Sheikh Suleiman walked into the office of Ambassador Quasquas, they exchanged pleasantries and the Sheikh took his seat as he made himself comfortable.

Ambassador Quasquas then welcomed Sheikh Suleiman to his office. Ambassador Quasquas was a former Ambassador of the Republic of Kitan to Turkey, and now appointed as the national electoral commissioner.

"We're here to indicate interest in the forthcoming election," said Sheikh Zurumi.

"Are you running for governorship or your deputy, Engineer Habu Kanti is the person running?" asked Amb. Quasquas.

Engineer Habu Kanti interjected and reminded the ambassador they're quite aware he conducts only governorship and other local elections in this country, and they aren't talking of the governorship election.

"Then which of the elections are you here for?" asked Amb. Quasquas.

"The presidential election, of course!" exclaimed Sheikh Zurumi.

"What, presidential election?" asked Amb. Quasquas.

Engineer Habu Kanti interjected again and told the ambassador the Sheikh is clear about what he wants, that they're about the presidential election and nothing else.

Ambassador Quasquas finds this topic to be quite thorny, yet insists he only gets involve in governorship and other elections in the country and doesn't involve himself in anything that relates to presidential elections.

"But President Ambo Hussein did say in his speech that the democratic process for the office of the President has been declared open," said Sheikh Zurumi.

The electoral commissioner looked at them and rhetorically asked them if they think the President really meant what he said.

Engineer Habu Kanti dug his heel in and said if the President said it just to make the world see him as leader who appreciates democracy, then they would let the world know he's a liar.

"But we don't have any form for presidential elections, and I'll have to speak with the President about this," said Amb. Quasquas.

"Ok, we'll be here next week Tuesday to pick up the form," said Sheikh Zurumi.

Moments after they left, the National Electoral Commissioner called President Ambo to discuss the visit of Sheikh Suleiman Zurumi, a man who could possibly be the President's nemesis.

"Hello Ambassador, how're you?" asked President Ambo.

"Mr. President, Sheikh Suleiman Zurumi just left my office, he came to pick up the form for the presidential elections," said Amb. Quasquas.

President Ambo laughed, but the laughter dissipated quickly with the frown that followed. He then asked the electoral commissioner what made Sheikh Suleiman think the office of the President is vacant.

Ambassador Quasquas toned down his voice and spoke calmly to avoid being in the President's crosshairs. "They said you declared the electoral process open, during your Silver jubilee speech," said Amb. Quasquas.

Funnily, President Ambo didn't even bother putting a sock on it, he just smiled and said his comments were mere stunts, and he wasn't serious about that.

Ambassador Quasquas was now between a rock and a hard place, and needed a neat way of extricating himself from this quagmire. He then asked the President what he should tell the Sheikh if they come back as they've promised.

"Don't worry, get the forms for the presidential elections ready and give it to them, but there won't be an election when the time comes," said President Ambo.

"Mr. President, you mean I should just continue with the whole process as if there will be an election?" asked Amb. Quasquas.

President Ambo concurred and urged the electoral commissioner to carry on with the presidential election, and he then said he knows what to do when the time comes.

"Ok, thank you Mr. President," said Amb. Quasquas.

The response of the United States Foreign Secretary to General Ambo's Speech.

Allan Hill: Today the United States wishes to express support for the people of the Republic of Kitan. As you all know, the speech by General Ambo to make Kitan a democratic nation has been noted by the United States, and as a result of this the United States and its Allies will give every support necessary to help the Republic of Kitan transit to a fully democratic nation. However, we wish to encourage the President not to renege on his word, because it will put a question mark on his credibility.

Six Months after indicating his interest in the presidential election, Sheikh Suleiman Zurumi called Hassan Mustapha to request for an opportunity to take part in the TV program, "the political viewpoint".

"Hello, is that Kitan Broadcasting Service?" asked Sheikh Zurumi.

"Yes, this is Hassan Mustapha speaking," he replied.

"Good, this is Sheikh Suleiman, I'm calling from Abidkitan," said Sheikh Zurumi.

"Sheikh, I know you, what can we do for you?" asked Hassan.

"I want to participate in the program you're hosting," said Sheikh Zurumi.

Hassan Mustapha reminded the Sheikh he anchors two programs and asked which of them the Sheikh intends to be a part of.

"The political viewpoint," said Sheikh Zurumi.

Hassan Mustapha reminded the Sheikh that guests on the program aren't allowed to use words that are considered rude to the President of the Republic of Kitan.

The Sheikh told Hassan Mustapha he has registered his interest to run in the presidential election and wants to sell his manifesto to the people of Kitan.

"Then you're welcome to be my guest on the program "the political viewpoint," said Hassan.

Sheikh Zurumi thanked the programme host for giving him the opportunity, but before they end the phone conversation. Hassan Mustapha had to officially inform the Sheikh he'll be his guest next week Thursday, so urged him to come prepared with his manifesto.

Aasim returns from Germany and delays returning to office as the Kitan's head of military intelligence.

President Ambo got the hint of Aasim's return from Germany and decided to track him down, but he obviously isn't going to give him a pat on the back, rather to vent. "Aasim, where are you heading off to this morning?" asked President Ambo.

Aasim didn't even bat an eyelid, neither was he remorseful over going AWOL, he just gave it straight and said he's going to the football field to train.

"After talking to you the other time about returning to head my military intelligence unit, your way of telling me no, was to travel to Germany to join your girlfriend, wasn't it?" said President Ambo.

Aasim quickly corrected his dad and said Nicole isn't his girl friend, she's his fiancée, and his dad knows it.

"Does that matter, why did you run off to her when you've work to do?" asked President Ambo.

"Dad, the truth is, I'm avoiding a situation where you and I might have misunderstanding," said Aasim.

President Ambo looked straight into Aasim and asked how, and what misunderstanding he's talking about.

Aasim confessed to his dad that there are lots of killings going on, and he doesn't want to be associated with that in anyway.

"Have I asked you to kill anybody, what's your problem then?" asked President Ambo.

Aasim remained hesitant and asked how he expects him to rush back to the military having full knowledge of the lurid details of their impunity. President Ambo insists his children must be strategically positioned to help to keep him secure and that's why he wants him back.

Aasim saw the trajectory of the conversation, and realised his dad is using moral suasion on him, he had to wriggle himself out of his clutches. He then urged his dad to give him some time to assess whether returning to the military is something he can do.

President Ambo knew what it meant to give Aasim the latitude of time, he quickly reminded Aasim that the last time they spoke about this, he requested for some time and the week after, he ran off to Germany.

"But I'm here now, though I still need some time to ruminate on your propositions, and I'm doing that painstakingly," said Aasim.

President Ambo started walked away from Aasim, but not without reminding him to learn being useful to his dad.

It's time for Nawal to return to school. She walked into the living room where her mum was seated and watching the news, she then told her she's set to leave.

"Oh, so quick, why don't you stay a couple of days more? After all this is your students' week," said Aisha.

"I've to go, my girls are waiting for me," said Nawal.

"What do you mean by your 'girls', who're they?" asked Aisha. Realising she's speaking to her mum, Nawal quickly corrected herself and said she meant to say her friends are expecting her to return because they've got a lot to do.

"Has your dad settled you?" asked Aisha.

Nawal reminded her mum that her dad doesn't give her cash, and all he does is transfer money to her account.

"Then, has he done that?" asked Aisha.

"Yes, he has, where's he? I need to let him know I'm leaving, and my flight will be due within the hour," said Nawal.

Umar walked into the conversation and overhead his sister talking about a flight that's due within the hour. "What do you mean your flight? And don't tell me you're travelling by public transport," he asked.

"Yes of course, and that's what I intend to do," replied Nawal.

Umar thinks her sister is really foolish for her naivety, and then questioned her judgement of denying herself the enjoyment of the privileges that comes with being the daughter of the President.

Nawal is controlled by her mindset of the secular world, funny enough she is studying in Turkey but aligns herself to the secular aspect of the Turkish society. "There isn't anything new with being the President's daughter, I love hanging around people," said Nawal.

Umar remained amused by his sister perception of life, he then asked why she enjoys looking like an ordinary person on the street, when she already has a silver spoon in her mouth.

She stunningly insists nothing makes her different from the common man on the street, aside this unnecessary display of flamboyance and showiness, which is the result of wealth accrued from oppressed masses.

Umar shook his head in pity for his sister, yet reminded her, he perhaps likes the puffiness, the splurge and the splashiness that's attached to the silver spoon in his own mouth, if his sister doesn't appreciate hers.

"Enough of this debate Umar, your sister just said her flight is within the hour," said Aisha.

"It seems like Aasim's ideology has gotten a hold of her mentality," said Umar.

"Leave Aasim out of this, you're free to remain inside your cocoon as the son of Mr. President, but my flight is due, and I need see dad," said Nawal. She left her brother and proceeded to see her dad, and immediately she stepped in President Ambo asked her if she's ready to leave for school.

"Yes dad, and my flight will be due within the hour," said Nawal.

President Ambo insists he still doesn't like Nawal's idea of taking public fight to Turkey, he then asked of Colonel Abdullah's whereabouts so he could take her to the airport.

Nawal seem not too keen for her security, she didn't hesitate to let her dad know, she has arranged for a special cab to take her to the airport. Sadly, her penchant for freedom has gone too far, and this makes a mockery out of the office of the president.

"What, do I hear you say, a cab? You've two cars, and a driver to yourself, so why would you need a cab?" asked President Ambo. Nawal seem to have overstepped the mark, and this got her dad irked, yet she insists she just love being simple whenever she's in the midst of people.

"You aren't leaving this house except Colonel Abdallah takes you to the airport," said President Ambo.

"But you know this isn't what I want?" asked Nawal.

President Ambo admonished her for making a mess of her privileges and reminded her she's beginning to share in Aasim's recklessness.

"Dad you know I don't like it when you interfere in my affairs like this," she protested.

President Ambo's love for his only daughter means her tantrums gets to him because she has her way of getting at her dad. Despite his sanctions, the President still has a soft spot for his daughter, so he'd to cheer her up. "Tell Colonel Abdallah to take you to the airport, it's for your own good," said President Ambo.

"Ok, as it pleases your majesty," said Nawal. She then walked to the living room as she waits for Colonel Abdallah.

"What did he say?" asked Umar.

"Who?" asked Nawal.

"Dad of course, did he support your travelling with a public transport?" asked Umar.

Nawal insists her debate with her dad isn't about public flight, he just don't want her to take a cab to the airport.

"Ok, I wish you a safe journey," said Umar.

Nawal then went downstairs to Colonel Abdallah and left for school.

CHAPTER
TWO
The Exile

Sheikh Zurumi is taking part in the political talk show "the political viewpoint," anchored by Hassan Mustapha. Interestingly, this talk-show only hosts governorship candidates and those contesting in other local elections, aside electoral aspirants, this show host government ministers keeping the people informed about the activities of government.

Hassan Mustapha: Viewers we're into another edition of your favourite program the political viewpoint, I'm your regular host Hassan Mustapha. In today's broadcast we're bringing you the leader of the Democratic Alliance Party of Kitan a popular and though controversial figure, to air his view on the politics of our dear nation.

Hassan Mustapha: I'm your host Hassan Mustapha, Sheikh Suleiman Zurumi you're welcome.

"Viewers at home thank you for watching," said Sheikh Zurumi.

"Tell us about your party manifesto, our viewers are keen to hear from you," said Hassan.

Sheikh Zurumi: We the Democratic Alliance Party, has only one mission, and that mission is to bring an end to dictatorial rule in our beloved nation.

Hassan Mustapha turned to the Sheikh and asked him to tell the viewers how his manifesto translates into a better life for the citizens of the Republic of Kitan.

Sheikh Zurumi: There are lots of things we want to do for our people, but first we must move the ownership of this nation from the hands of one man and his family to the hands of the people.

"Ok, please continue," said Hassan.

Sheikh Zurumi continued and said that it's only when the citizens decides who governs them that the life of every citizen of Kitan will matter, and they'll all have a say on how they should be governed.

Hassan Mustapha: But the President of the Republic of Kitan has done marvellously well for the people, through free education, free housing schemes and a whole lot more. How does your party intend to do more than what our President has done already?

Sheikh Zurumi: The schools you talked about, the houses and everything you've mentioned are all the properties of the people of the Republic of Kitan. This shouldn't be considered a favour.

Hassan Mustapha: What will the political landscape be like if your party happens to win the upcoming election?

Sheikh Zurumi: The political landscape will be democratic, in which the people decide on every matter affecting them.

Hassan Mustapha: Sheikh, give us your final word as we round off this program.

Sheikh Zurumi: People of Kitan, look around the Middle East, the days of dictatorship are over, it's time you decide how our country should be run.

Hassan Mustapha: Sheikh, thank you for coming, viewers that's all for today until same time next week.

After watching Sheikh Suleiman's interview on the television, President Ambo Hussein was filled with rage and sent his guards to arrest his uncle, Sheikh Abdul Hussein who's the Director of Kitan Broadcasting Corporation. He also ordered the arrest of the host of the TV program the "Political Viewpoint," Hassan Mustapha.

Sheikh Abdul's arrest didn't only leave him on the back foot, it came to him as a shock because the benignity of his political theocracy.

Colonel Abdallah waited calmly for the Sheikh while he prays in the mosque and immediately Sheikh Abdul steps out of the mosque, Colonel Abdallah walked up to him. "Sheikh Abdul, good evening" he said.

"Colonel, where you going with your Presidential guards, are you making an arrest in the mosque?" asked Sheik Abdul.

"I'm sorry Sheikh, it's you I've come for, Mr. President wants you," said Colonel Abdallah.

"Me? Wait a minute, and you're coming to me with Presidential guards?" asked Sheikh Abdul.

"Yeah, it's just routine, nothing more," said Colonel Abdallah.

Sheikh Abdul didn't buy Colonels Abdullah's excuses, and his efforts to assuage the Sheikh of his concerns didn't do the job either. The Sheikh then insists that's if it's nothing, why then didn't Colonel Abdallah give him a phone call to let him know the President wants' him. He then reached for his phone to call President Ambo and inquire what the arrest is all about.

Colonel Abdallah prevented the Sheikh from making any phone calls, and said he's sorry, the orders from the President include denying him access to phone calls, and that includes a phone call to Mr. President.

"Are you aware that President Ambo is my nephew? Ok then, let me speak to my son," said Sheikh Abdul.

"Sheikh Ali will hear about this later, you aren't allowed to make calls," said Colonel Abdallah.

The Sheikh chuckled with a nod, he then muttered under his breath and said this isn't a mere invitation, it's an arrest. "Are you out to embarrass me or what?" asked Sheikh Abdul.

Colonel Abdallah knew he's dealing with the President's uncle, he then pleaded with the Sheikh, saying he has no hand in this. He assured the Sheikh he's just following orders and to be frank, he was quite surprised when he was ordered to arrest the Sheikh.

"What about my car, should I drive behind you or what?" asked Sheikh Abdul.

"I'll join you in your car, while my men will come behind us," said Colonel Abdallah.

An hour later, Sheikh Abdul was brought before Mr. President. "What's the meaning of this?" asked Sheikh Abdul.

"Uncle, I gave you and your family the opportunity to enjoy with me but you're now taking side with my enemies," said President Ambo.

"My son, why're you doing this? You're my blood, I can't work against you," replied Sheikh Abdul.

President Ambo picked up the remote control and told him to watch this if he's pretending not to know what he has done, he then played back Hassan Mustapha's interview with Sheikh Suleiman Zurumi.

"What! Why should Hassan grant an interview of this nature without consulting me?" said Sheikh Abdul.

"Uncle, don't pretend you don't know, because you're meant to vet their program line up," said President Ambo.

Sheikh Abdul then asked the President to give him a minute so he could find Hassan Mustapha and let him know he shouldn't have aired such an interview. He then promised to discipline Hassan Mustapha for this.

"You're going nowhere, Uncle. Hassan Mustapha will join you in the cell soon," said President Ambo.

Hassan Mustapha was marched in as the President and his uncle argues. "Mr. President, they said you want to see me," said Hassan Mustapha.

Sheikh Abdul was still speaking through the bars of the cell where he was locked up, and he then asked Hassan why he granted the interview.

Hassan Mustapha didn't hesitate to ask the Sheikh what interview he's talking about. Sheikh Abdul spoke with quite a low voice as he points out to Mustapha, he's referring to the interview with Sheikh Suleiman. He then expressed his disappointment with Mustapha for not clarifying with him before going ahead with the interview. Everyone knows the three wise monkeys that embody the proverbial principle of see no evil, hear no evil, and speak no evil. That sadly, is about to unravel before the eyes of this old uncle of Mr President. The President then turned to Hassan Mustapha to make his case, even though there's nothing altruistic about this brouhaha.

"Welcome Mr. TV presenter, I sent for you, please join your director in the prison cell," said the President.

Hassan Mustapha apologised to the President, saying he's sorry, yet said he doesn't understand what he' has done wrong. President Ambo was quite upfront as he pointed out to Hassan Mustapha that he brought Sheikh Suleiman Zurumi to insult him before the people of the Republic of Kitan.

"No Mr. President, you know I wouldn't do a thing like that," said Hassan.

"But you just did, by giving him the one opportunity he has been looking for, the Television," said President Ambo.

Hassan Mustapha's excuses didn't do the job of persuading this livid President, and sadly there's no need grasping on straws any further because this is about to precipitate into a grim end.

"But Mr President, during your Silver jubilee broadcast, you said the opposition party is free to campaign through whatever channel it deems fit," said Hassan.

President Ambo became highly incensed. "Where's the signed document authorising you to do that?" asked President Ambo.

"I'm sorry Mr. President, and I never knew this interview would irk you," said Hassan. President Ambo looked away as he told Hassan Mustapha, now he knows, and he won't live to repeat this mistake. The President then took a pistol from one of his guards and pointed it at Hassan.

Sheikh Abdul interjected immediately, and pleaded with Mr. President, and he begged him not to shoot, Hassan Mustapha joined in the plea, and sadly, the President fired three shots at Hassan Mustapha.

"Oh no, Mr. President I'm sorry," said Hassan. The President looked away, without any change in his disposition that showed he has just taken a life, and moments later, Hassan Mustapha took his last breath then died, and lights out.

Sheikh Abdul was quite open mouthed as he watched President Ambo waste Hassan Mustapha and he didn't hesitate to let the President know it hasn't come to this, and none of this is intentional.

President Ambo remained unperturbed, and as far he's concerned, it was as if a fly has just been wasted. He then turned to Sheikh

Abdul and called him, Uncle. "You're my blood, and I won't kill you because you're my blood, but I'll send you very far away," said President Ambo.

Sheikh Abdul pleaded with the President and urged him not to do this. "I'm your old uncle who has worked with you, in all sincerity," said Sheikh Abdul.

President Ambo then asked his uncle to choose any country of choice, Saudi Arabia, Quarter, Turkey, Egypt or any country he likes to live, but he doesn't want to see him ever again. Bent on keeping his promise of offering his son the position of the Director of Kitan's Broadcasting Service, and now that this moment of schadenfreude has presented itself, President Ambo Hussein will do nothing but exploit it.

The President then left his uncle behind bars and went into his office and came back minutes later, he came back with a cheque in his hand. He then told his uncle this is a cheque of Two million dollars, he handed it to him and asked him to just take it and leave the country.

"Mr. President, I'm an eighty-six years old man, how can I cope, and what about my family?" asked Sheikh Abdul.

President Ambo assured his uncle that his children will be safe in the Republic of Kitan. He promised him nothing will happen to them as long as his uncle doesn't give bad publicity to his government from wherever he chooses to reside.

"What does that mean, I don't understand?" asked Sheikh Abdul.

"The day you say anything negative about my government from whatever country you're, that day your children will beg for their lives," said President Ambo.

Sheikh Abdul was taken over by this ominous silence, and looked lost in this sudden debacle that has just befallen him. He then reminded his nephew that there are other ways of handling this, before he proceeded to beg him, saying he doesn't want to leave his homeland.

President Ambo stretched his hand as he hands the cheque to his uncle despite his uncle's earlier refusal to take the cheque. "Take this cheque and leave now, or else, I'll send you away empty handed," said President Ambo.

Sheikh Abdul suddenly felt so drained, and had no choice but to collect the cheque and subtly reminded the President that this isn't a good send forth. The Sheikh took the cheque and left.

Sheikh Abdul went to his eldest son, Sheikh Ali, who's the same age with the President to inform him of the unfortunate decision of Mr. President.

Sheikh Ali saw his dad and suddenly realised something is off, he then asked his dad what the problem was and pointed out to his dad, he's looking pale.

"My son, walk with me," said Sheikh Abdul. They then walked into the back garden for a time alone, and he then took time to inform his son he has been banished.

"Banished, I don't understand, how dad?" asked Sheikh Ali.

Sheikh Abdul had to hit the nail on the head, and said the President asked him to leave the country to anywhere, and he gave him this. He then dipped his hand into his pocket and brought out the cheque and showed it to his son.

"This is strange, what did you do to deserve this from Ambo?" asked Sheikh Ali.

Sheikh Abdul had to narrate how things got to this point, and said the President got angry over the TV interview Hassan Mustapha granted to Sheikh Suleiman. Sheikh Ali exclaimed and said he did watch the interview and immediately knew President Ambo wouldn't like it yet insisted the President has taken this too far.

Sheikh Abdul then muttered under his breath, and said Hassan Mustapha is dead.

"What! He presented a program about two hours ago, and that can't be," said Sheikh Ali.

Sheikh Ali was gobsmacked with the too many revelations his dad was bringing to him, but his dad nodded and reminded his son that Hassan Mustapha died in his presence about forty minutes ago.

"Is it because of this interview?" asked Sheikh Ali.

"Yes, of course, he felt we're taking sides with his enemy," said Sheikh Abdul.

Sheikh Ali couldn't help but remind his dad that it was Hassan Mustapha that hosted the interview, and asked what that got to do with him, that he has to be banished.

Sheikh Abdul ruminated on his conversation with the President even as he reminisces on the gruesomeness of their meeting. He told his son he's the director of the broadcasting corporation, and the President thinks he should have known about it. "I told him I didn't, but he refused to believe me," said Sheikh Abdul.

Sheikh Ali couldn't bear to see his cousin treat his dad like a piece of dirt, he then stood up and told his dad to wait, so he could speak to President Ambo.

He then went over see President Ambo over the punishment he meted on his dad. President Ambo didn't even give room for any exchange of pleasantries, he went on to ask Sheikh Ali why he has come to see him.

"Ambo, when did you start asking me what I'm doing in your office?" asked Sheikh Ali.

"Ali, are you calling me Ambo, or Mr. President?" asked President Ambo.

"Ambo, I know you're the President of the Republic of Kitan, you don't need to remind me about that," said Sheikh Ali.

"I said, stop calling me Ambo, I'm Mr. President," said President Ambo.

Sheikh Ali insists he has called the President by his name right from their childhood, and even the morning of the same day, he called him, Ambo. "Why the sudden change, is it because of my father?" asked Sheikh Ali.

"Yes, your father has joined my enemies to work against me, and I won't forgive him, or do you intend to ruffle feathers with me?"

"Before now, when we're in public I call you Mr. President, and when we're alone I call you by your name, but you changed the whole thing just because you want to punish my dad, your uncle?" Sheikh Ali.

President Ambo reminded Sheikh Ali they're still cousins, brothers actually, but he should know he wouldn't tolerate anyone trying to undermine his authority.

Sheikh Ali felt lost, as his cousin allowed his heat to be awash with frivolous accusations. "Where does this misconception of adding us to your imaginary enemies come from?" asked Sheikh Ali.

President Ambo cautioned Sheikh Ali and urged him to stop making flippant remarks against him in his office and insists that won't be tolerated.

"You and I are sixty-year-old men and my dad is eighty-six, why not allow him live out the rest of his life here in Kitan where he belongs?" said Sheikh Ali.

President Ambo reminded Sheikh Ali he can't make him reverse the decision concerning his dad. Sheikh Ali decided it's best to set aside the fiery exchanges, he then sat down, in an attempt to plead with President to change course. He reminded the President they've been loyal to him and have never in anyway betrayed him. "I've put my life on the line for you, and why're you doing this?" he asked.

"Because I'm the President, and also, because I've the power," replied President Ambo.

Sheikh Ali was shocked at the President's response. "You mean because you've the power?" asked Sheikh Ali.

"I'm a lion, this is my territory, and the audacity is mine," said President Ambo.

Sheikh Ali went mum for a while, as his instinct told him this isn't just about Hassan Mustapha, it's rather a premeditated decision, and sadly his dad is in the crosshairs of the President. He then subtly asked the President if he has been looking for an opportunity to punish his family, even when they laugh and eat together as brothers.

"I've had enough of your nonsense, leave before I ask my guards to walk you out, and tell your dad I give him just twenty-four hours to pack his bags," said President Ambo.

"Ambo, it's a shame you're doing this to us, your flesh and blood," said Sheikh Ali.

President Ambo reminded Ali that his dad shouldn't have put himself in this conundrum. "Ambo, even if my dad has found himself in this quagmire or conundrum as you call it, I expect that you apply some discretion for the sake of family," said Sheikh Ali.

President Ambo stood up and said he has exhausted every possibility for discretion on this matter, he then ordered Sheikh Ali to leave his office.

"Ok, ok, I'm already on my way," said Sheik Ali.

Sheikh Ali left President Ambo and went back home, depressed and angry. His dad, who has hoped for good news was quick to ask how the whole thing went, and what President Ambo said.

"Ambo is crazy; he told me he's doing this because he has the power to do whatever he likes," said Sheikh Ali.

Sheikh Abdul looked on in surprise, and muttered to himself, and asking what has the world turned into. After all, his nephew, whom he has given all the needed support to stay in power has turned on him in such an uncanny manner. Sadly, it was quite obvious that his uncle wasn't even offered a chalice, yet his nephew accused him of drinking the chalice and punished him for that.

"Dad, don't worry you'll be fine, you should go to Qatar and stay, their government will take care of you. At least, they know you as the uncle to the President of the Republic of Kitan," said Sheikh Ali.

Sheikh Abdul was lost in thought as to his life in exile going forward, and he serendipitously gave an unsettling smile, then said Ambo is now a plague and the wickedness embedded in his underbelly is showing through his brazen impunity.

Sheikh Ali couldn't hold back his concerns of how incendiary he finds the President' remarks and said President Ambo's political grandstanding of calling himself the lion of Kitan, adds a new colouration to the mix.

"What about your mum, how'll she cope?" asked Sheikh Abdul.

"I'll speak to mum," said Sheikh Ali.

Sheikh Ali went to his mum, Aminat, to keep her abreast of his dad's debacle. He met his mum knitting a sweater for her grand-daughter which is her usual hobby, then sat beside her.

"Mum, how're you doing?" asked Sheikh Ali.

"My son I'm fine, I saw your wife at the women centre, but we didn't have time to talk, how's she?" asked Aminat.

"She's fine, but she wasn't home as at the time I left," said Sheikh Ali.

His mum then asked Sheikh Ali if he came to the mosque for prayers and decided to drop by to say hello to them.

Sheikh Ali subtly shook his head in refutation and said he has come to see her because his dad has a little problem.

"Your dad seems ok, that's him sitting in the back garden. What's the problem about?" asked Aminat.

Sheikh Ali toned down his voice as he told his mum his dad has been banished by Ambo.

The news was quite shocking enough that it left Aminat spooked. She thought her son was having a laugh, as she asked her son, "what sort of joke is that?" After all, Ambo is his dad's nephew.

Sheikh Ali's facial disposition didn't reflect a man making jokes. Such a joke will be quite an expensive one, and to buttress the seriousness of the situation, he told his mum that President Ambo has killed Hassan Mustapha for granting an interview to Sheikh Suleiman, and now, he's banishing his dad for the same offence.

"What! Are you telling me Hassan Mustapha is dead?" asked Aminat. "Yes, of course, he killed him in dad's presence," said Sheikh Ali.

Aminat stopped what she was doing and insists someone needs to talk some sense into Ambo, she then turned to her son and urged him to talk to President Ambo. Sadly, she was more disappointed when Sheikh Ali told her he has gone to him and talked with him, but he ordered him out.

Aminat insists that the lack of benignity in the manner with which President Ambo rules his people, she knew he would turn on them one day. She just doesn't know how and when, unfortunately her husband never saw this coming.

"He has been ruling the people with an iron fist, and one day the people will turn on him just as it's all over the Middle East," said Sheikh Ali.

This is a sad day for this family, Aminat couldn't get her head around this sudden quagmire that came upon them, she then asked Sheikh Ali what his dad intends do about it.

"Dad will leave for Qatar tomorrow; you can go with him immediately or possibly join him a week later," said Sheikh Ali.

Aminat fought back tears, as she exclaimed that Ambo has just shattered the little peace they're enjoying in this home. She proceeded to say President Ambo has killed a lot of people and has destroyed a lot of families and has now turned on his uncle. This family have largely been equivocal about the brutal acts of this President, they've stood by him through thick and thin, and sadly, the chickens have now come home to roost.

"Mum, this nation has morphed into the most bizarre of times," said Sheikh Ali.

Aminat placed her hand on her cheek, as she imagines leaving her homeland for a life with her husband in exile. Yet, she couldn't get her head around why a mere interview should result in the death of Hassan Mustapha. She chuckled and said Ambo Hussein's horrible polemics has plunged Kitan into a land soaked with blood, and then asked, who knows what he'll do next. She then said her husband should leave the next day, while she will join him a week later.

"Mum, don't worry, you'll be fine. Dad will leave tomorrow," said Sheikh Ali. After having a conversation with his mum, Sheikh Ali joined his dad at the garden.

"Dad, mum will join you a week from now, I'll bring her to Qatar," said Sheikh Ali.

"Please, you'll take me round the town tonight; let me see this city of Ansarouh one more time," said Sheikh Abdul.

Sheikh Ali became methodical, and suddenly put his contingencies into action, he immediately assured his dad, he will be giving a press statement on the matter immediately he leaves for Qatar.

"No, don't do that, my son. He'll hurt you badly if you try that," said Sheikh Abdul.

Sheikh Ali seems to be ready for a grandstanding with President Ambo, he insists he doesn't care what follows but the world needs to know about the evil inside President Ambo. Sadly, Sheikh Abdul wasn't mincing words when he advised his son to stay away. He told his son, the President categorically warned him never to say anything negative about his government from any country he resides, else his children will beg for their lives.

"Ambo has now resorted to threats," said Sheikh Ali.

Sheikh Abdul exposed the grim realities before them, and made it clear to his son that those threats from President Ambo aren't empty. The President's Uncle was more of the pious rather than being classed as the pitiless, as precipitated by his political the-ocracy, which make him quite a contrasting character from his nephew. "He's bloodthirsty, and I saw it in his eyes, don't fall into his trap," Sheikh Abdul warned.

"Ok then, I'll do as you've said," said Sheikh Ali.

Sheikh Ali then nods in affirmation to his dad and said it's now obvious that the days that have come upon them are evil. He however assured his dad, he'll be careful with Ambo and if not for himself, but for his children. Yet, his dad's stunning remark was that no one forced Ambo to transit to civil rule, and he sees no reason why the innocent would bear the brunt of President Ambo's political stunts.

The next morning Sheikh Abdul had to leave his fond memories behind as he left the Republic of Kitan for Qatar where he lived in exile and sadly, the only adult in the room has just been kicked out and scapegoated. His wife joined him in exile a week later, and Umar was appointed to replace Sheikh Abdul.

President Ambo walked out of his office and handed a letter to Umar, and he then asked him to open it.

Umar opened the letter and realised his dad had just fulfilled a promise he made to him in time past. "Oh dad, you made it happen, thank you," said Umar.

President Ambo smiled, displaying a cheeky grin that's nothing but a tale of sweet and sour, he then reminded his son of his promise to throw his uncle away to make the space for him. Funnily, he could contrive no more conspiracy against his uncle, all he has left is to cook something up.

"Dad, when am I starting?" asked Umar.

"It's there, it' clearly stated in your letter," replied President Ambo.

"Oh, thank you dad, I can't wait to start," said Umar.

A month after Umar's resumption of office, he was busy narrating to his sibling about his conquest in the office in one of the weekends, while he was in the company of his siblings in his dad's living room. Sadly, Aasim wasn't particularly thrilled about his brother's narratives; he then asked Umar how he felt about his new employment, "Oh, check me out in my executive office, my excitements can't be quantified," said Umar.

"I guess you're aware that an old man, and dad's uncle to be precise, was shamefully disgraced and sent into exile, just because dad wants' to create this position for you?" asked Aasim. Interestingly, Aasim's comment didn't do anything to wipe the smirk off Umar's face, as Umar remained unperturbed and told Aasim he doesn't need anyone reminding about how the job came about.

Aasim pressed on Umar and suggested he shouldn't have taken the job, and perhaps asked their dad to create another vacancy for him. Umar suddenly seemed to realise the job he just got has been tainted and dripping with the blood of the innocent. He then told Aasim he never thought of it that way, yet he reminded Aasim he wouldn't want to be like him that's never willing to take whatever opportunity their dad offers unblinkingly.

"Umar, you're my brother, I'll only tell you the truth," said Aasim.

"What's your truth, Aasim? Is it to make us see dad as a bad person," asked Umar?

Aasim smiled and said he doesn't have a different truth aside from the one truth, and that truth is that the man their dad sent to exile suffered so much unwarranted heart break and shame, but none of his siblings seem to care.

"I get your point but there's nothing I can do about that for now, I just have to go along with dad," said Umar.

"You feel this way because you've ran out of boxes," said Aasim.

Umar muttered and said it is, what it is.

Aasim interjected "Oh, que sera sera, I suppose?" asked Aasim.

"Yeah, what will be, will be," said Umar, he then stood up from his seat and left Aasim to continue sulking over sheikh Abdul's treatment.

CHAPTER

THREE

Blood on your hands

Two years after undergoing a successful surgery, Sadeq felt the need to call his dad, to inform him he's visiting his mum to demand answers.

After their usual exchange of pleasantries, Asif Qadri inquired of how Sadeq is fairing in Tunisia.

"Dad, we're fine, just that things haven't fully settled since the uprising in Tunisia. Asif Qadri went on to ask Sadeq about his wife, Rukiyat.

"She's fine, dad, but there's something I'll like to discuss with you," said Sadeq. Asif Qadri became curious and asked what it was his son wants to discuss with him. His dad was all ears, as he listened keenly to what his son had to say.

Sadeq knew this conversation is a grey area for his dad, yet he went on to inform his dad he wants to visit his mum so she could give him answers to some nagging questions that has been bugging his mind for years.

"What questions are you talking about?" asked Asif Qadri.

Sadeq reminded his dad that these questions are personal to him, and they depend on how he felt about them. He tried as much as he can to present his quest for answers in the most convincing way he could.

Asif Qadri didn't hesitate to restate his earlier position on this matter, but this time he went on to ask his son not to be foolish, and then urged him not to dare because President Ambo is a bloodthirsty monster.

"Dad, I can't back down now, my mind is made up," said Sadeq.

Asif Qadri realised his son's mind is made up, yet this is a spell binding trip that will leave him without sleep. Sadly, Asif is now boxed in the corner, so he resorted to pleading with his son. Asif Qadri knew too well that not all leaves are vegetables, some are herbs, and herbs are more potent, and sadly, he considers this president to be a herb. He reminded Sadeq not to mistake a herb for a vegetable, that they may look alike but a herb is a hundred times more potent than a vegetable, and insists, Ambo isn't what people think he is.

Sadeq is convinced he's man enough to sort things out with his mum, he then pleaded with his dad, begging him to let him do this.

Asif Qadri's voice cracked immediately, which reflects his desperation to stop his son from going ahead with this audacious move. He them muttered and said to himself. "How can I watch my son walk into his grave, son I'm begging you, don't do this," said Asif.

"Dad my mind is made up," said Sadeq.

Asif Qadri understands what this means, allowing his son to visit the wife of President Ambo, even though the woman is his mum, could unravel before his very eyes. This could immediately bring the past back to life and place him in the crosshairs of President Ambo. "Do you know this action could lead to my death, you're about to take away the little peace I'm enjoying," said Asif Qadri.

Sadeq insisted President Ambo Hussein isn't anything compared to a hornet's nest, and reminded his dad that all Ambo does is just issue empty threats.

Asif Qadri is now helpless after all effort to change the course of this conversation failed; he then asked his son when intends to make this trip to the Republic of Kitan.

"That will be next week Tuesday," said Sadeq.

"Ok, I wish you well," said Asif Qadri.

The next day Sadeq's dad called his son's wife, Rukiyat, to see if there's a way he could use her to persuade her husband from going ahead.

"Hello my daughter, how're you?" asked Asif Qadri.

"Baba, I'm fine," said Rukiyat.

Asif Qadri asked her how she's doing, and then asked if she's free to talk. Rukiyat replied to her father in-law that she'll be going out in thirty minutes time but she's free to talk for now.

"Ok, that'll be fine, and did your husband tell you he's visiting the Republic of Kitan to speak with his mum," asked Asif Qadri.

Rukiyat nodded in affirmation, even though she was on phone with her father in-law, and said she's quite aware of the move and thinks it's a good idea. At least, it's time for his mum to look at him in the eyes and tell him why she has been avoiding him.

Asif Qadri interjected and pleaded with Rukiyat, reminding her if she wants her husband alive, then she shouldn't allow Sadeq make the trip.

"But why! His mum won't eat him up. It's just talk, nothing more," said Rukiyat.

Asif Qadri smiled at Rukiyat's naivety, he then muttered, and said it isn't just talk, then insists Sadeq's mum has been doing all she can to keep him away from Ambo Hussein, that's why she's avoiding Sadeq.

"I think if he gets the answers he needs, it'll help him to move on," said Rukiyat.

Asif Qadri continues to insist Sadeq won't get any answer. He narrated to Rukiyat how President Ambo collected his wife thirty-six years ago when Sadeq was just four years old, not because he was weak or witless, he did let it go because every strife with Ambo Hussein ends with blood being shed.

Interestingly, Asif Qadri was able to get through to Rukiyat, and break her resolve for answers. She then asked her father in-law what he wants her to do at this point.

"Please do whatever you can to stop him, I beg you," said Asif Qadri.

Rukiyat is now confused as to how to go about constraining her husband from making this planned spellbinding trip. She advised her father in-law not to get his hopes up, and reminded him Sadeq is stubborn, particularly when his mind is set on something. Yet promised to do all she could to stop the trip from going ahead.

"Thank you, my child," said Asif Qadri.

Days later, President Ambo and his family members were seated in his living room chatting, in one of those family times.

Aasim's character flaw is his inability to keep to himself, the views of the citizens concerning his dad. Truth be told, Aasim is the go-to-person in this family, but his unshakable and self abasing character is bound to set him on a collision course with his dad. He took the liberty of the family time to let his dad know that most of the people in Kitan, are feeling he isn't sincere with his election pledge.

"Who told you that rubbish?" asked President Ambo.

Aasim looked away yet told his dad the news is all over town, he even went on to remind his dad they're aware of the fact that his dad is being accused of Hassan Mustapha's death.

President Ambo flared up and asked Aasim if he's taking advantage of the father-son time he spends with his family as an opportunity to insult him.

Aisha had to tone the temperature and immediately turned to Aasim and asked him to apologize to his dad.

"I'm sorry, dad. Though, Umar said he saw you kill Hassan Mustapha," said Aasim. Funnily, it seems like Aasim's apology wasn't quite an apology but an opportunity to lay bare the lurid details of his dad's acts before every member of his family. This news came to Aisha as a shock, it was as if she was hit by a ton of bricks, she then turned to her husband and asked if what Aasim just said is true.

Malik interjected and reminded his mum that Hassan Mustapha deserved to die. Aisha didn't hesitate to put Malik in his place. "Shut your mouth, how do you know who deserves to die and who should live?" she asked.

Aisha then shifted her focus to her husband, reminding him his hands are soaked in so much blood. "I hope our children don't suffer for our sins," said Aisha.

Malik interjected again and reminded his mum she's unnecessarily making a mountain out of a mole hill because his dad never said he did it.

"His silence has answered my question, and I know your dad more than you may think," said Aisha.

"But if he did it, then it's one of those things a man needs to do to keep his government intact," said Malik.

Aisha couldn't allay her fears concerning the future, she just muttered and said her own worry is why her husband wouldn't be like other Arab nations that treat their citizens well and humane.

Aasim cuts in and said the only reason Qatar and other Arab nations are still maintaining relationships with the Republic of Kitan is because that's the only way they can influence this nation positively into doing things aright.

President Ambo suddenly felt this meeting is creeping into critiquing his government, and he then flared up again at Aasim. "Are you insinuating these nations rule their people better than myself, is that what your friends are telling you?" asked President Ambo. Funnily, this meeting is now divided, and Malik had to take side with his dad, and said his problem in all this is what Aasim was doing with these low lives in this city.

"They are my friends, and we play football together," replied Aasim. Malik chuckled at his brother's relative naivety and asked how is it he called these guys his friends even when they hate him so much?

"They don't hate me, they like me because I like them, but they hate you because you hate them as well," said Aasim.

The President became infuriated with the direction of this conversation, and he then stood up and left. "Enough of this talk, you've just chased your dad away," said Aisha.

Aasim wanted to leave a parting word for his brother and said Malik should know he has helped so many citizens of the Republic of Kitan into so many football clubs abroad.

Malik shrugged of Aasim's claim, saying that's his business, he then stood up and retired to his flat.

Days after her conversation with her father-in-law, Rukiyat had being cracking her head on how to go about stopping Sadeq from paying his scheduled visit to the Republic of Kitan. She then walked up to her husband and said she's beginning to have second thoughts about this trip. He stopped what he was doing and paid rapt attention.

"What about it?" asked Sadeq.

She crossed her hand around his neck, and said she thinks going to see her mum inside the presidential palace is risky.

Sadeq was lost as to his wife's sudden change of heart, he reminded her she supported this move whole heartedly the other day and asked why the sudden change.

"Nothing, I just felt you should have a rethink," she said.

Sadeq was riled by this new turn of events and felt his wife didn't just suddenly become pessimistic about the trip, he quickly asked if his dad put her up for this.

Rukiyat didn't give a straight response to this question, rather said she was cautiously optimistic before now, but she's now pessimistic about the whole thing. She insists this isn't about who put her to this, it's about how fatal the trip could be.

"Did my dad call you? A simple yes or no will suffice," asked Sadeq.

Rukiyat nodded in affirmation, yet she urged her husband to have a rethink about this whole trip.

Sadeq wasn't quite convinced that a rethink is what he needed at this point, he insists his dad has gotten the answer he needs to move on, he also needed his own answer, and he must hear it directly from his mum.

"Why don't you do this some other time in the future, maybe at a more perfect time?" asked Rukiyat. Sadeq was quite stubborn, he insisted there's never a perfect time, and he just needed to do this and move on.

"If you're determined about doing this, then suit yourself, but I pray it doesn't turn out to be as your dad fears," said Rukiyat.

Four days after insisting on the trip to visit his mum, Sadeq travelled to the Republic of Kitan, and was stopped at the security post in the Presidential Villa.

"Hello, good afternoon," said Sadeq.

He then proceeded to say he's here to see Mrs Aisha Hussein. The Presidential guard then asked Sadeq if he's related to Aisha, because he bears some resemblance.

Sadeq replied and said she's his aunt, but just as the guard began probing further Aasim drove past by and saw Sadeq and stopped. After all, Aasim has a perfect resemblance with Sadeq, because they both look like their mum, just that Aasim is a bit younger in looks.

Colonel Abdallah was some distance away, and later joined his man who's speaking with Sadeq, but the guard turned to Aasim and got him involved. "Aasim, he's here to see your mum," said the guard. Funnily, the moment Colonel Abdallah set his sight on Sadeq he knew who he was, despite falsely describing Aisha as his aunt. Aasim also sensed who he was and suddenly took over the conversation, and that prevented the guards from making further inquiries into his motives.

"Excuse me; I don't know why you look so much like me, even though you're older than I am," said Aasim.

"I'm Sadeq," he replied.

"Which Sadeq? I hope it's not what I'm thinking?" asked Aasim. The Presidential guard watched as Sadeq laughed, and then asked Aasim what's it he's thinking, their meeting was quite friendly, and they seem to have bonded immediately. Though, Sadeq didn't explicitly introduce himself, yet they've managed to communicate some important details to each other without making it so audibly, to leave a hint.

Colonel Abdallah then asked Aasim to please let his mum know about this visitor, while he waits at the security post for clearance.

"No need waiting here, let him come with me," said Aasim.

"Are you giving him the all clear?" asked Colonel Abdallah.

Aasim insists, Sadeq isn't a security risk, he then urged the guards to let him in. Colonel Abdallah turns to Sadeq, and said he can go with Aasim, even though they insisted on taking down his information for security clearance purposes.

After going through security checks, they drove into the presidential compound, with Aasim in the front while Sadeq's car followed from behind. They then continued their conversation. "Are you Sadeq, my mother's first son?" asked Aasim.

"Yes, I'm," said Sadeq. They shook hands, and actually did a brief catch-up, but Sadeq had to save the catching-up for later. Funnily, they look alike, similar built, in height and body structure, and even the facial bearings are just the same. Aasim was filled with so much joy, he chatted with Sadeq as if they've known each other forever...

"Why haven't you come around all these years? We've heard of you, but haven't seen you," said Aasim.

"Hmm, then we'll have some more catching up to do, but is your mum in?" asked Sadeq.

"Yes, she is, and she must be happy to see you," replied Aasim. He left Sadeq and quickly walked upstairs to inform his mum.

Serendipitously, he met his dad seated beside his mum, and President Ambo then asked Aasim why his face was wreathed in smiles, and then proceeded to ask what the excitement was.

Aasim was keen not to spoil the surprise, he then asked his mum to guess what. "Aasim, I'm not up for your guess game," Aisha replied reluctantly.

"Your son is here, I mean Sadeq," said Aasim.

"What! What's he doing here?" asked Aisha. She immediately rushed downstairs to meet him. Aasim on the other hand was quite disappointed with his mum's reaction to the news, and he then followed his mum from behind. "What's going on, aren't you happy he came to see us?" asked Aasim.

She saw Sadeq looking so handsome because she hadn't seen him for the last twenty years. "Oh, my son!" she exclaimed.

Sadeq wasn't having any of it, he canned his emotion for his mum. After all he sees her on television more often than not. He stopped his mum from giving him a hug. "No, don't touch me please," said Sadeq.

President Ambo stood up from his seat in anger and immediately walked downstairs to confront Sadeq. He looked at Sadeq, and the more he looked at Sadeq his penchant for blood increased, he then told Sadeq that the fly that loves the scent of a corpse will definitely follow the corpse to the grave, but this time, the corpse isn't going into the grave, but the fly will.

Sadeq turned to President Ambo and said he's not here for him. "I'm only here to get some answers from my mother, and I'll leave your house immediately," he replied.

"I warned you not to ever come near my wife or near my house, but you refused," said President Ambo.

"Allow me to see my mum and leave," said Sadeq. He then turned to his mum who's already overwhelmed and crying yet finding it difficult to say a word. "Mum, why have you been avoiding me? I need an answer," asked Sadeq.

"My son please calm down, you don't understand, it's more complicated than you think," said Aisha.

President Ambo left them, he then walked into his bedroom took his pistol and came downstairs. "I warned you, but you wouldn't listen," said President Ambo.

Aasim saw his dad with a gun and immediately intervened, and sadly, Aasim is a jolly good fellow, but has no idea of the depth of the inner workings of his dad's heart. "Dad, he has done nothing to you, this is between him and mum," said Aasim.

President Ambo then walked up to Sadeq and fired three shots at him. "With this you'll not bother me anymore, good riddance!" said President Ambo.

Dad, no, stop, stop," said Aasim. It was already too late, as the gun went off, and Sadeq slumped and died on the spot.

Aisha fell on Sadeq's lifeless body, and held him tightly, and wept, as she begs her son not to leave her. "Oh, my worst nightmare has come true, why did you do this to my son, Ambo," she screamed and wept.

Aasim couldn't believe his eyes, it was all like a movie before him, he quickly turned to his dad in anger. "Dad this is bad, you've no right to be killing people because you're the President," said Aasim.

It was as if President Ambo hasn't had his fill of blood, he turned and then pointed his gun at Aasim. "One more word from you, I'll kill you right here and right now, you're of no use to me. At least I've two good sons I can trust, just say a word, and put me to test now," yelled President Ambo.

Aisha left Sadeq's lifeless body, she then rushed and stood between the gun and Aasim. "Just kill me and let my son be, do it, enough of your bullying, kill me and get it over with," Aisha screamed.

President Ambo then brought down his gun and went into his office to make a phone call. "Abdallah, where are you?" he asked.

"I'm here, in the villa, Mr President," replied Colonel Abdallah. It didn't take long before Colonel Abdallah answered to the President's call. President Ambo immediately asked the Colonel to take Sadeq's body out of his premises. "Go and dump it with his dad, let him know I killed him for coming close to my wife, and because I considered him a trespasser," said President Ambo.

Colonel Abdallah and four of his soldiers took Sadeq's corpse to his father. When they got to Asif Qadri's house, they knocked the door but there wasn't any response.

"Colonel, I don't think he's at home," said Zahed.

"Where then will he be?" asked Colonel Abdallah.

Zahed asked around, and walked back to the Colonel, and said he just learnt that Asif Qadri is a Bureau De Change businessman.

"Where does he transact his business?" asked Colonel Abdallah. Zahed then said Asif Qadri has a shop in the central market. "Ok, let's go there," said Colonel Abdallah. They all returned to their vehicles and drove to the central market.

Thirty Minutes later, they located Asif Qadri, Colonel Abdallah then walked up to him and said they want to have a word with him. Asif Qadri saw Colonel Abdallah and his men and immediately realised these are President Ambo Hussein's guards. "You're Ambo Hussein's guards, aren't you?" he asked.

"Yes, I am, and we're here to see you," replied Colonel Abdallah

Asif Qadri suddenly became worried about Sadeq's safety, that ominous feeing suddenly overwhelmed him and the first thought that came to his mind was that Sadeq have been arrested. "Is anything the matter?" asked Asif Qadri.

"We brought Sadeq's corpse to you," said Colonel Abdallah.

"What! No, no, no, this can't be true; oh, my worst nightmare has just befallen me," cried Asif Qadri.

"President Ambo said I should tell you he killed him for coming close to his wife," said Colonel Abdallah.

Asif Qadri cried, and said Ambo Hussein promised to kill his only child and he just did.

"Come and take his corpse," said Colonel Abdallah.

Asif Qadri refused to go with Colonel Abdallah and his men, he urged them to return the corpse to Ambo, so he could feast on it. At this point neighbours around Asif Qadri's shop are beginning to gather because of his weeping.

"Sorry I don't take orders from you," said Colonel Abdallah. He then ordered Zahed and Jaifer to go into the van and drag the corpse down here. Zahed and Jaifer both corporals in the army, went into the Van and dragged Sadeq's corpse on the ground to Asif Qadri's shop. Asif Qadri was shocked to see his son's corpse being dragged on the ground. "Is it my son that you're dragging like a thief?" asked Asif Qadri.

Onlookers were mortified by the sight of the corpse being dragged on the ground. "That's your son Sadeq, we're leaving," said Colonel Abdallah.

They left the corpse and returned to their vehicles and left.

"No, Ambo has to kill me," said Asif Qadri. It was quite an eerie scene that attracted sympathetic on-lookers, Asif Qadri then got some help from people around to put his son's corpse inside his car and drove off, following the Colonel to the presidential villa.

"The guard at the gate stopped Asif Qadri. "You aren't allowed to come in here," said Kunafis.

"Why? I'm returning my son's corpse to President Ambo," said Asif Qadri.

Kunafis prevented Asif from continuing into the presidential villa. Kunafis reminded Asif this isn't a cemetery and ordered him to go back now. Since Kunafis refused him entry into the presidential villa, Asif Qadri had no choice but to alight from his car, he then began screaming. "Ambo, come and finish what you started," said Asif Qadri.

President Ambo was attracted by the noise, and he looked through the window, and saw Asif Qadri. "I knew this fool will walk into his death," said President Ambo.

Colonel Abdallah went upstairs and reported back to the President that they've handed the corpse to his father.

"Did you know he followed you here?" asked President Ambo.

"Yes sir, but he was stopped at the gate," said Colonel Abdallah.

President Ambo turned to Colonel Abdallah, and said he was attracted by Asif Qadri's noise, he then ordered the Colonel to go and put him out of his misery.

Colonel Abdallah was lost as to what President Ambo meant by asking him to go and put Asif Qadri out of his misery. He obviously wasn't asking Colonel Abdallah to go and give Asif Qadri a pat on the back and a pack of chocolate, he's instructing him to do something grim. "Mr. President, I don't understand," said Colonel Abdallah.

"Kill him and call the council to come and take their bodies away," said President Ambo.

Colonel Abdallah cringed inside him, but he didn't show it to the President that he wasn't comfortable with this order, this kind of assignment will make even the devil himself to feel some crawling on his skin. After all, he's a soldier, and carrying out orders, and killings, is what he's trained to do irrespective of his displeasure about the said assignment. "Ok, Mr. President," said Colonel Abdallah. At this time Aisha locked herself in her room, and crying her eyes out, and had no knowledge her husband is going the extra mile to close a chapter in her life.

Moments later, Zahed walked to Colonel Abdallah as he came downstairs. "Colonel, did you call me?" asked Zahed.

"Yes, follow me," said Colonel Abdallah. They both walked to the gate, and he opened fire on Asif Qadri and killed him.

Immediately after Colonel Abdallah shot and killed Asif Qadri. Kunafis, who was the guard that stopped Asif Qadri by the gate, then asked. "Sir, what do we do with these corpses?"

Colonel Abdallah instructed Kunafis to call the council to come and take the corpses away.

Aisha locked herself up in her bedroom that day and cried all through the day. President Ambo tried earlier but didn't get a response, and he came back again and knocked asking her to open the door.

"Go away; just go away because I hate you so much," said Aisha.

"Darling, please, just open the door," said President Ambo.

Aisha had lost her voice from sobbing; her grief is beyond comprehension. All she could do was mutter in her cracked and broken voice asking Ambo Hussein to allow her to grieve the loss of her son, and that she's presently as feeble as a feather in the wind.

"Darling I'm sorry, the boy and his dad were giving me a headache," said President Ambo.

"Your endearments won't get you anywhere," said Aisha.

"But we need to put this behind us," said President Ambo.

Aisha reminded her husband that the pain he has caused her is ineffable, she proceeded to say, it's like a sharp dagger has been pierced through her heart.

President Ambo continued knocking as he insisted "The boy underestimated my power," he said.

"You killed them because you know there's nothing I can do about it, but remember, your doom will soon come, I promise you," said Aisha.

"Aisha, I did this for you and the kids," he said.

"Enough of your ingenuity, your action is likened to an arsonist shutting the door against his victim to prevent them from escaping fire while pretending to call neighbours for help," said Aisha.

Sadly, humility isn't President Ambo's thing. He became enraged with his wife and said likening him to an arsonist reduces him to a weakling and that's quite disrespectful. He stopped knocking the door and left in anger.

Rukiyat was distraught after her husband didn't return to Tunisia that day and decided to call Asif Qadri maybe he might have an idea of Sadeq's whereabouts. She couldn't reach Asif Qadri either, and finally, she decided to call an employee of Asif Qadri.

"Hello Basal," said Rukiyat.

"Rukiyat, how're you?" asked Basal.

"I'm fine, why is your voice like this?" asked Rukiyat.

"Are you on your way?" asked Basal.

Rukiyat was lost as to what Basal was getting at. "On my way to where?" replied Rukiyat.

"On your way to Kitan of course! Will you remain in Tunisia when your husband just died?" said Basal.

"Who died! My husband left here this morning to Kitan, how can you say, he died?" asked Rukiyat.

Basal managed to inform Rukiyat that President Ambo Hussein killed Sadeq and his dad today, "They are both dead," said Basal.

"What, Asif? No..., (She cried). The grim reality of this doomed trip to the presidential villa has just dawned on Rukiyat, and things have unfolded just as Asif Qadri had feared. His hunch nagged him, and he did all he could to stand in the way, yet his son insisted on going ahead with the trip.

Basal then told Rukiyat he has been crying all day, and that's why his voice is like this. He suddenly realised there's no response from the other end of the phone. Sadly, Rukiyat has suddenly lost herself, the news was too grim that it deafened her, and made her dumb. She has suddenly gone cuckoo. "Rukiyat, are you there?" he asked.

"No, leave me alone, I can't talk," said Rukiyat. She screamed and threw her phone on the floor, crying.

A day after the death of Sadeq and his dad, Aisha was still crying over the death of Sadeq. She was seated in a corner of the living room, in a manner that shows she wants to be left alone, and the ambience around her is likened to a graveyard silence. "Ambo you killed my son, you said you'll do it and you actually did," said Aisha.

"My darling I'm sorry, the boy wanted to dare me to see what I'll do," said President Ambo.

"And you did what you promised you'll do to him, didn't you?" asked Aisha.

President Ambo insisted he had to act because he's a man of his word, and he takes his promises seriously.

Aisha wasn't in the mood for a conversation with her husband, all she could do was remind her husband that his mannerism and disposition towards her son is one of violent antipathy. Malik interjected in his attempt to absolve his dad of any wrongdoing. "Mum, though I wasn't around when the whole thing happened, but dad did the right thing," said Malik. "Shut up, Malik. Do you think you're an inch as valuable to me as Sadeq, no mother messes with their first son," said Aisha.

Malik didn't hesitate to remind his mum of the hypocrisy in her statement, he then asked her, if she loves Sadeq this much why then did she abandon him.

"Your dad promised to kill him, so I had to cut all ties with him just to keep him safe. Do you know what it feels like to abandon my son just because I don't want my husband to trace his calls, then find his location and kill him?" asked Aisha.

Malik insisted his dad has warned Sadeq not to come close to his wife. Malik's feelings about people as disposable kind of winds his mum up, and sadly, Malik remained an unwavering defender of his dad's fatal posturing, and his being flunkey is a new mix thrown into the broth.

"Your dad warned him not to come close to a stranger or his mother, don't you know he had every right to be with me whenever he felt like it?" asked Aisha.

Malik continued in his insensitivity by restating his earlier position that his dad was just protecting his own.

"Your dad is your hero, isn't he? The strange thing is that the wicked usually enjoy in their wickedness but just wait and see the end of the wicked," said Aisha.

President Ambo was sitting adjacent to his wife, he got irked as she talks about the possible end for a wicked person, and he then stood up angrily. "Aisha, you mean you want me to end in shame, maybe you will join that foolish son of yours in the grave?" he retorted.

Aisha stood up and charged at the President, this time she's holding nothing back as she takes the fight to him. She urged him to go for his pistol and shoot her because that's what he does best. "For your information, I'm no longer trapped in a vortex of fear," said Aisha.

President Ambo stood up to leave, particularly now that Aisha has switched from being on the defence to being on the attack. He took steps to leave but Aisha was on his face. "You know I'll do it, don't make me kill you," said President Ambo.

"The day you killed my son, was the day your journey to perdition started," said Aisha.

President Ambo realised he just crossed the line with his wife, he then pleaded with her and said he has tried to assuage her pains by letting her know his actions against her son weren't intentional. Aisha looked away, as she makes it clear to him that his argument is a puerile one, and she won't fall for it.

Funnily, President Ambo's apology was kind of toxic for Aisha to assimilate, and she isn't ready to dine with this devil any longer, and that got President Ambo pissed. "Your ill-feelings towards me, over the death of your stupid son have turned you into a dissenting voice in my home and I won't take it," said President Ambo.

Malik sensed his mum and dad are at each other's throat, he quickly intervened before things gets messy for the family. "Dad, it's okay, it hasn't come to that," said Malik.

Aisha turned to Malik and asked him to leave his dad alone because his thirst for blood is likened to a child on a sugar rush, and that incandescent rage will put his dad in a precarious situation.

President Ambo became quite furious at his wife's unforgiving spirit, he then accused her of taking the posture of a brawler in his home, and assured Aisha he's having none of that.

Aisha didn't bat an eyelid, after all, she has taken the fear off her eyes, and she took it upon herself to liberate her family from this terror within. She unflinchingly made it clear that she has had enough of his bullying, "Shoot me, and get it over with," said Aisha.

President Ambo stopped and cautioned Aisha. Don't push me, Aisha," he said. They continued bantering but engaging in banter isn't something the President finds to be soothing, yet, he seemed to have lost his ability to blow smoke out his ears this time. After all, Aisha wasn't in a mood for moonlighting, more so the boat is already rocked.

"Your wickedness has gone ubiquitous, it has gone suffuse, and soon it would consume you," said Aisha.

President Ambo looked on as his wife paced up and down, yet felt the need not to inflame her any further with his incandescent rhetoric. He just subtly gave her a parting banter, saying she's suffering from a common-sense melt-down before walking away, and left Aisha to continue sulking over her loss. Aisha followed him and continued to terrorise him with the words of her mouth.

"Your smugness that disapproves of basic civility will consume you," she said.

President Ambo saw a new Aisha that he has never seen before, even his threading softly, softly hasn't dissuaded her from engaging him in a further tiff. He then turned to Aisha with the look of a man begging to be heard and said he's cautiously optimistic that there's certain inevitability about the future of his family if they don't put the past behind them and work together as a family. Asking her to put the death of her first son behind her after boastfully taking his life is a big ask for Aisha, and she didn't hesitate to remind her husband, his eyes are too close together, that's why he can't see the obvious.

A week after the death of Sadeq and his dad, Aasim visited the Grand Imam of Ansarouh, the nation's capital. President Ambo is now on a mission of damage control, after his dramatic gun-pointing act at his son and wife.

"Aasim, you're here!" exclaimed the Imam.

"Yes, Sheikh, you requested I see you, so here I am," replied Aasim.

The Sheikh asked Aasim to take his seat and make himself comfortable, he then used his hand in gesture to show Aasim to his seat. I spoke to your dad after my conversation with you.

Aasim looked the Imam in the eyes, and unblinkingly, but subtly reminded him. "The killing of my stepbrother and his dad, and turning his gun on me, is a grave sin and something my dad shouldn't get away with," said Aasim.

The Imam spoke softly and said he understands Aasim's animosity but reminded Aasim that he has made President Ambo understand the gravity of his action.

"I think I've had enough of my dad. Presently, I'm ready to split heirs with my dad, maybe it's time we part ways," said Aasim.

The Imam understands he has a daunting task ahead of him, mending relations particularly where too much water has gone under the bridge might need more than mere luck but a dint of hard work. He quickly interjected. "That's why I asked you to see me because it's time to mend your relationship with your dad," said the Imam.

Aasim didn't bat an eyelid before letting the Imam know there's nothing to mend, after all, his dad considers him a renegade. Aasim then fixed his gaze at the Imam and asked if his dad is right to consider him a rebel.

"No, you aren't, you're just a child on a different path," said the Imam.

Aasim stated the obvious division in the family and laid it bare to the Imam that his dad seems more comfortable with his brothers around him.

"Aasim, no matter how uncomfortable the actions of our parents are, they still deserve to be respected," said the Imam.

Aasim looked at the Imam in awe and questioned the reasonableness of his logic. He quickly asked the Imam if he's implying President Ambo deserves reverence, a man on a killing spree, and then muttered, saying his dad should earn his respect not demand it.

Aasim's criticalness didn't deter the Imam because the Imam made his position clear that he understands that President Ambo is turning his home into a smouldering cauldron yet insisted that Aasim had no choice but to respect his dad.

Aasim was spooked by the Imam's insistence that his reverence for his dad takes priority. "Are you buoying up his actions or what?" asked Aasim.

The Imam stood up and came back moments later, he then sat opposite Aasim, and said two wrongs can't make a right, just that, there isn't any need rousing his dad's anger any further.

"Hmm, you mean my dad should continue kicking the cans down the road. Isn't it?" asked Aasim.

"No, not at all! Your dad's action isn't a rude awakening. I saw this coming but didn't expect things to be this ugly," said the Imam.

"Peering into the future," said Aasim.

"What about the future?" asked the Imam.

"Nothing, but if the cynical schemes of an ambitious man like my dad plays out, then expect more heads to roll," said Aasim. It's now glaringly obvious that Aasim's emphatic refusal to work for his dad wasn't well received by his dad, and the simmering anger precipitated by this blatant disrespect might spell doom for Aasim.

The Imam urged Aasim not to irk his dad any further, so he doesn't go kicking off. "Why do we keep pushing this matter down the pipe? And presently we seem to be running out of pipes," said Aasim.

"I understand your worries, which explains who you truly are, and that's your personality in an unflattering light," said the Imam.

"I wish I could do more, and I expect my dad to be more gracious to the people," said Aasim.

The Imam noted to Aasim that his reputation as a charitable person precedes him, he then urged Aasim to always remember one thing.

"Hmm, thank you, but what's that one thing?" asked Aasim.

Instead of mentioning the one thing he talked about, the Imam proceeded to let Aasim know he likes him, he likes Aasim's benevolence, his benignity and his heart for charity.

"Aren't you the one who told me hospitality saves even from death?" said Aasim.

The Imam laughed, yet asked Aasim when he discussed the relationship between hospitality and death with him, because he doesn't seem to remember having such conversation with him.

Aasim smiled with this showiness that's masked by a grin, he then reminded the Imam that it was when he was just six years old, when he gave his new football to Maman after he saw Maman using a plastic container in place of a football.

Then Imam took a deep breath, as he travelled down memory lane down to his encounter with Aasim when Aasim was just six years old. "Hmm, now I remember, you do have a good memory," said the Imam.

The Imam now realised he once sowed a seed in Aasim, this seed is words of wisdom that was sown into the heart of a six years old, which he so cherished, and being hospitable and charitable are virtues humanity should pursue.

"Aasim, your dad would need you in time to come, I urge you to stay in close proximity with your dad," said the Imam.

"How! You know I can't be a part of a government that sheds the blood of its citizens," said Aasim.

The Imam spoke in riddles, yet allowed Aasim some latitude, and reminded him he mustn't be a part of his dad's government, yet he mustn't stay away from his dad.

Aasim still didn't understand in certain terms what the Imam is getting at, and he didn't hesitate to ask, if there's something the Imam isn't telling him that he needed to know, because if he plays no role in his dad's government, then he shouldn't have any need to stay around his dad.

"That's just my message for you," said the Imam.

"Ok, thank you, I think I should get going," said Aasim.

"Thanks for coming," said the Imam.

Days later, the President noticed Aasim has been unusually absent, since his close encounter with his dad. They haven't seen each other since the day he killed Sadeq and pointed a gun at him.

Malik walked into his dad's office for other purposes, but President Ambo set aside his conversation with Malik and asked him about his brother, Aasim. "I haven't seen Aasim since last night, but he seems to be inside his flat," said Malik.

President Ambo muttered under his breath and said Aasim seems to be avoiding him.

Malik asked his dad what he expected from Aasim and reminded him that pointing a gun at somebody and expecting that person to remain your friend is a big ask.

President Ambo wasn't in any way remorseful over his imploding act, he boasts to Malik saying Aasim is lucky to be alive because he could've been dead by now.

"Dad, I've supported you in everything, but turning on your family isn't a good idea," said Malik.

President Ambo couldn't hide his prejudices against Aasim, as he opened up to Malik that his brother is driving him crazy and his love for Aasim has waned.

"Dad, don't expect him to behave like us, we were exposed to different ways of life," said Malik.

President Ambo felt the excuse of what lifestyle his children were exposed to is a lame one, and he wasn't buying it, he then made himself clear that he didn't send Aasim to study abroad only for him to come back and ruffle feathers with him.

"Dad, you've to go about this with care if you don't want your family to implode," said Malik.

President Ambo laughed and had this lasting smirk on his face. "Implode! That's laughable, unless there's more than meets the eye," said President Ambo.

"Dad, I suggest you give him some space to allow him come to terms with the death of Sadeq," said Malik.

President Ambo felt this whole grieving thing is merely a ruse, and reminded Malik, his brother has got no reason to grieve over the death of an impostor who seeks to steal their inheritance.

"I still can't get my head around why Sadeq choose to act like a fly that follows the corpse to the grave, and Sadeq should have stayed away from mum," said Malik.

President Ambo made a light joke about the brutishness of his act and said, Sadeq provoked the manifestation of his wild side and that isn't the most idyllic thing to do.

The next day, President Ambo went to Aasim's flat to see if he's inside, and to look for a way to pull him back to himself. The President stood by the door and pressed the doorbell. "Who's it at the door?" asked Aasim.

"It's me, your father," he replied.

Aasim opened the door, and then asked. "Dad, what can I do for you?" asked Aasim.

President Ambo was quick to demand reverence from his son, in his usual striking manner. "Have you greeted me, or have we seen each other today?" asked President Ambo.

Aasim wasn't up for his dad's forceful solicitation of reverence, he subtly pointed out who's doing the encroaching. "You'll have to wait for me to come to your flat first before demanding that I greet you," said Aasim.

"You know you're rude, you're very rude, and won't you ask me to come in, to at least find out why I'm here," asked President Ambo.

Aasim remained cautious because he's obviously aware that his dad is a highly inflammable character with quite a temper that characterizes him as very volatile. He assured his dad that if there's anything that connects them to each other, he'll check with him later. Aasim turned to leave and said he would like some privacy.

President Ambo brought out a letter and gave it to Aasim and told him that's his appointment letter.

"What appointment are you talking about?" asked Aasim.

President Ambo took Aasim's disdain on the chin, after all, his mission was to warm up to Aasim whom he thinks wrongly casted him as a murderer defined by blood and guts. "Why don't you open the letter before asking your dad questions?" asked President Ambo.

Aasim took the letter and opened it, and after reading, he turned to his dad, and asked why this sudden appointment. Convinced that his dad finds him insufferable, he remained cautious, and he reiterated to his dad that he only promised him he'll think about the appointment. He then proceeded to remind his dad that the content of this letter can't endear his dad to him.

"I want you to start tomorrow as the head of this country's military intelligence," said President Ambo.

Aasim dropped the bombshell and said he's sorry, that he'll be leaving for Europe later today, because he's still reeling from the dizzy effects of his dad's action the other day.

"What do you mean by that, and who did you discussed this with?" asked President Ambo.

Aasim interjected and asked who he should've discussed the matter with. "You should've discussed it with me," said President Ambo.

"Sorry Mr. President, but these your platitudes won't reconcile the ruptured relationship between us," said Aasim.

President Ambo's frustration got the best of him, and he lashed out and said he's tired of Aasim's unending twists and turns and Aasim's actions are affecting his ability to muster a serious clout from the people.

Aasim's understanding of true leadership is that power comes from the people, and he reminded his dad that his attempt of seeking to circumvent reality through exclusionary political style doesn't keep the people down forever.

"I'm only trying to leverage on the fact that you're closer to the people than your brothers and use your help to get the people to love their president," said President Ambo.

The smirk in Aasim's face says otherwise, because he felt his dad is merely blowing smoke and could end up holding the hat. He pointed out to his dad that he set his family on the garden path the very day he killed Sadeq "You killed my brother right before my eyes and turned your gun on me, which means you can kill anyone," said Aasim.

President Ambo subtly reminded Aasim, that Sadeq isn't his brother, and urged him to refrain from such utterance.

"He's my brother, we share a perfect resemblance, and we share good hearts, maybe these qualities are alien to you because we got them from mum," said Aasim.

His brothers' unwavering fealty for their dad is what's lacking in Aasim's relationship with his dad; and securing his son's unquestionable loyalty is a tall order.

President Ambo realised his conversation with Aasim seems to be going nowhere, and Aasim is taking advantage of this conversation to get under his skin. He then turned to leave but reminded Aasim he has to assume duty tomorrow. President Ambo suddenly stopped to get Aasim's affirmation about his resuming work the next day.

"Dad, my flight is tonight, permit me to go and start packing my things," said Aasim.

"I know if you get to Europe, you'll tell them you saw your dad shoot somebody, so I forbid you from travelling," said President Ambo.

Aasim decided to hit the nail on the head by recusing himself from his dad's government and told his dad working for him won't work because his dad can't use him to kill innocent people.

"Who is asking you to kill? Working in the military is an honour to you," said President Ambo.

Aasim needed to let his dad know what he's wishing for by reiterating that if he works in the military and discovers his dad is doing something wrong, he isn't going to cover it up. He proceeded to urge him to let him be, particularly now that he knows what will be at stake if he returns to his role in the military.

President Ambo wanted to walk away but sounded a note of caution, expressing his frustration as he told Aasim he's tired of fiddling with him. Although, he needed Aasim to help endear the President to the people, but President Ambo's showy display of power is standing in the way. Whenever the opportunity for his arbitrary use of power arises, his disposition becomes unpredictable, and likened to a child on a sugar rush. Now that his dad opened the door into the conversation of getting the people to love their President, Aasim took advantage of it to remind his dad that his ideology about governance is the vicious, debilitating factor that won't endear the President to the people.

"I didn't come here to be lectured, and I advise you to check your utterances," said President Ambo.

"The worst you will do is to kill me, you've already attempted to, but I won't put my conscience in dilemma in an attempt to work for you," said Aasim.

"Enough of this, you're becoming too emboldened, and don't make me go murky and muddy with you," President Ambo threatened.

"Your brazenness has earned you the sobriquet 'The lion of Kitan'," said Aasim.

President Ambo seemed quite enraged by his son's disrespect, he immediately cautioned Aasim with his roaring and quite distinct anger. "Enough of your grandstanding, you've become unmannerly and churlish, I'll soon go brutish on you, if you don't curb your tongue," raged President Ambo left in anger.

Later that night, Aasim was stopped from making his trip to Germany by the Immigration officer at the airport. The Immigration officer pleaded with Aasim and told him he can't let him through.

Aasim wasn't quite sure of what the reason might be, he then asked the Immigration Officer what the problem is and reminded him he doesn't want to miss his flight. The Immigration Officer didn't say much, after all, he's just a messenger. He pointed Aasim to the big guns upstairs, and told him the Comptroller General will want to see him.

"Is it, Kabir Yau?" asked Aasim.

"Yes, he is in the office waiting for you," said the Immigration Officer.

Aasim stretched his hand forth to collect his travel documents, as he asked the Immigration Officer to give him his documents.

"I'm sorry, I can't, I'll take it to him, and he will hand it over to you himself," said the Immigration Officer.

The refusal to hand him his travel documents got Aasim spooked, he then muttered as he fixed his gaze at the Immigration Officer and said this joke has become uninteresting. "Let's go to your comptroller general," said Aasim.

They walked into the Comptroller General's office.

Immediately Aasim set his foot in the big man's office and requested to know what's going on. The Comptroller General went straight on to apologise to Aasim and made it clear that they can't allow him continue his trip to Germany.

"Why won't I continue my trip to Germany?" asked Aasim.

The Comptroller General is now in an awkward position as he pleaded with Aasim a second time that he's very sorry, his hands are tied.

"Your hands aren't tied, and if they're, you wouldn't be holding my travel documents," Aasim retorted.

Comptroller General was forced to open up to Aasim that it's an order from above and there's nothing he can do about it. It's now glaringly obvious to Aasim that a third hand is now involved in this matter and someone from above is pulling the Comptroller General's strings.

"I know my dad put you into doing this, but I want you to say it clearly," said Aasim.

Comptroller general nodded in affirmation yet said he wouldn't want to incur the President's wrath.

"Ok, I understand, but give me my travel documents, and let me go back," said Aasim.

"Aasim I can't, we're instructed to seize it from you," said the Comptroller General.

Aasim then asked him specifically if his dad ordered them to retrieve his documents from him. "Aasim, I'm sorry, I know you're a nice person but I'm afraid of what your dad could do to me, if I disobey him," said the Comptroller General.

Aasim had no choice but to return, after all, his dad knows full well, how best to clip his wings.

The next morning, Aasim confronted his dad over the seizure of his travel documents. Interestingly, he didn't consider the need for pleasantries immediately he walked into his dad's office, rather he went on to ask his dad why he asked the immigration officers to seize his travel documents.

"Because I want you to know who is in charge here," said President Ambo.

Aasim reminded his dad that he can't coerce him into working for him unblinkingly. President Ambo suddenly toned down the rhetoric and decided to go softly on Aasim owing to the fact that he spooked him the night before. "I want you to use your military and non-military acquaintances to garner support for your father's government," said President Ambo.

Aasim looked on and was amazed at his dad's childlike obsession for power and said true leadership does not flourish from the serial acts of betrayal, sleaze and brazen impunity.

"That's utter nonsense; give me one genuine reason why you shouldn't work for me?" asked President Ambo.

Aasim didn't bat an eyelid and he didn't mask his response either, as he just went on to tell his dad the way it is. "Your government is repressive and there are too many killings," said Aasim.

"No, because you feel it's right for the people to say whatever they like about my government," said President Ambo.

"Free speech is a right that can't be shirked," said Aasim.

"Have I killed you?" asked President Ambo.

The President just shot himself on the foot for asking the question he just asked. After all, he's asking the very person had had wanted to kill weeks back. Aasim had to put the record straight, and told his dad, he killed his brother, and wanted to kill him. "I know you're still looking for a perfect opportunity to kill me," said Aasim.

"I'm the lion here and you don't have a say, where lions are, no other animal has a say," said President Ambo.

Aasim quickly address the impunity in his dad's heart. He reminded his dad that sometimes the Hyenas do take lions by surprise in which the brazenness and the audacity of the lion will come to an end.

"Are you telling me, you'll take my government down by surprise?" asked President Ambo.

"That's not what we're talking about, I need my passport," said Aasim.

President Ambo turned away from Aasim and said this discussion is over, he then ordered Aasim to leave now, or else he'll ask Abdallah to throw him into the cell.

Aasim had to leave his dad's office yet left him a parting word as he said it's the manner in which he leads the people, that makes power and wealth ephemeral, but this isn't over.

A week later Sheikh Suleiman travelled to the United States and granted a press interview, where he talked about the politics in the Republic of Kitan and even referenced the death of Sadeq and his dad, Asif Qadri.

"Good evening viewers, I'm Ashley Morgan. Today, I'll be inter-viewing Sheikh Suleiman Zurumi, the Presidential aspirant of the Democratic Alliance Party in the Republic of Kitan," she said.

"Sheikh Suleiman, you're welcome," she said.

"Thank you for having me," said Sheikh Suleiman.

"Sheikh, tell us about the resolve of President Ambo Hussein to return the Republic of Kitan to a true democracy," asked Ashley.

"The citizens of the Republic of Kitan are hesitant and call the President's resolve into question, though I'm glad the world is watching to see if he'll stand by his words," said Sheikh Suleiman.

"Sheikh, you seem to be in doubt about this whole political process in which you're a part of, why would you call the President's resolve into question?" asked Ashley.

Sheikh Zurumi exposed President Ambo to the world and said the immediate disappearance of Hassan Mustapha after he invited him to feature in his programme as a guest tells it all.

"You can't be certain for sure that President Ambo had a hand in the disappearance of Hassan Mustapha," asked Ashley.

"Ashley, this isn't rumour, Hassan Mustapha was marched out of his office by the presidential guards in the presence of his colleagues just after the show in which I was a guest," said Sheikh Suleiman.

Ashley Morgan was left bemused by the Sheikh's claim and asked if Hassan Mustapha's disappearance was because he gave him a platform to reach the people.

"Yes, of course!" exclaimed the Sheikh.

"But you've indicated interest to run for president and President Ambo hasn't stopped you from running?" asked Ashley.

"The tell-tale signs are there, the world should watch out," the Sheikh warned.

"Ok, what sign in particular? Our viewers would like to know the tell-tale signs you just talked about," asked Ashley.

"A President who killed his stepson as well as his dad, in an attempt to protect his throne is a monster the world should place under close watch," said Sheikh Suleiman.

"Sheikh Zurumi, thank you for coming," said Ashley.

"Thank you," said Sheikh Suleiman.

President Ambo listened to Sheikh Suleiman Zurumi's comments about him, and this got the President spiting fire and thunder. Hours later, President Ambo sat down in his living room and was still sulking and didn't stop fuming, insisting this Sheikh is beginning to take him for a ride, and he won't get away with this.

Aisha looked at him with the look of a woman who has no mercy to offer and unsuspecting character. "You think you're still invincible, the world is beginning to know who you're," said Aisha.

"Don't worry, by the time I finish with Sheikh Suleiman, you'll know I'm still invincible," said President Ambo.

Aisha isn't just poking fun at her husband, she's rather extending her message of ill luck, she looked at him, then reiterated that the blood of her son is still on him, and the blood of that innocent boy will expose him.

"I know you're saying all these because of Sadeq, but I've told you I'm sorry," said President Ambo.

"What has Asif Qadri done to you to deserve this, you took his wife away from him, killed his only child and then killed him, and you think it will all go away just like that?" asked Aisha.

"The boy tried my patience that was why I killed him," said President Ambo.

"And if I've stayed back, you would've shot Aasim, wouldn't you?" asked Aisha.

"Yes, I would've shot him in a manner that he'll either spend the rest of his silly life on a wheelchair or even die," said President Ambo.

Aisha looked away and said, she called him a wicked person before, but it's now glaringly obvious that he's a monster. She made it clear to her husband that his actions did nothing but put a wedge between him and Aasim.

"Enough of your hawkish rhetoric, Aisha," said President Ambo.

"There isn't any sense of escapism in this, your grandiosity has only burnt the bridge between you and your son Aasim," said Aisha.

President Ambo didn't see Aasim to be of any real concern, after all, he can do with him as he pleases, he then urged Aisha to allow him worry about his relationship Aasim.

"Ok then, but I advise you worry more for yourself," said Aisha. She then stood up and left, but as she took steps to leave, President Ambo yelled, instructing her not to walk out on him, yet she ignored him went away.

Minutes later, Nawal returns from school, this time she came roaring, taking the fight to her dad for killing Sadeq.

Nawal walked into the house just as her mum left her dad in the bedroom and walked to the living room. "Oh, Nawal, you're here, and you didn't tell me you're on your way," asked Aisha.

Nawal wasn't particularly interested in pleasantries this time and the platitudes of informing her parents she's returning from school. "Yes mum, I'm just coming from school," replied Nawal.

"But you travelled to school just a month ago, have you forgotten you're travelling from Turkey?" asked Aisha.

"Yes mum, I'm schooling in Turkey, but I just can't remain in Turkey while dad was busy killing Sadeq and his dad," said Nawal.

Aisha pointed Nawal to the bedroom telling her to ask her dad about his atrocities. Nawal continued her fiery outburst saying their dad never even gave them the opportunity to meet Sadeq, insisting he's their stepbrother.

Aisha had to explain her motive for leaving Sadeq in the shadows, and out of her life. She told Nawal she kept Sadeq away all these years because her dad promised to kill him, and now he just did.

Nawal reiterated that her mum can't absolve herself now that her plans have gone up in smoke, insisting if she knew her dad wanted to kill Sadeq why didn't she spill the beans. At least they would've gotten involved and possibly prevented this incident from happening.

Aisha became emotional and said she never saw this coming, and sadly, she thought she could handle it on her own.

"Mum, you're a party to all these crimes, if you marry a man who goes about killing innocent people, then you'll share in his guilt," said Nawal.

Nawal altruistic view on blame sharing sent Aisha scampering for cover, as she quickly pointed out to Nawal that her children are witness to the fact that she doesn't agree with the President when it comes to hurting innocent people.

"Where's dad? I want him to look into my eyes and tell me why he did such a terrible thing," said Nawal.

"Your dad is in the bedroom, go and meet him," said Aisha.

Nawal knocked the door to her dad's bedroom but before he opened his mouth to let her in, she barged into her dad's bedroom, and without the platitudes of pleasantries she asked.

"Dad, why?" asked Nawal.

"Nawal, you're supposed to be in school, in Turkey, and by the way, have you greeted me?" he asked.

Nawal took advantage of the latitude allowed her by her parents as the baby of the house to bad mouth her dad. She flounced around her dad's bedroom and insisted she can't greet him for such a crime, and asked why he killed Sadeq. "What sort of dastardly act of blood and guts is that?" asked Nawal.

"Are you questioning me or what, what has come over you?" asked President Ambo.

Nawal stopped flouncing, she stood and gazed at her dad, she then replied, saying nothing came over her but killing a man and his son is the greatest crime against humanity.

President Ambo wasn't quite ready for this conversation, yet decided to go slow on his daughter by letting her know he warned Sadeq, he didn't want to see him anywhere near his wife.

"But the woman in question is his mother, were you denied access to your own mother?" asked Nawal.

"I'm getting bored of this conversation, and you'll have to leave my room," said President Ambo.

"Dad, I'll hold this sin against you for life, and I won't forgive you for this," said Nawal.

Sadly, President Ambo isn't a dark horse of some sort, and his penchant for violence isn't a secret, but he's now realising how worried sick his family members are over his sickening thirst for blood. Faced with the rude awakening that Sadeq has fans within his household, meant he took the right decision to take him out before he warms up to his children and steal what belongs to them.

President Ambo turned to Nawal and said he's saving his inheritance for his children, and Sadeq could've wormed his way into his home and he had to prevent that.

"What are you preventing? This act is sickening, I'm truly sick to my stomach." She then took a deep breath. "In fact, you aren't human," said Nawal.

President Ambo got up angrily from bed, and after all, he has had enough of this discourtesy from his daughter. "Then, what am I?" he asked.

Nawal angrily walked away from her dad's bedroom but left him a parting remark. "You're a monster, and a menace," said Nawal.

CHAPTER

FOUR

The clean up

Two weeks later.

President Ambo walked up to Colonel Abdallah in one of his evening walkabouts; he then called the Colonel aside and asked. "How effective are you as a presidential guard?" asked President Ambo.

Serendipitously, being closely associated with President Ambo means fostering the cult of Ambo Hussein, and it's obvious that only the buccaneers in this republic participate in the inner workings of this President's affairs.

"Mr. President I'm lost, I don't understand what you're talking about," said Colonel Abdallah.

President Ambo asked the Colonel what's it that's difficult to understand, and proceeded to ask if he truly understands the concept of being a bodyguard to the number one citizen.

"Sorry Mr. President, please make it easier for me to understand," said Colonel Abdallah.

"You want a layman's explanation because you're actually a layman, isn't it? Maybe I'll get another head guard," President Ambo threatened.

Colonel Abdallah then pleaded with the President and said all he wanted is for him to make things a bit clearer to avoid mistakes.

President Ambo had to hit the nail on the head, and made it look like it's nothing out of the ordinary, and reminded the Colonel that being his bodyguard also requires him to take care of the enemies of the President.

"Now I get you, but which set of enemies are you particular about?" asked Colonel Abdallah.

President Ambo subtly told the Colonel that he's particularly interested in his political enemies posing a threat to his presidential seat, and insists he wants their threats neutralized.

"Mr. President, please give me a list of those you consider an enemy," said Colonel Abdallah.

President Ambo turned to leave, but walked back and reminded the Colonel of the fact that he mustn't leave traces that leads to him because these are behind the scene activities. Sheikh Suleiman Zurumi's interview in the United States has set President Ambo on a revenge mission, and his penchant for revenge has gotten the best of him because he felt denigrated by the Sheikh.

Colonel Abdallah smiled. "Mr. President, you chose me because they call me the perfect finisher," he said.

"Yes, I remember, but I'm surprised to see you waiting for me to make this request before you start acting," said President Ambo.

"Mr. President, don't worry, very soon you will have no enemies," replied Col. Abdallah.

A week later, President Ambo called Colonel Abdallah aside for a second time, and gave him a list of those he considers his enemies. He made it clear to the Colonel that these are those that have indicated interest in contesting for presidency yet urged him not to apply the same method for the cleanup process.

"Some of them will be implicated and sentenced to death, some will die by accident and others, in the hands of their girlfriends," said Col Abdallah.

President Ambo smiled, though with a fake smirk on his face. "That's perfect, at least I can trust you with this, but make sure Aasim doesn't know of this," said President Ambo.

The comment about Aasim being kept in the dark is a twist thrown into the mix, Colonel Abdallah looked lost as he reminded the President that Aasim is his son and can't be his enemy. Funnily, the President is only making sure, that no one throws a spanner in this mission.

President Ambo couldn't make his son look like the enemy, but he insisted that Aasim's Western lifestyle is drawing his household backwards, and he could blow the whole thing out if he knows about this.

"Western lifestyle? I don't understand," said Col. Abdallah.

President Ambo took his time to let Colonel Abdallah know that Aasim is someone he shouldn't touch with a ten-foot barge pole because here in the Middle East, people have respect for their parents, but that's lacking in the West.

"Ok, I'll keep it from him," said Col. Abdallah.

President Ambo turned to leave, but he then muttered and said at least there won't be anyone trying to take away his presidency from him after this clean up.

The next day Colonel Abdallah took two soldiers from the guards under his command as the head of presidential guard, and formed the Code Z. Firstly, he'd to let them know what they are getting into, he then went downstairs and called Hamza by himself.

"Sir," replied Hamza.

"I want you and Abba to meet me in my office now," said Col. Abdallah.

"Yes sir," said Hamza.

Minutes later, Hamza and Abba were in the Colonel's office, and he then stopped what he was doing and shut the file on his desk.

"I've selected the two of you for an important task, and the reason why I selected you is because you're both single and this mission is called Code Z," said Colonel Abdallah.

"Sir, what's the mission about?" asked Hamza.

"Shut up, I'm still talking, and it's because you're both single the tendency to be in a merry state of mind and reveal what you do to your wives will not happen. This is the reason I choose you, and can I trust you?" asked Colonel Abdallah.

"Yes sir," said Abba.

"Yes sir," said Hamza.

Colonel Abdallah informed them that there are certain people they'll have to take out, but they'll start with Sheikh Suleiman Zurumi in Abidkitan. Though, they won't kill him directly, but they'll set him up.

"How do we go about it sir?" asked Hamza.

"Get a gun that has never been documented, use it to kill somebody, and hide the gun in a place where it can be linked to the Sheikh," said Col. Abdallah.

"Yes sir," said Colonel Abdallah.

Colonel Abdallah assured Hamza and Abba they'll be handsomely rewarded yet took his time to remind them that if there's any mistake in this mission, they're dead, and if this secret is leaked, they're dead as well. The Colonel did a good job of extending the penalty of any failure of this mission to their families, so they now know that snitching will cost them their lives, and those of their aged parents.

"Yes sir," said Abba.

"Yes sir," said Hamza.

A week later, in other to make the setup a perfect one, Hamza and Abba spent days in Abidkitan putting Sheikh Suleiman Zurumi under surveillance, during which they observed him having a quarrelled with his mechanic.

Hamza turned to Abba and said they now have what they wanted, and it's time to strike. If they kill the mechanic, the Sheikh will be blamed for it, and a lot of people will believe he actually did it because of the animosity between them.

"When do we put things in motion?" asked Abba.

"Let's do it tonight, but that'll be in his shop when there won't be any eyewitness," said Hamza.

"Ok, that will be good," said Abba.

"Please, make sure you leave no prints on the gun," said Hamza.

That night they went to the mechanic's workshop and killed Awalu, the mechanic who publicly had a minor misunderstanding with Sheikh Suleiman Zurumi. The evening of the next day when the Sheikh was in the mosque for prayers, they went and hid the gun in his car.

It didn't take long after the gun was securely placed in the Sheikh's car, the Police Commissioner, Nasiru Dazi who has assisted the President to do his dirty jobs swings into action.

Nasiru Dazi was hinted to act, he called Sani, one of his officers and said intelligence reaching him seems to suggest Sheikh Suleiman Zurumi was behind the death of Awalu.

"Sir, do we pay him a visit?" asked Inspector Sani.

"Don't use the words "pay him a visit," the Sheikh is a big fish, and the world is watching," said Nasir Dazi.

"Sir, what do we do then?" asked Inspector Sani.

"Use words like, "let's invite him for questioning," said Nasir Dazi.

"Sir, do we invite him for questioning?" asked Inspector Sani.

"Yes, and once you arrest him don't allow him the privilege of going into his house to sort himself out," said Nasir Dazi.

"Sir, do we put him in handcuffs?" asked Inspector Sani.

"If you like, you can bring him in without handcuffs, but make sure he doesn't go into his car or enter anywhere," said Nasir Dazi.

"Ok sir," said Inspector Sani. The Inspector left and took three of his men to make the arrest.

Inspector Sani walks up to the Sheikh as he leaves the mosque. "Sheikh, good afternoon," said the inspector.

"Inspector, how're you, I hope we're safe?" Sheikh Suleiman jocularly asked.

"Yes Sheikh, you're safe, just that you're wanted at the station for questioning," said Inspector Sani.

Sheikh Suleiman was shocked to hear he's being invited for questioning and then asked what sort of joke this is.

The inspector's face isn't that of a man making jokes, he respectfully made his mission clear to the Sheikh, and said he isn't here for joke, and they're questioning him over the death of Awalu.

"Which Awalu are you talking about?" asked the Sheikh.

Inspector Sani told the Sheikh they're questioning him over the death of Awalu, his Mechanic.

"What! Is Awalu dead? But I saw him two days ago, and what has the death of Awalu got to do with me?" asked Sheikh Suleiman.

Inspector Sani told the Sheikh that eyes witnesses reported a misunderstanding between him and Awalu a day before he was shot dead.

Sheikh Suleiman became critical of this police team, sensing something quite sinister is fishing he immediately resorted to caution. He then said this is one of their jokes, but he isn't going with them without an arrest warrant.

Inspector Sani wasn't ready for any dawdling, he brought out the arrest warrant, and handed it to the Sheikh, and said this is the warrant for his arrest, and urged him to get going.

Sheikh Suleiman didn't move an inch, he took his time to peruse the warrant and realised all the I's were dotted, and T's, crossed, and then decided to go with them. "Hmm, you came prepared, ok, let's go," said Sheikh Suleiman.

The Sheikh followed the Inspector and his men to the Police station. While in the interrogation room the police engaged in a confession seeking interrogation, but the Sheikh didn't admit to any wrongdoing, then a search warrant was issued. This whole drama is happening so thick and fast, and the Sheikh is grappling with finding the appropriate response to his debacle.

While in the Sheikh's house for the search, Inspector Sani informed his men on places to focus their search. "Idris, search these areas, Mahi search these rooms, and Hauwa follow me," said Inspector Sani.

Sheikh Suleiman insists his hands are clean, saying they won't find anything because he has no knowledge of the crime he's being accused of. Sadly, this Sheikh have no idea the inner workings of President Ambo Hussein's government will catch up with him after stepping on the feet of the buccaneers of the Republic of Kitan.

Inspector Sani shunned the Sheikh, asking him to allow them do their job, and after pretending to search the entire house and finding nothing incriminating the Sheikh.

"Let's return to the station, so you can tell them there's nothing associating me to this crime," said Sheikh Suleiman.

"Hmm, let's search your cars," said Inspector Sani. They began searching his cars.

"What will you find in the car, if you can't find anything in my house?" asked Sheikh Suleiman.

Minutes later, the Inspector brought out the gun. "What's this?" asked Inspector Sani.

Sheikh Suleiman was shocked to see Inspector Sani dangling the gun in front of him and asking what this is.

"No, this can't be true, and this must be a set up," said Sheikh Suleiman.

"Is this your gun and do you've a license for this pistol?" asked Inspector Sani.

Sheikh Suleiman exclaimed and remained open-mouthed and insists this isn't his gun and questioned how the gun got inside his car.

Inspector Sani looked at the Sheikh with this filthy smirk on his face and said to the Sheikh that if this is the gun that killed Awalu, then he'll have to explain himself to the court.

Sheikh Suleiman then muttered and said "now I get it, this is the hand work of Ambo Hussein."

They left and returned to the police station, and a week later the prosecutor charged the Sheikh with the murder of Awalu.

After the arrest of Sheikh Suleiman, Code Z turned their attention to Sheikh Kazmi Nasir the presidential candidate of Kitan's labour Party.

Hamza went to the mechanic that works on Sheikh Kazmi Nasir's car. "Hello, you're Mallami, aren't you?" asked Hamza.

"Yes, I am, who wants to know, and is anything the matter?" asked Mallami.

This mechanic is known for being upfront, and never on the back foot, but his character flaw is the only one thing that puts him off, and that's his disdain for ceaseless flattery.

"You live here in Abidkitan opposite the bakery," said Hamza.

"How do you know where I live and what do you want from me?" asked Mallami.

Now that they have succeeded in getting his attention, Abba called Mallami aside, and softly told him a friend has a job for him.

"Which friend are you talking about, is it your friend or mine?" asked Mallami.

"Yes of course! It's mine we're talking about, and he's quite rich," said Abba.

Mallami was taken aback to hear this, he then asked if this rich friend knows a lowly Soul like him. Sadly, this mechanics' life is about to go up in smoke, and his encounter with these devils might be a turning point of his life. "Yes, he knows you, and that's why he sent us to you," said Abba.

"Ok, what job does he want me to do for him, is his car faulty?" asked Mallami.

Hamza whispered to Mallami and said this isn't about his friend's car, but they actually want him to disconnect the brake in Sheikh Kazmi Nasir's car.

"What! I can't do that, the Sheikh is a good man, and even the Almighty Allah won't forgive me," said Mallami.

"Mallami, don't worry, the Almighty Allah will forgive you but if you don't do it your wife and children will die, and Allah won't forgive you then," said Hamza.

"No, I can't do this to Sheikh Kazmi, his blood won't be on me, and you can't deceive me about the Almighty Allah's mercy, everyone knows the Almighty Allah forbids spilling innocent blood," said Mallami.

Hamza's patience is already growing thing, he then asked Mallami if he prefer to die. Interestingly, Mallami proved to be more than a bargain for this pair who would've killed him anyway even if he'd obliged to do their bidding for them.

"Yes, but you can't make me kill another man," said Mallami.

"Ok then," said Hamza. He brought a pistol and shot him twice on the head and Mallami died right there and then. Unfortunately, this mechanic is just a collateral damage in the scheme of things as Ambo Hussein re-enact himself.

"No, why did you do that? We should've convinced him a little more, maybe he would've accepted to do it," said Abba.

Hamza muttered, saying they don't need Mallami anymore, and after all, they still would've killed him after the assignment because he has seen their faces.

"Then how do we execute our plan?" asked Abba.

"We go for plan B," said Hamza.

Abba looked at Hamza and then complained he never told him they have a plan B. Hamza turned to Abba and smiled then said he just came up with it the moment he realised the mechanic was stalling. Abba then asked what the plan B was.

"I'll get a truck and crush Sheikh Kazmi Nasir's car with him inside his car, and it'll still look like an accident," said Hamza.

Abba stepped away from the mechanics' corpse, and said that wouldn't be a bad idea but they would need Sheikh Kazmi Nasir's itinerary to perfectly execute this.

"Yes, that'll enable us know the spot the accident will occur," said Hamza.

A week later, Sheikh Kazmi Nasir's car was crushed by a truck descending a steep hill in what was thought to be an accident, in which the driver of the truck couldn't be found.

After the death of Kazmi Nasir, and Sheikh Suleiman in custody for murder, Code Z turned their attention to Engineer Habu Kanti.

Days later, Safayat and her seven years old younger brother Bashir were tailed by Code Z and abducted in a quiet part of the market by men in balaclavas.

Hamza was wearing a balaclava "Come on, get in the car," he said.

"Leave me alone, I don't know you, leave me," said Safayat.

Abba quietly showed her a gun and spoke in a whisper. "Shush, if you make noise I'll kill you, and then kill your brother.

Safayat became quite terrified and pleaded with the men not to hurt them. They fearfully got in the car.

Immediately they had Safayat and her brother secured in the car, Abba brought out a piece of cloth, and then asked them to shut their eyes.

"Please, please don't hurt us, what are you going to do to us?" asked Safayat.

"If you stay calm, we won't hurt you, just don't make any noise," promised Hamza. They stayed calm and Abba tied their eyes with the piece of cloth, and the car drove some fairly long distance into a compound.

Abba then asked them to get down from the car, Safayat and Bashir alighted from the car, with their eyes still tied. Abba then advised Safayat and her brother to work gently so they don't stumble. "Where are we, please where are we?" asked Safayat. Sadly, seven-year-old Bashir was already crying.

Immediately they alighted from the car, Hamza urged them not to make a noise, and used his hand to cover Bashir's mouth, and just as they entered the house, he untied the cloth that was over their eyes.

Now that Safayat is able to see, she didn't hesitate to ask why these men in balaclavas brought them inside this house.

Hamza and Abba still had their balaclavas on when Hamza turned to Safayat and told her they want her to do something for them.

"What's it? Let us go please," said Safayat.

"You work for that politician, Engineer Habu Kanti, isn't it?" asked Hamza.

"Yes, but why're you asking?" she asked.

Abba brought out a small bottle containing a liquid substance and told Safayat that all they want from her is for her to administer this in Engineer Habu Kanti's food.

"No," she screamed. "I'm a good person, and I can't do that," said Safayat.

Hamza brought out a pistol and threatened Safayat, threatening to kill her and kill her brother right now.

"No, please, please, don't kill us," she pleads.

"Ok listen, we'll let you go and we'll keep your brother here, if you put this in Engineer Habu Kanti's food we'll release Bashir," said Abba.

"Please don't hurt my brother," said Safayat.

While still inside the room, with the car parked in a well fenced isolated compound, Abba urged her to just do what they asked of her, and promised, her brother will be safe. Safayat understands the ramification of being a killer, and she's sadly, being thrown into the deep end of blood and guts. "I'll be stoned to death; if people find out I killed Engineer Kanti," said Safayat.

"No, not all, the engineer won't die, he'll only suffer a stomach upset," said Abba.

"It's a lie, you want to use me to commit murder, and I'll be stoned to death, you know this," insists Safayat.

"Don't worry, the way this drug works, I promise you people won't know you're responsible," said Hamza. Safayat continued to plead with Hamza and Abba, urging them to let her and her brother off the hook, but Abba who seems to have run out of patience then yelled, enough of this talking. Abba quickly grabbed Safayat, tied her eyes, and they dragged her back to the car.

Bashir cried aloud. "Leave my sister, bring my sister back," said Bashir.

"Leave me, where's my brother? Please don't hurt my brother," said Safayat.

They drove off and took her back to town but before they allow her get out of the car, Abba assured her if she fails to do it, she'll see her brother's corpse on the very spot they were abducted. Hamza then untied her eyes yet reminded her that if she tells this to anyone, they'll kill her brother.

That night Safayat had to make a choice between her brother and her boss, whose house she lives in. It was like choosing between the devil and the deep blue sea, and after a deep thought and her fear for her brother's safety she then decided to empty the liquid inside her boss's glass of water. By mid night, Engineer Habu Kanti died of heart failure and by morning, Bashir, Safayat's younger brother was released unhurt.

The trial of Sheikh Suleiman Zurumi was watched around the world because he's a known figure, and sadly, the court process which was meant to make the killing of Sheikh Suleiman Zurumi genuine, was more of a theatrical show and a charade.

The Defence and the prosecuting counsel make their final submission.

Salem Othman (The defence Counsel): My lord, based on what the prosecuting counsel has presented, the accused has no case to answer. The forensic evidence was fabricated, incorrect and was handled by an agent of the state and not by an independent expert. As such this evidence should be inadmissible in this honourable court. My client should be discharged and acquitted by this court because the prosecution had led no credible evidence linking the accused to the alleged crime. Consequently, I urge the court to sustain the no case submission to discharge and acquit the defendant at this stage.

Nurud Sallam (The prosecution): My lord, we've placed oral and documentary evidence before this honourable court, and what's left for the defence counsel to do is to open his case. I insist that the prosecution has led credible evidence through the ten witnesses and the firearm responsible for the death of Awalu Tahir that has been presented to this honourable court.

The court was adjourned till the following week for judgement, and a week later, the court reconvened.

The Judge's ruling: After a thorough review of this case based on the evidence placed before me, I find the accused guilty of murder, and he's hereby sentenced to death by hanging.

A week later the sentence was hurriedly carried out, and there was fear and terror in the political clan in the Republic of Kitan. Even the self-proclaimed political labyrinths in the land are now scampering for safety. Funnily, all the presidential aspirants in the country had serendipitously been neutralised. It's glaringly obvious that even when no one is speaking out, fingers of accusation are pointed at President Ambo.

Days later, after the Hanging of Sheikh Suleiman Zurumi, Governor Labaran khan and his daughter Nafisat were in a conversation.

"Nafisat, I'm still talking to you, and where are you up to?" asked Governor Khan.

"Dad, I'm going to see Nawal; she came in two days back," said Nafisat.

Governor Khan didn't hesitate to ask his daughter why she's sounding as if she doesn't know Nawal has been in town days before.

"I knew she was in town, in fact we arrived Kitan together," said Nafisat.

Governor Khan has suddenly developed cold feet, and sadly his daughter's friendship with President Ambo's daughter seems to be a hand full for him particularly now that the brutishness of the president has sent a chill down the spines of most politicians.

He reminded his daughter she was with Nawal days before. "Do you've to pay her a visit?" asked Governor Khan.

Nafisat sensed a sudden apathy from her dad, towards her relationship with Nawal, sometimes her dad mutters under his breath but doesn't hit the nail on the head. "What's it dad? You suddenly seem not to be comfortable with my friendship with Nawal," asked Nafisat.

"I try as much as possible to stay far from President Ambo, and I expect you to do same with Nawal," he said.

Nafisat seem not to understand her dad's dilemma as she reminded her dad, he seems to have forgotten it was Nawal who convinced her dad to make him the governor of Shambihya. Governor Khan admitted that it was his daughter's friendship with Nawal that gave him this job, but Ambo isn't a man to be close to.

Nafisat's naivety meant she isn't following her dad's concern; she then turned and fixed her gaze on her dad and asked him what it was that President Ambo Hussein did to him that he suddenly dreads him this much.

"Didn't you hear of the death of Sheikh Suleiman Zurumi, don't you know he was set up?" asked Governor Khan.

Nafisat didn't hesitate to let her dad know that what he just said is common knowledge, and not something he should take to heart. She then echoed that everybody in Kitan knew Sheikh Suleiman Zurumi was set up and killed.

"What if it's me that fell into his trap; don't you think he will do same to me?" ask Governor Khan.

Nafisat is her dad's only child, and after her mum died of cancer ten years ago, she has always had her ways with her dad. She reminded him that everyone knew Ambo Hussein to be a devil that deserves using a long spoon to dine with yet urged her dad not to be this afraid.

"All other Governors stay clear from his path, and I just felt I should do same," said Governor Khan.

"Dad, but that shouldn't stop me from seeing my friend," she replied.

Governor Khan had no choice but to let his daughter have her way, his only parting word for his daughter is for her to be careful whenever she pays a visit to the President's house.

"You're right dad, the death of Sheikh Suleiman Zurumi is enough to cause jitters for any politician in Kitan," said Nafisat.

Governor Khan was quite sympathetic with the dead Sheikh Suleiman, and said the Sheikh was loved by everyone, and his death sent a strong message to citizens of his beloved nation.

"Dad, I'm leaving, I'll ask the driver to take me to the presidential villa," she said.

Her dad still sounded his note of caution one more time and urged her to be back in three hours time, just to keep Nafisat on a tight leash.

141

CHAPTER

FIVE

The diplomatic row

President Ambo in his crooked mind devised various killing means with which to neutralize every perceived threat. Unbeknown to President Ambo, the prying eyes of the international community weren't asleep, and the serendipity behind the mysterious deaths of all the presidential aspirants makes foolish of his wisdom. It didn't take long before the world began to react, and this time, they aren't crying wolf. They are reacting to the death of Sheikh Suleiman and other politically motivated deaths in Kitan. The first of such reaction was from foreign Secretary of the United States, who issued a press statement.

Alan Hill: Today the United States and its Allies wishes to state that the level of human right abuses and politically motivated killings in the Republic of Kitan is now alarming. There's no explanation for the mysterious deaths of these three presidential aspirants within a space of three months, and it's now a concern to the international community.

Therefore, the world wouldn't just sit on their hands and do nothing about this. We'll be in touch with our European Allies to come up with a robust response to these grave atrocities committed by this repressive regime.

Anne Bradford: I'm with the Daily Green newspaper, will the United States withdraw it ambassador from the Republic of Kitan?

Alan Hill: For now, our embassies will remain open to enable us continue to hold constructive talks with the government of the Republic of Kitan to see how we can bring these grave atrocities to an end.

Julie Pane: I'm with the TWRR news; we learnt from your earlier press statement that the ambassador of the United States is being recalled from Kitan, how can the embassies be opened without an ambassador?

Alan Hill: Yes, the ambassador was invited by the foreign office for briefing on how to engage as these dangerous trends unfolds in the Republic of Kitan, and when this briefing is over the ambas-sador will return.

Sarah Cox: I'm with the Waterfall press; will sanctions be part of the response from the United States?

Alan Hill: I must say the United States is weighing all options and at the moment sanctions aren't off the table. However, we'll apply the best option that helps to achieve our desired objective, and one that'll be beneficial to the people of the Republic of Kitan, I'll take only one more question.

Owen Johnson: I'm with the Box news, will the United States use its allies in the Middle East to pressure President Ambo Hussein into doing the right thing?

Alan Hill: The United States is already in contact with its Allies in the Middle East, and we're seeking ways to pressure President Ambo Hussein into doing what's right, but our long-term goal is helping the Republic of Kitan transit to a true democracy. Thank you.

President Ambo was filled with rage after watching the reaction of the United States foreign secretary on TWRR news, and he immediately convened an emergency meeting with his foreign minister and special advisers.

"I believe by now, most of you must've watched the press interview Alan Hill gave," said President Ambo. The President quickly played back the interview to refresh their memory.

Brigadier Sale Mai who's Kitan's head of military protested in anger after watching the clip, sadly he's had the privilege of watching the press statement before this meeting. "What's the meaning of this?" he asked. He then quickly took side with the President, making a mockery of Allan Hill, and saying he goofed up because his accusation lacked merit.

"Can you see that?" asked President Ambo.

Baha Aliyu, who's the foreign secretary apologised and quickly pointed out to the President that the British foreign secretary is making a press statement on the same issue as they speak.

President Ambo muttered and said these people are trying his patience. He immediately switched channel to watch the press statement from the British foreign secretary currently taking place. Interestingly, President Ambo likes stirring the broth but hates what it turns into when stirred. He quickly turned to the foreign secretary and instructed him to make a speech asking the international community not to meddle with the internal affairs of the Republic of Kitan. Baha Aliyu understands the inner workings of diplomacy, he quickly advised against any action that might be considered brash.

"Mr. President lets handle this with caution, maybe we should summon their ambassador to express our displeasure and then if they continue, we'll go a step further," said Baha Aliyu.

After summoning the United States Ambassador for a meeting, Baha Aliyu felt the need to take things a bit further.

Mr Baha Aliyu makes a press statement.

People of Kitan, it has come to our notice that the United States and its Allies have chosen to meddle in the internal affairs of the Republic of Kitan. We've always considered our Western Allies as our friends and treated them with respect, unfortunately they've decided to cast aspersions on our government without bothering to find out if what they called facts are true or not. However, we wish to state that our subtle approach in dealing with international affairs shouldn't be taken for cowardice, thank you.

The furore over the deaths of Presidential candidates in the Republic of Kitan continued to reverberate, and this has resulted in the United Nations Secretary General making a press statement.

Jean Black: The United Nations finds the spate of killings of Presidential candidates in the Republic of Kitan, as an act that can no longer be tolerated in a civilised world as ours.

Consequently, the United Nation Human Right Council will hold sessions which will commence as soon as possible to review the human right abuses in the Republic of Kitan in which victims of human right abuses will give testimonies of their experiences.

A week later, Malik, the eldest son of President Ambo, who's the minister for Finance received a call from the World Bank.

Malik picked up the call and it was Tracy Williams from the World Bank. "Hello Tracy, how're you?" he asked.

Immediately after their exchange of pleasantries, Malik went straight to discuss the intentions of his dad's government.

"I'm fine Tracy, when is the transfer taking place?" he asked.

"The transfer? That's why I'm calling you," she said.

"That's good then, I'll want the transfer done today," replied Malik.

Tracy Williams apologised to Malik, saying she's sorry the World Bank couldn't go through with the development loan his country requested.

"What do you mean by you couldn't go through with the loan? This loan has been approved, and all that was left is to effect the transfer," said Malik.

Tracy Williams applied a conciliatory tone, yet hinted Malik that this is down to the bank's board, and has nothing to do with her, and said the development loan was cancelled the previous night, during the meeting of the Board of the World Bank.

Malik exclaimed and felt insulted because he finds this decision to be quite squawky, before asking Tracy if she's thinks it's possible that a loan that has been approved and gone through all the necessary processes can be withdrawn just like that.

Tracy Williams decided to be upfront with Malik as opposed to being on the back foot in this matter, she reminded Malik that provided the transfer of funds hasn't taken place, then the Board can withhold the funds.

"This is a breach, and why did they do this?" asked Malik.

"The Republic of Kitan has a poor human rights record and the World Bank doesn't support a nation where the citizens are killed by their leader," said Tracy.

"What do you mean by this? Stop saying what you know nothing about," said Malik.

Tracy Williams said she isn't disillusioned on this subject, yet she quickly pointed out to Malik and said it isn't her saying, but the notoriety of his dad's government is all over the headlines.

Malik decided to soft pedal, thinking he could sweet talk her into getting the board to revisit the loan, he softly told her their government relied on this loan to fund the building of a new rail line from Abidkitan to Ansarouh.

"I'm sorry, but that's the decision of the World Bank," said Tracy.

Malik decided not to play the loser's card with Tracy any longer, particularly now that the World Bank has aligned with his dad's enemies. He then asked Tracy if this whole hysteria has metamorphosed into some kind of fraternal resentment. Tracy Williams is equally a politician of some sort, as she said the world has chosen not to sit on their hands, they've chosen to take collective action.

"Ok, let me get back to the President and inform him of this new development," said Malik.

"Ok Malik, I've to go," she said.

Immediately after his phone conversation with Tracy Williams, Malik stood from his seat and asked his driver to take him to the President's office.

Malik walked into his dad's office. "Dad, I just finished speaking with Tracy Williams," he said.

"Ok, when is she transferring the funds for our speed rail project?" asked President Ambo.

Malik suddenly gave a sobering look as he informed his dad that they've cancelled the loan even after the loan has been approved and processed. Sadly, the world could see right through President Ambo's disguise, and the chickens have come home to roost. The news of the cancellation of the loan spooked President Ambo, and he didn't hesitate to question if Tracy is okay, and why she would do such a thing.

"Dad, this isn't Tracy, it's the Bank's Board that took the decision," said Malik.

"Why, that's what I'm asking, why did they take such an insensitive action? asked President Ambo.

Malik had to go for the reported speech approach particularly now that the international community has given his dad the middle finger. "They said they can't support us because of our human rights record," said Malik.

"What nonsense?" asked President Ambo.

"Dad, with the present crude oil glut in the market, how do we fund the speed rail project without this loan?" asked Malik.

President Ambo didn't need to be lectured about where to point his finger of accusation, as he didn't bat an eyelid before saying the United States and their European Allies are behind this, and he knew they have the World Bank in their pocket.

"But dad, do we really need the loan, we're a rich nation?" said Malik.

"Malik, we need the loan, the fiscal bubble you're seeing is a fragile one," said President Ambo. This isn't a country that's suffering economic free fall, yet Malik has now been intimated that even rich nations still need loans for developmental projects. He then proceeded to ask his dad how he intends to address the interference from the West, because they're prying so much into their internal affairs.

President Ambo isn't just willing to talk tough, he has chosen to match his words with action, and he has now decided that the West can't be his enemy and remain in his country, he's therefore sending them packing.

"Ok, that's a good idea," said President Ambo.

President Ambo invites his Foreign Minister to his office immediately after Malik left.

"Good morning Mr. President," said Baha Aliyu.

"Baha, I sent for you because we can't be taken for fools," said President Ambo.

"Mr. President, I don't understand, who's taking us for fools?" asked Baha Aliyu.

President Ambo informed Baha that the development loan he requested from the World Bank that's meant for the nation's speed rail project has just been cancelled after approval. This whole kerfuffle might even get worse before it gets better. Baha Aliyu always had his hat of diplomacy on as he suggested to President Ambo that it's advisable for the minister for finance to organise a meeting with the President of the World Bank.

The President ruled out Malik's involvement, and said his son Malik doesn't have the stamina to withstand these people. "Then you should arrange for the meeting yourself, and persuade him to reconsider the decision," said Baha.

President Ambo was upfront in sharing with all who cared to hear including Baha that the United States is behind all these.

"Yes Mr. President, you're right, but what do we do?" asked Baha.

President Ambo yelled and said he'll send them a strong message, so they know he's not to be toyed with.

Baha Aliyu didn't think a brash response will do the trick of bringing the West back to the table, he quickly reminded President Ambo that a tit for tat shouldn't be the best way out of these ruptured relations.

President Ambo said he doesn't care, and after all, he has just been insulted and he isn't having any of it. He then instructed Baha Aliyu to give a press statement on the matter.

"What should I say, Mr. President?" asked Baha.

"I want the United States and its Allies to leave the Republic of Kitan within twenty-four hours," said President Ambo.

"Persona non grata? No, Mr President, some of these nations apply strict reciprocity, while others could respond in a manner tougher than we may expect," said Baha.

"Baha, I'm the President, just do what I've asked, forget about your personal magnetism," said President Ambo.

"Ok Mr. President, I'll do that immediately," said Baha.

Heaving around in his ocean like a whale, it's obvious that this President is in a state of cognitive dissonance. Even at that, he'll never acquiescence the move to stay calm in the face of international rebuke, particularly now that the horse has bolted. It didn't take long after his meeting with President Ambo, requesting he asks the United States and its Western Allies to leave his country, Baha Aliyu issued a press statement.

Baha Aliyu: Citizens of Kitan, today our country has just been denied the needed funds necessary to finance our speed rail project.

This Speed rail is supposed to run from Abidkitan to Ansarouh, to bring development to our nation. The World Bank called the minister for finance this morning to tell him the development loan which has been approved and has passed through all the necessary processes have been cancelled. As we all know, this is the hand work of the United States and its European Allies, and we wish to say enough is enough. However, the government of the Republic of Kitan gives the United States and its European allies just twenty-four hours to leave our country, thank you.

Now that President Ambo had fanned the flames of a ruptured relationship with the international community, the West have decided to reciprocate in a tit for tat as Baha had feared.

The United States and her Western Allies froze all the assets of the Republic of Kitan in their respective countries and rolled out a list of sanctions against the Republic of Kitan.

Alan Hill: Today, the United States has rolled out a list of sanctions against the Republic of Kitan. Henceforth, all the assets including bank accounts of the Republic of Kitan in the United States has been frozen with immediate effect. I know our European Allies are thinking of doing the same until President Ambo Hussein learn to rule his people in an acceptable manner. Thank you.

With the Republic of Kitan being blacklisted and sanctioned by the international community, the nation's stock market has crashed and investors are selling off and moving their investment some-where else. A move that has quite a chilling effect on the nation's economy, and those lingering and hoping for a dead cat bounce seemed to have misjudged the precariousness of the situation.

A week later, Aasim walked into his dad's office to inform his dad that his account has just been frozen.

President Ambo looked at his son with his masked professionally detached hysteria. "What has that got to do with me?" asked President Ambo.

Aasim was quite upset to find himself sharing in his dad's karma and told his dad this has everything to do with him because he's being punished because of his dad's actions.

President Ambo rebuked Aasim for crying wolf and reminded him he isn't the only one whose account was frozen. After all, accounts belonging to his brothers were also frozen, but he's the only one making a fuss about this whole thing.

"You know the truth, dad. Malik and Umar have most of their assets in the Middle East, their assets in the West are close to nothing, I'm the only person that has all my assets in Europe," said Aasim.

"That's the price you pay for turning yourself into a European, marrying a European woman, and leaving all your assets in Europe," said President Ambo.

"So, you don't care about what happens to my assets?" asked Aasim. Aasim insists he has no reason to share in his dad's karma because his hands are clean, and interestingly, you just don't dance with the devil and walk away, you can't. People always think they can, but they can't, and in this case, Aasim's sin is that of his association with his dad, and his dad's cavalier attitude says it all.

"Why would I care, when you equally don't care about working with me?" asked President.

"I get it," said Aasim.

President Ambo reminded Aasim that his brothers were wise to have most of their assets in the Arab nations where their assets would be safe. He insisted that if Aasim had listened, his assets would've been safe.

Sadly, Aasim felt was his dad was deflecting from the crux of the matter, and he's now taking a mickey out of him, and felt there's no need continuing this conversation. Yet, reminded his dad that the location of his assets should be a decision he alone should make. He then turned around and left his dad's office.

Now that the world has a clearer picture of the blood and guts associated with President Ambo's government, he felt it's time for a charm offensive to see if he can change perception about his government. The heart of this President is filled with too many deceitful schemes, and this time, he needed to pull one off his sleeve. President Ambo then walked up to Colonel Abdallah and said it's time for damage control.

"In what area, Mr. President?" asked Colonel Abdallah.

"Colonel, I want you to help me put up a rally that will counter international perceptions about my government," said President Ambo.

"Mr. President, I can't put up a rally against you," said Colonel Abdallah.

"No, this wouldn't be a rally against me; rather, it'll be for me," said President Ambo.

Colonel Abdallah listened keenly to understand what's expected of him because he knows too well, the penalty for error. He then asked the President how he wants the rally to appear.

"I'll release one million dollars for the rally; just gather people from various cities chanting support for me," said President Ambo.

"Where do you want them to hold the rally?" asked Colonel Abdallah.

President Ambo wants this theatrical display of emotion for him to be carefully orchestrated and well choreographed in a manner that will make it seem real to those prying eyes that allowed themselves to be deceived. He told the Colonel that he wants the rally to start from somewhere and end at the city's' central square so he could come and address them.

"Ok Mr. President, Code Z will handle it perfectly," said Colonel Abdallah.

Colonel Abdallah had to set up a new task for Code Z, and that will be organising a one million solidarity march in support for President Ambo.

"Hamza, where's Abba?" asked Colonel Abdallah.

"He's on guard at the gate," said Hamza.

Colonel Abdallah then instructed Hamza to go and get Abba, and said he wants to see the two of them in his office because there's an assignment for Code Z.

Few minutes later Hamza and Abba were in the Colonel's office. "We're here, sir," said Hamza.

Colonel Abdallah began by saying he must commend them for their good job with the enemies of Mr. President, after all, they've earned their stripes.

"Thank you, sir," said Abba.

Colonel Abdallah then informed them that the President has just voted one million dollars for a solidarity march in support of his continuing in office. He then instructed them to get somebody to lead the campaign.

"What's the campaign about, sir?" asked Abba.

Colonel Abdallah had to lecture them as he advised them to get somebody that's loved by the people, to gather people together to chant support for the President.

"Sir, when do you want this to happen?" asked Abba.

"Latest next week, go to town, use your old tricks and get somebody to do it," said Colonel Abdallah.

"Ok sir," said Hamza.

Code Z swung into action immediately, but their first assignment is getting the right person to spear head the solidarity march. Unfortunately, this move is just meant to stop the bleed but not to heal the wound because the country's reputation is already in tatters, all the President wants is just to stop further sanctions.

Hamza and Abba's first act was to arrest a journalist whose son was popular and commands respect among the people.

Days later, Code Z went for Tammim Ibrahim, who was the son of the arrested journalist. His dad was arrested for offensive posts against the government. Hamza called Tammim and told him they want to have a word with him.

"What word do you've to say to me, after arresting my dad innocently?" asked Tammim.

"I suppose you're aware we have your dad in our custody?" asked Abba.

Tammim is the son of a journalist, he obviously knows about some of the mischief of these two, and it's no longer news that they came to his house and took his dad forcefully.

"If you can help us, then we'll release your dad, or else he'll be tried for treason and you know what that means," said Hamza. Sadly, the arrest of his dad was a leverage to make Tammim do their bidding.

"Who'll trust you guys? A lot of people have idea of the dirty jobs you guys do. At least, you know I'm the son of a journalist," said Tammim.

"You're not supposed to trust me, but I give you my word," said Hamza.

"Ok then, what's it you want me to do?" asked Tammim.

Hamza spoke softly to Tammim, saying everyone knew him to be outspoken, and the people love him, and they want him to organize a rally in support for President Ambo. This request didn't only come as a stinker to Tammim, it actually spooked him, organising a rally for a man he has protested against all his life is a no brainer.

"No, not in my lifetime will I do a thing like that," said Tammim.

Abba didn't mince his words as he replied Tammim and reminded him his dad will be a dead man if he doesn't and that he'll be tried for treason and hanged publicly with his body on display, dangling for all to see.

Tammim became quite afraid over his dad's fate, he knows for sure these guys aren't blowing smoke, and these guys are nothing, but the horse men of death. "Does it mean you used my dad's arrest as a bait just to get at me?" asked Tammim.

"Yes, what do you think? But we'll finance everything, and reward you handsomely," said Hamza.

Behind this reward is a big stick to weep Tammim into line, and choosing either of the carrot or the stick places Tammim between the rock and a hard place because the carrot and stick are both ghastly, and he unfortunately must choose either or both.

Abba gave Tammim a phone number and urged him to give them a call if he's ready to do as asked, and urged him to make haste because his dad's life is hanging on a tread.

Tammim suddenly said he doesn't think this is something he can do. He then attempted walking away angrily.

Sadly, he's dealing with people who are nothing but a semblance of evil.

"Then consider your dad dead, not just dead, but to the amusement of the crowd," said Hamza.

Throughout that night Tammim was plagued and couldn't get over the thought of his dad's body dangling on display, and in full glare for the world to see. Sadly, the fear of what might befall his dad broke Tammim's resolve because these two crooks gave him quite a scare. Tammim got up quite early, with his eye glued to the wall clock until it was 8.am that morning. He then dialled the phone number Abba gave him. "Hello Sergeant Abba, it's me Tammim," he said.

"Tammim, are you ready for us?" asked Abba.

"Yes, I'm ready, but one day the Almighty Allah will reward you for your actions," said Tammim.

"Shut up and meet me opposite the trade centre so we can talk further," said Abba.

Hamza was standing beside Abba when Tammim's phone call came in, and after their conversation Hamza asked Abba whom it was he was speaking with.

"It's Tammim, that mouthy young man," said Abba.

"What's it about him and is he ready for us?" asked Hamza.

"Of course, he's ready, because he doesn't want to see his dad's body dangling on display," said Abba.

"That's good, so what's next?" asked Hamza.

"Let's go, I told him to meet us opposite the trade centre," said Abba. They drove off immediately, and twenty-five minutes later they were at the trade centre waiting for Tammim. It didn't take long before Tammim showed up. "Oh, here you're?" he asked.

"Yes, but what you're asking me to do is very evil and you know I'll be hated by all for doing this, but I'll do it for my dad," said Tammim.

"Don't worry my friend, you'll make lots money," said Abba.

Hamza had to lecture Tammim on what's expected of him, and the nature of the assignment, and said they want him to get some people to join him organize this solidarity march.

"How will it work?" asked Tammim.

Hamza reminded Tammim that the President will release one million dollars to him and his men to share to as many people that are willing to attend this rally.

Abba reminded Tammim they'll give him the money two days to the day of the rally, and urged him not to leave town once he collects the money, and any attempt to escape with the money will bring death for him and his dad.

Tammim didn't hesitate to remind this pair that the money is blood money, and advised them not to worry, then told them he's only doing this for his dad.

"The title of the rally is one million solidarity march for President Ambo Hussein," said Hamza.

Tammim didn't hesitate to let them know that a lot of people won't come, and pursuing a target number of one million people is an overreach.

Hamza is a man who believes money does magic, he didn't hesitate to dismiss Tammim's concern and said with money people will come even if they don't like the President. He then urged Tammim to make sure he shares enough money to them.

Tammim don't want to give the evil pair an opportunity for an excuse that will make them kill his dad, he had to hit the nail on the head and said he can't gather one million people because that will be an overstatement.

"No, at least we need about one hundred thousand people, which will be from about ten cities," said Hamza.

"We'll be marching to the central square, I suppose?" asked Tammim.

Hamza smiled and nodded his head in affirmation and said cameras will be there to film the whole thing for the world to see. Abba urged Tammim to make sure he says nice things about the President, and after the rally his dad will be released immediately.

After setting things in motion with Tammim, Hamza went to the Colonel's office, and reported back, saying everything is ready.

"What's ready?" asked Colonel Abdallah.

"The one million solidarity march in support for our President," said Hamza.

"Ok that's good, and when is it happening?" asked Colonel Abdallah.

"That will be next week Thursday, about ten days from now.

"Ok, I'll get the money ready to enable him mobilise people for the rally," said Colonel Abdallah.

"Ok sir," said Hamza.

The day of the one million solidarity march for President Ambo Hussein is here with Tammim leading the pack as they march and chants support for the President.

Tammim: Today, we the citizens of the Republic of Kitan have gathered here to express our support for President Ambo Hussein. We say we're happy with the work you're doing, and for that we're asking you to continue with your job as the President of our beloved nation. Tammim then turned to the crowd, "who do we want?"

Crowd of supporters: Ambo Hussein, Ambo Hussein, Ambo Hussein.

"What do we want to say to Ambo Hussein?" asked Tammim.

Crowd: Continue being our president.

"Again," asked Tammim.

Crowd: Continue being our president.

President Ambo's motorcade drove out of the presidential villa to the central square as he moves to grace his supporters. On arrival, he alighted from his car beaming with a smile like that of a child on a sugar rush. He then took the microphone to make a speech.

President Ambo: Thank you people of the Republic of Kitan, I must say I'm overwhelmed by the solidarity you've just displayed. Today, you've proved your love and support for the world to see, I believe the press are here to cover this happy moment in the history of our dear nation.

Therefore, I wish to remind my friends and those who chose to be my enemies that the people of the Republic of Kitan have come to ask from their heart, that I Ambo Hussein should continue being their President.

People of Kitan, I appreciate this great gesture. Thank you.

Tammim has received so many death threats for organising such a rally in favour of Ambo Hussein, yet he went ahead, and sadly, he has been bullied into drinking this Kool-Aid that turned him into the enemy of the people.

By the evening of the same day, Tammim came for his dad, and Hamza was quite upfront with him this time as he praised Tammim and said he did a good job.

Tammim wasn't up for any corrupt flattery and went straight on to request his dad's release from Hamza.

"You deserve to be complemented," said Hamza.

"I don't need your compliment, just hand my dad over to me," said Tammim.

"Ok follow me," said Hamza.

Tammim followed Hamza and they went to one of the cells in the presidential villa, and immediately Tammim sighted his dad through the bars of the cell, he asked his dad if he's ok. Al-Gailani, Tammim's dad quickly asked his son what he was doing here, and sadly, he has been in the dark and has no knowledge his son had pact with the devil.

"Nothing dad, I've come to secure your release," said Tammim.

"What did you tell them that's making them to release me just like that?" asked Al-Gailani. Suddenly, the hinges of the door of Al-Gailani's cell squeaks as the door was opened, and Tammim's dad was released. Tammim knew he had crossed the line to secure his dad's release, and he wasn't proud of it.

"Dad we'll talk about that later, when we get home," said Tammim. The moment Tammim and his dad drove out of the President's secured neighbourhood; they noticed they were being followed.

"Look behind you, that car seems to be following us," said Al-Gailani.

"I noticed it," said Tammim.

"Oh, you knew and never said anything about it, when did you noticed we were being followed?" asked Al-Gailani.

Tammim told his dad he knew they were being followed about ten minutes back, and he's been keenly watching the stalker through his rear-view mirror.

Al-Gailani sensed this stalking is unto something grim and sinister, he quickly suggested they call the police, but Tammim muttered under his breath, and said he knew it will come to this. Tammim's comment seemed to ring an alarm bell in his dad's head, and he quickly interjected to know what concern it was that his son just talked about.

"What will come to this, what are you talking about, and what have you done?

"Nothing dad, I only did what I've to do to secure your release, and that's why death threats were coming," said Tammim.

Al-Gailani was taken over by despair, and he quickly asked his son what it was he did to secure his release, and who it was that wants his son dead. Sadly, before Al-Gailani finished speaking, Tammim was shot twice, and the assailant sped off. Tammim's speech slurred as he told his dad he did what he could to prevent Ambo Hussein from killing him, he then apologised to his dad before taking his last breath.

Al-Gailani was thrown into confusion, and it was as if his world just ended. "Tammim, Tammim, what did you do to deserve this, oh God, who has been planning to destroy me?" asked Al-Gailani, and unfortunately Tammim died right in his dad's arms.

Months later, the Foreign Minister of the Republic of Kitan issued a press statement.

Baha Aliyu: We wish to state that the Republic of Kitan will no longer take part in the United Nations Human Rights Council sessions examining our purported human rights abuses.

I must say the West has been politicizing everything that concerns the United Nation and its human rights campaign, particularly when it comes to our dear nation, the Republic of Kitan because they have the United Nations in their pocket. We have observed double standards in both their dealings and in the reports of the human rights watch.

Therefore, we will not continue in this spectacle where citizens who have one thing or the other against our government are being paid to make frivolous accusations against us in the form of witness testimonies.

I must make this clear to our friends and to those who chose to see the Republic of Kitan as an enemy, that we will never be bound by any resolution adopted by the council. Thank you.

CHAPTER

SIX

The Military Coup

While the diplomatic row persists, an ex-military chief in the country who is an in-law to the late Sheikh Suleiman Zurumi decided to stage a coup, to oust President Ambo Hussein from power. It's like President Ambo Hussein has an axe to grind with a lot more people than he thinks. While a number of military chiefs were on official mission in Tunisia during the Arab League Security Council.

Retired Brigadier Mumtaz took advantage of this foreign assignment to call some serving military chiefs for a covert meeting. "You're all welcome, and I know you must all be wondering why we're meeting here in Tunisia, as opposed to the Republic of Kitan. I must say it's because of the nature of the assignment on the ground," said Rtd. Brigadier Mumtaz.

Brigadier Bachakar was in the meeting and also a serving Military Chief, he paused for a while. "Hmm Brigadier, from what you're insinuating this meeting is against the state, I suppose?" asked Brigadier Bachakar.

"What if someone sees us gathering here, you know President Ambo has eyes everywhere?" Colonel Salman.

Retired Brigadier Mumtaz nodded in affirmation and said the meeting is against President Ambo, but not against the people of the Republic of Kitan, because it's about liberation. More so, it's taking place at night, and no one will see them here in Tunisia.

"Brigadiers, I'm sorry I've a family and I don't think getting involved in this, is right," said Colonel Salihu.

Colonel Salman turned to Colonel Salihu and urged him to calm down because everyone in this meeting has a family they truly care about.

"Brigadier Bachakar, you served under me, and you know I'm not a careless person and if I must ask, who will help this country if not you and I?" asked Rtd. Brigadier Mumtaz.

Brigadier Bachakar turned to retired Brigadier Mumtaz and said he understands the Retired Brigadier when he said this isn't about them, but about the citizens of their country. "What do you want me to do," asked Brigadier Bachakar.

Brigadier Mumtaz laid bare his strategy and said he'll bring in arms from his foreign friends around the world who are in support of this assignment. He then left Brigadier Bachakar to take charge of deployment of logistics.

Colonel Salman was quite up for this action, but then asked the Brigadiers about what the next line of action should be in case things didn't go as plan.

Brigadier Mumtaz had to hit the nail on the head, and said everyone in attendance should know that President Ambo won't spare them if things go south. He then urged them to all prepare their minds to die.

Colonel Salihu has been on the back foot since he was made aware of the purpose of the meeting because he considered himself the underdog in this whole arrangement. "Brigadier, I've a family and I want to be there for them, and I don't think I've good feelings about this," said Colonel Salihu.

Colonel Salman who's a fellow Colonel quickly interjected in a bid to assuage his fellow Colonel of his concerns, urged Colonel Salihu to look at the bright side of things, and reminded him they all want to be with their families as well.

Colonel Salihu didn't like the bandwagon effect and reminded Colonel Salman that the Brigadiers children are all grown up so they won't feel it much, but his own kids are still tender and he doesn't want to leave them at the mercy of another man.

Retired Brigadier Mumtaz had to step in, and said he equally love to be alive, and if this Military Coup succeeds, he wouldn't want to be in government and he's only here to contribute to the liberation of his dear country. Brigadier Bachakar urged all his serving military personnel to look at this from the bright side, and that he'll begin to pick those that will do the job with them.

"We'll reconvene this meeting in a month's time, to review progress and how prepared we're," said Rtd. Brigadier Mumtaz. He then turned to Colonel Salihu and told him he trusted him that's why he involved him in this, and then urged him to be happy about being a part of this assignment.

Aasim has maintained a safe distance from his dad, but his inability to travel has been quite nerve wrecking for him. He then decided it's time to revisit the issue a second time, to request the return of his passport and travel documents.

"Aasim, what are you doing in my office, have you come to tell me when you wish to resume your appointment?" asked President Ambo.

Aasim was prepared for his dad's usual one liner and responded with his own one liner and said they will only talk about his resumption to duty if his dad hands over his travel documents to him.

"Why should I do that, answer me, Aasim?" asked President Ambo.

Aasim mumbled and said he wants his passport because it's his, and not his dad's. Interestingly, President Ambo felt it's best for Aasim to be on his toes by giving him the run around, insisting he already told him his travel documents aren't with him.

"You know I know it's with you, so why should I believe you?" asked Aasim.

"Because you've got no choice than to believe me," replied President Ambo.

Aasim had to find a way of pressuring his dad to return his travel documents, he then told him his fiancée isn't feeling fine, and he needed to go and see her. President Ambo in turn accused Aasim of itching to run off to Germany to tell his German fiancée he saw his dad kill people, and she will encourage him to tell it to the press.

"What I discuss with my fiancée is my business, and it has got nothing to do with you," said Aasim.

"I want you to change your mind and join your father in building this nation," said President Ambo.

Aasim had a lot of animosity towards his dad and doesn't hesitate to get them off his chest whenever he'd the chance. "You should've thought about that before pointing a gun at me after killing my brother right before my eyes," said Aasim.

President Ambo toned down his hard stance as he puts away his posture of a cavalier before asking Aasim why is it he finds it difficult to move past the gun-pointing incident?

"Some things are just too difficult to forget," said Aasim.

"Why don't you get a wife from Kitan, or even Tunisia, Qatar, Egypt or any Arab nation, any woman at all, just point her and you'll have her, and why must it be an European woman?" asked President Ambo.

"Love is blind they say, nobody decides who they fall in love with," said Aasim.

President Ambo dismissed Aasim's 'love is blind' cliché as utter nonsense, and said it's possible to have feelings for someone, but it behoves on Aasim to decide whether or not to go along with the pulse of his heart. Moreover, things of the heart can be deceitful.

"Give me my passport because I need to be with my woman," said Aasim.

"Your choice of woman, why is that? I don't think it's because European women are more fastidious, maybe you prefer them because they are salacious and I hate that appetite of yours," said President Ambo.

Aasim becomes uncomfortable as his dad winds him up by describing his fiancée as salacious, and sadly, his dad is beginning to do his head in. He quickly protested even as he watched his utterances to avoid his dad turning on him. "Why're you hounding me? There's nothing hinky about my appetite, just give me my passport," said Aasim.

President Ambo suddenly became bored and said this conversation is over for now, he then urged Aasim to ask for his passport where he left it.

Aasim sensed that the conversation has suddenly turned thorny, he then reminded his dad that this isn't over, because he'll either point his gun at him again or he gives him his travel documents. As he took some steps in his attempt to walk out of his dad's office. "Hey, hey, (he growled) come, please come," his dad said in a softer tone.

"Why the sudden change in tone?" asked Aasim.

"What happened to us? I mean, you and me," asked President Ambo.

"Nothing, just that we are, who we are," said Aasim.

"No, I want my sweet little boy back, that innocent and obedient Aasim, is all I wanted," said President Ambo.

Aasim understands too well that his dad is playing on his emotions, and this sudden soft tone is a smoke screen. "That's the Aasim standing before you, I only consolidated on the qualities you just mentioned," said Aasim.

"No, not at all, what I have now for a son is an impostor, the real Aasim went to Europe to study and never came back, the person that returned from Europe is quite a different person," he growled.

"Dad, people change!" exclaim Aasim.

He felt the need not to continue along this path with his dad, because he thinks there's no need to continue grasping at straws when the opportunity to do what's right is glaring to all.

"No, father-son relationship remains the same, irrespective of the son's age, meaning I'm still in charge here," said President Ambo.

"I guess you know, a wall isn't just one brick," said Aasim.

President Ambo got upset and stood up in anger, as he pointed out to Aasim that his comment was quite insulting.

Aasim had to step aside for calm, and yet insisted he's coming back for his passport before walking away in anger.

Aasim's German fiancée isn't feeling too well, and she has been nagging him to death to return to Germany. This would have been easy for anyone, but sadly, Aasim's dad had his travel documents tucked away, and he's now in a bind and sorting himself out of his present conundrum is now a tall order. After his failed attempt to retrieve his travel documents from his dad who seems hell bent on having him in the military, Aasim had to call his fiancée to plead for time. "Hey Nicole, what's up?" asked Aasim.

"I told you I haven't been feeling well," she replied.

Aasim interjected and asked Nicole if she has been able to see a doctor as they discussed two hours earlier. Nicole affirmed she did, and she's just finished with her doctor before hitting the nail on the head as she asked about the outcome of his meeting with his dad.

"I'm still having some trouble with my dad, and I'll join you immediately I get it sorted," he said.

"What do you want me to do, sit down and wait for eternity or what?" asked Nicole. This lady isn't just having a migraine, she's lovesick, and her so called fiancée is held hostage by his dad. Sadly, the further Aasim dug his hill the dirtier it gets.

"Baby, I'll join you soon and everything will be perfect," said Aasim.

Nicole heard a knock on the door and had to end the conversation, she then told Aasim they'll talk later.

Aasim called Maman, a native of the Republic of Kitan who plays for a German Division One club. Aasim was instrumental in helping Maman leave the country to Germany where he's now based through his help.

"I'm fine, Maman, how's Germany?" asked Aasim.

"I'm fine, but what are you still doing in Kitan? You should be here by now," said Maman.

Aasim told Maman not to worry that he'll come over to Germany when the time is right but for now, he's ironing out some issues with his dad. Maman informed Aasim he saw Nicole a day before and she wasn't feeling too well, he then asked Aasim if he's aware of this.

"Yes, she told me about it and I would've been in Germany, just that my dad seized my travel documents," said Aasim.

"Why's he doing that?" asked Maman.

Aasim opened up to his friend, Maman, saying his dad wants him to head his military intelligence unit and he declined the offer.

Maman seemed to be following the happenings in the Republic of Kitan much more than Aasim does as he was quick to remind Aasim that the President mentioned Aasim's appointment in his silver jubilee speech. Maman was upfront in reminding Aasim that the offer is a good one and asked why he is refusing the job. He had to make it clear to Maman that he ditched mediocrity and have chosen to live his life on his own terms.

"You and I know why, there are lots of human rights abuses going on and I wouldn't want to be part of it," said Aasim.

"Now I get it, you aren't like your brothers who just join the flow," said Maman.

Aasim understands too well that his brothers were trapped in their dad's vortex, and said his brothers are doing their best, just that they can't help it.

"Aasim, I owe everything I'm today to you, you picked me from the gutter and brought me to Germany, just as you've done for so many poor people in Kitan. Please, don't think we aren't seeing the sacrifices you're making for the poor," said Maman. Aasim smiled and said he has come to understand that the good life isn't for one person, and the world will be a much better place when that good life is shared with others. Maman made it clear to Aasim that this isn't just some form of corrupt flattery, and said he's just expressing how a lot of guys feel about the good things he's doing for them.

Retired Brigadier Mumtaz is being briefed by his inside men to enable him to ascertain how soon the Military coup will be executed. This is their second meeting in Tunisia, and it's happening in the dark of the night.

"Officers, you're all welcome, we're gathered here today because plans like this aren't meant to be dragged out for too long, so

Brigadier Bachakar please brief us on the level of preparation," said Rtd. Brigadier Mumtaz.

"Officers, everything is set as we speak, we already have an inside man in the intelligence unit, another in armoury and another in the television and radio broadcasting station," said Brigadier Bachakar.

"What about the presidency?" asked Rtd. Brigadier Mumtaz.

"I'll be with the President the moment the action kicks off and I'll take him on myself, but before then, I'll use one of our Armoury maintenance personnel to disarm the tanks in the presidential palace," said Brigadier Bachakar.

"I'll make sure the armoury in the state capital is out of use the moment the action begins," said Colonel Salman.

"One of my sergeants will take care of the broadcasting services, he will take it and then I'll move in with my men to make the broadcast," said Colonel Salihu.

Retired Brigadier Mumtaz held onto his altruistic view and urged the officers to make this a bloodless coup if things go as plan, he then gave a nod and said he's happy with the strategy in place so far. Colonel Salihu interjected and asked the Brigadier about the shipment of the ammunitions he promised.

Retired Brigadier Mumtaz informed the officers the shipment has already arrived, and Brigadier Bachakar has already seen them, so there won't be any problem with logistics.

Brigadier Bachakar had to give the final briefing and reminded the officers this operation will take place in the next two weeks, and it will be on Friday immediately President Ambo returns from Mosque. He then urged then to meet in the week following for final assessment and then wish each other well.

"Officers, thank you for coming and until we meet again next week, I wish you all well," said Rtd. Brigadier Mumtaz.

The solidarity march that was meant to deceive the world ended up in the ultimate ambiguity because the reputational bleed didn't stop, rather the Arab league has just suspended the Republic of Kitan. Sadly, this news is going to hit him hard below the belt, much more than a ton of rock will do, suffice to say that the Arab League is President Ambo's last bastion of hope. Malik paid a visit to his dad's office to discuss the business of governance.

"Malik, transfer $20,000 to Nawal's account," said President Ambo.

"What's she doing with all this cash? Last month you asked me to transfer $30,000 to her which I did," said Malik.

President Ambo told Malik it doesn't matter, after all, they all know Nawal is extravagant, but she needs to be comfortable. Baha Aliyu walks in and apologised to the President and said he's sorry to bother him.

"No problem, what's it, Baha?" asked President Ambo.

Baha Aliyu handed the President a letter and urged him to take a look at the letter he just received.

President Ambo collected the letter from Baha and read through. "What! How can the Arab League do this to me?" asked the President.

"I don't believe this, why should they join the West to work against us?" asked Baha.

Malik looked on as his dad and Baha expressed their anger over what the Arab League had done but no specific mention of what it was the Arab league has done. "Dad, what is it?" asked Malik. Baha Aliyu then turned to Malik and said they've been suspended from the Arab league. Malik then collects the letter from his dad so he also could see for himself, the content of the letter. "Why, let me have a look at that," said Malik.

President Ambo muttered and said this is a stab, but he'll sort it out. Baha Aliyu quickly suggested to the President to have a word with Sheikh Bin Sanalla. President Ambo's dilemma has turned into a multi-headed hydra rearing its ugly head from different directions, even the one million march in support for this president ended up with him being perceived as having his foot in his mouth.

"I'll do that right away," said President Ambo. He quickly reached for the phone and dialled Sheikh Bin Sanalla, the Secretary General of the Arab league.

"Hello Sheikh, how're you?" asked President Ambo.

"I'm fine Ambo, and how're you doing?" asked Sheikh Bin Sanalla.

"Sheikh, I'm not fine, and with the letter I just received, I must confess I'm not happy with you," said President Ambo.

Sheikh Bin Sanalla listened keenly to President Ambo, and then chuckled. He just gave his one liner, and said this isn't about the Arab League, rather it's about President Ambo Hussein and the way he's presenting the Arab people to the world.

President Ambo beats his chest and said he's a good leader and his people love him, and that was why a million citizens of the Republic of Kitan held a solidarity march asking him to continue in power.

Sheikh Bin Sanalla smiled and asked President Ambo if his assertion is really the truth or what he wants the international community to believe to be the truth.

"Sheikh, you're my friend and I want this decision to be reversed," said President Ambo.

Sheikh Bin Sanalla had to put on his hat of diplomacy of emotional detachment and said this isn't a decision he alone can reverse because the matter was put to a vote and a resolution was reached.

President Ambo was quite despaired of being left out all alone to dry, and the only people whom he though had his back have just given him the boot. "Why should the Arab league make me and my country the topic of discussion, instead of discussing about other more important issues?" asked President Ambo.

Sheikh Bin Sanalla maintained his one liner, as he reminds President Ambo, he's misrepresenting the Arab people before the world, and it's best to disassociate themselves from him.

President Ambo pleaded with the Sheikh, saying the Arab league and the Organisation of Islamic Countries are the only Allies he has got left, and begged him not to take that away from him. Sadly, under the present circumstance, Sheikh Bin Sanalla's hands are tied because the decision is the result of a vote, all he could do is to urge President Ambo to change his ways, and maybe his membership will be reconsidered.

"I'll discuss with other members of the Arab league for consideration on this issue," said President Ambo.

"Ok, thank you," said the Sheikh. They ended the conversation.

Two days later Malik walked into the President's office and sadly, his dad has tried to reach him earlier and has been unable to reach him on phone either. "Where were you? I've been trying to reach you," asked President Ambo.

"I was holding a meeting with the Progressive Youths of Kitan," said Malik.

"Ok, how did it go?" asked President Ambo.

"It went well, and I want to make them the new image of Kitan," said Malik.

"Good, I'll be paying a visit to Sheikh Bin Sanalla, and I want you to be there," said President Ambo.

"Is it over the Arab league suspension?" asked Malik.

President Ambo will need much more than a mere rabbit foot, to make this trip a success, and hence he will continue to grasp at straws that won't prevent him from heading down the garden path.

"Of course, yes, and we can't afford to stand alone because the world is a global village," said President Ambo.

"Ok, but aren't we supposed to see other members of the Arab league to garner support from them before we meet with the Sheikh?" asked Malik.

President Ambo' responded to Malik's suggestion, saying that wouldn't be a bad idea but it's best to start with the Sheikh so he could convince other members of the Arab league in advance before his visit. Sadly, this armchair diplomacy is all President Ambo Hussein has in his sleeve at this point, and he has to rely on hope for this to work.

Malik decided to think outside the box and asked his dad what next if this move fails. President Ambo looked away in sombreness and said that would rather be unfortunate because he wouldn't mind going to war with any Arab nation that aligns with the West against him.

"But they are your friends," said Malik.

President Ambo chuckled in his rather bizarre and haughty tone, saying of course they are his friends, yet they can be friends today and enemies tomorrow.

"What changed then?" asked Malik.

"Alliances!" exclaimed President Ambo.

The President smiled afterwards at his own logic of action, he then tried to rephrase in altruistic perspective, and said when people change alliances, they could quickly move away from being friends to becoming enemies.

"But I would advise we show some restraint," advised Malik.

President Ambo assumed a brash posture and insisted that restraint shouldn't mean allowing lily-livered sycophants to poke their fingers into his eyes. Malik urged his dad to exercise restraints because it wouldn't be wise warring a conflagration of enemies.

"Don't worry Malik, I'll play their games with them," said President Ambo.

"But wait a minute, dad! Don't you think your exiled uncle, Sheikh Abdul, is behind this decision by the Arab league?" asked Malik.

President Ambo arguably said he never thought of it, but there's a possibility his uncle is behind his troubles and promised to get to the bottom of this. Sheikh Abdul is now in President Ambo's crosshairs, and even if the President can't reach him because he's in exile, he can reach Sheikh Abdul's children. At least, his children are within Ambo Hussein's ambit, and this means double jeopardy for Sheikh Abdul.

Malik continued to fan the flames of his dad's volatile temper, as he went on to line his dad up against Sheikh Abdul with his prejudiced assertions. He insisted that the Sheikh is friend to most members of the Arab league, and he believes the Sheikh talked them into doing this.

Aisha came to see her husband for other reasons and overheard the mention of Sheikh Abduls' name as she walked in, she then turned to Malik and asked what it is about Sheikh Abdul and the Arab league.

Malik smiled funnily, saying he just told dad there's a high possibility his uncle is behind their suspension from the Arab league. Aisha wasn't pleased with what she just heard, she understands full well what it means for her husband to set his sight on Shiekh Abdul. She turned to Malik in a stunning rebuke that quickly wipes off the corrupt smirk in his face. "Where does this startling conclusion come from?" asked Aisha.

President Ambo has never failed to buoy Malik's illusory sentiment, and Aisha hasn't been impressed that her husband and her deluded son happened to be two peas in a pod. The President was quick to slap down Aisha's criticism of Malik, and said Malik isn't under interrogation here, and he has just given him a clue, which he intends to pursue.

"Malik, are you encouraging your dad to go after his cousins after sending their dad on exile?" asked Aisha.

"I never mentioned dad's cousins; I only talked about his uncle," said Malik.

"You know quite well that your dad will only hurt his cousins just to get at his uncle," said Aisha.

President Ambo seemed to have an ear full of Aisha's unsolicited intervention, he then rebuked his wife, saying he doesn't want her nagging in his office. He insisted that it's his prerogative to punish anyone just to get to whoever he wants. Aisha is no longer willing to leap in with full-throated support for this despot that has now suddenly become apocalyptic, and sadly she isn't ready to be shut up by this pair whose moral code she considers toxic. She turned to her husband and admonished him for his back-of-the-fag-packet approach when dealing with sensitive issues, she then urged him not to drag his family into this murky, muddy and rumbling current that has the possibility of sweeping the entire family away.

President Ambo isn't a man whose bluff can be called easily because of his ability to rise up to the occasion once his pride is at stake, he quickly reminded his wife that he Ambo, is the torrential current, and he alone decides how it rumbles.

Aisha remained statue-still, and refused to leave the matter alone, because turning on family members isn't just as easy as black and white, it's a grey area, and because it's grey, knowing when a line is crossed becomes quite difficult. After all, when the consequence comes, she will share in the karma. "I must confess, you and your son are heading on a slippery path," said Aisha.

"Mum, if they've a hand in this, then they should pay," said Malik.

Aisha turned to President Ambo again and said she doesn't think there will be a way out of this by the time he hits rock bottom. Sadly, this is the Presidents' office, but it's fast turning into a family circus, and Aisha seemed to have rolled up her sleeve and willing to take the plunge with her husband in fighting this out.

"Aisha, thank you for your unsolicited warnings, but if you desire to hit rock bottom, you'll do that alone," said President Ambo. Aisha turned to her son Malik, and said she hopes he wouldn't end up on bended knees before these people.

"Bended knees, how do you mean mum?" asked Malik.

"When your dad is absent and it's your turn to be the President, you'll need all these people to give you a voice and help you sit on the presidential seat, before you can think of consolidating power," said Aisha.

President Ambo shunned his wife asking her not to put fear into their son and urged her not to make Malik feel victimised.

"Why aren't you preparing your son for the realities of the future?" asked Aisha.

President Ambo insists on his legacy and making his son fearful about the future is a sign of weakness, and that he would rather victimise the people and drive them into their holes, than allow his son go before them on bended knees.

"So, this is it, I don't have a say on something that could impact on my family?" asked Aisha.

President Ambo seemed not to be having Aisha scuttle his business, he quickly reached for the phone and dialled Colonel Abdallah, but it was Hamza that picked up the phone, the President then asked him to put Colonel Abdallah on the phone.

"Mr. President, it's Colonel Abdallah on the phone," he said.

"Colonel, inform Ali, I want to see him immediately," said President Ambo.

"Is it Sheikh Ali, your cousin?" asked Colonel Abdallah.

"Which other Ali would I be talking about? You imbecile," said President Ambo.

"Ok Mr. President, I'll get him to see you immediately," said Colonel Abdallah.

"Good," said President Ambo.

Aisha couldn't help herself because things could get dirty, she then tried one last time to stop her husband from going ahead. "Ambo, turning on your cousins is like cutting off your last life-line," said Aisha.

President Ambo dismissed Aisha one last time and said his cousins have outlived their usefulness, and whatever happens to them will be of their own doing.

"Ok, suit yourself," said Aisha, as she walks away.

Two hours later, Sheikh Ali arrives at the presidential villa, and walked straight into President Ambo's office. "Ambo, why the urgency and I hope all is well?" asked Sheikh Ali.

President Ambo didn't hesitate to remind his cousin of the present situation, after all, the relationship between this pair has gone sour. Before now, when these two cousins disagree, all they do is knock a few doors then come around later smiling, but things have changed now. "I've told you to always address me as Mr. President, don't make a mess of my familiarity with you," said President Ambo.

"Ambo, did you bring me here just to remind me of how you should be addressed?" asked Sheikh Ali.

President Ambo quickly steered the conversation away and said he brought him here for other matters of concern, but also reminding Sheikh Ali that his indiscretions will no longer be tolerated. Sheikh Ali finds it quite difficult to choose the right adjective to describe President Ambo's current disposition towards him, yet he took the sarcasm on the chin.

"By the way, what's this matter of concern that would warrant my input?" asked Sheikh Ali.

"Ok, let me just cut to the chase, we've been suspended by the Arab League," said President Ambo.

Sheikh Ali was shocked and distraught to learn of the suspension from the Arab League, he then asked when this happened and also asked to know the reason for this harsh decision.

"That's why I called you, so you can tell me, because I believe you would know better," said President Ambo. Sadly, winning the hearts and minds of the members of the Arab League to get President Ambo's tail chopped off might be quite a tall order. Sheikh Ali is now lost as to the direction of travel of this conversation because President Ambo was speaking in riddles.

"Know better as how, and do you want me to reach out to the Arab league to inquire of the reason behind this harsh decision?" asked Sheikh Ali.

"No, that isn't what I meant; I'm of the opinion that you're aware of this decision before it was communicated to us," said President Ambo.

"How, am I a member of the Arab League or what are you insinuating?" asked Sheikh Ali.

"Maybe your dad is a member, and he orchestrated this decision as revenge," said President Ambo.

Sheikh Ali laughed and said he now knows why Malik gave him a stern look and couldn't even greet him as he walked in.

"Who greets a traitor? I just want you to know I'm aware of your dad's actions and I'll respond proportionately," said President Ambo.

"And you're sure my dad is behind this?" asked Sheikh Ali.

"Yes, of course, he's friend to most of these Arab League Sheikhs and I won't take it from him.

Sheikh Ali smiled as he asked President Ambo what's it that makes him think his dad is a psychotic and vengeful person. He sensed President Ambo is at it again and just as he lashed out and sent his dad on exile over nothing, he's about doing same over his suspension from the Arab League. After all, if you want to kill a dog give it a bad name and hang him, maybe that's President Ambo's new trick.

"How would I know?" asked President Ambo.

"Sorry to disappoint you Ambo, my dad has been sick for the past two months, so how'll he be able to orchestrate this revenge?" asked Sheikh Ali.

President Ambo understands that diplomacy happens just by words of mouth, particularly for an elder statesman like Sheikh Abdul, he quickly reminded Sheikh Ali that being sick doesn't stop his dad from making calls to his Arab League friends or visiting them to discuss his intention.

"Sorry Ambo, my dad has been in a coma for the past two months," said Sheikh Ali. The Sheikh handed his phone to President Ambo, and then showed him messages between his mum and him, as well as the pictures of Sheikh Abdul in hospital.

President Ambo read through the messages, and spent a few minutes looking at the pictures. "When did this happen?" asked President Ambo.

"My dad fell sick the moment you sent him on exile, you actually broke his heart, and for some time now he's in a state of coma. He only regained consciousness this morning, and I don't even know if he'll get out of this alive," said Sheikh Ali.

President Ambo suddenly became sombre after Sheikh Ali sent him on a guilt trip. "But you never told me he was sick, maybe I would have given him amnesty," said President Ambo.

"You never cared about the pain others go through from your actions, we just want to be left alone. Please sort yourself out with the Arab League, we don't have a hand in it," said Sheikh Ali.

Just as Sheikh Ali turned to leave President Ambo reminded him he'll still investigate the Sheikh's story to be sure he just told him the truth.

"Ambo, you can investigate for all you care, just sort yourself out and I beg to leave," said Sheikh Ali.

"Ok, but if I've a reason to bring you back here, I'll do it without hesitation," said President Ambo.

"Suit yourself, Ambo," Sheikh Ali said, and then left.

Furious President Ambo continued his phony investigation on his uncle's possible influence on the Arab Leagues' decision. He then put a phone call across to his exiled uncle, Sheikh Abdul.

"Hello Uncle," said President Ambo.

"Hello Ambo, how're you my son?" asked Sheikh Abdul.

"Uncle, do you've a hand in this?" asked President Ambo.

"A hand in what? I don't seem to be following," asked Sheikh Abdul.

Funnily, Sheikh Ali felt President Ambo's accusations are all nonsense, and didn't bother to give it thought, and neither did he bother to hint his dad of his conversation with Ambo Hussein. Sadly, Sheikh Ali had no idea President Ambo is bent on pursuing this further.

"I'm asking you if you've a hand in the decision of the Arab league, at least you're aware I'm well briefed of your political theocracy," said President Ambo.

Sheikh Abdul understand his nephew is accusing him of treason, so he quickly asked President Ambo what makes him think he would do a thing like that, and funny enough, he wouldn't do that to his nephew, and not to anyone.

President Ambo is consumed by his double standards, and he isn't making a crapshoot when he gave his uncle the subtle reminder. "I suppose you know what will happen if I find out you encouraged the Arab league to punish me?" said President Ambo.

Sheikh Abdul smiled at this finger pointing by his nephew, and then chuckled, before he reminded President Ambo that he's an elder statesman who knows what's at stake. "I'm an old man, Ambo, and I think I've enough wisdom not to put you to the test," said Sheikh Abdul.

President Ambo dug his heel deep while winding his uncle up as he accused him of cronyism, even as he took aim at his uncle by reminding him his old man's wisdom doesn't exonerate him from scrutiny.

"Your dad and I are brothers, and do you remember your first steps as a child learning how to walk happened in my house? So, I wouldn't involve myself with those against you," said Sheikh Abdul.

"Yes uncle, that was why I didn't give you the same punishment as Hassan, I gave you money and an opportunity to live out the rest of your life abroad.

"Ambo, do you remember you spent your holidays in my house while you were a student?" asked Sheikh Abdul.

"Yes uncle, and you don't need to remind me of all that, because I'm the President now," said President Ambo.

"Do you remember I enrolled you into the military?" asked Sheikh Abdul.

President Ambo's personal vanity means he couldn't stomach any more reminders of his past by his uncle, so he needed to wriggle himself out of this conversation, and quickly urged his uncle to stop toying with his emotion. "Uncle, you're beginning to irritate me, and I advise you to stay out of my way," said President Ambo.

"Even though I'm abroad, I know you're listening to my conversations, my phone calls and watching my movements, I won't put my children in danger," said Sheikh Abdul.

Sheikh Abdul now has a taste of President Ambo's dexterity in his thirst for blood, and unwittingly associating with this President is like romancing with the devil, and sadly, you will get the knock when you're most vulnerable.

"What about those secret face to face conversations you're holding? I don't have access to them," said President Ambo.

"Mr. President, why don't you allow your old uncle enjoy some peace?" asked Sheikh.

"Ok, I'll leave you for now, but I'm watching you Uncle," said President Ambo.

Interestingly, the Arab League has chosen to cut ties over blind support for this despot and reversing this move on a whim will be quite a tall order, but instead of looking inward, this President seem to prefer the goose chase.

It's time for the final meeting before the military coup that's intended to bring President Ambo's government down swings into action. The officers were all gathered in their secret meeting point, away from the prying eyes of President Ambo Hussein.

Retired Brigadier Mumtaz thank all the officers for coming and said the day's meeting is more about wishing each other farewell and to also conclude on the deployment of logistics.

"Everything is ready, arms are already deployed to the various locations for easy access, and all our inside men have been well briefed," said Brigadier Bachakar.

Retired Brigadier Mumtaz insists on ensuring the coup isn't mired by blood and guts and reminded his officers, they must all remember that this action isn't out of spite or malice but out of love for their nation.

"Where will our assembly point be in case we fail?" asked Colonel Salihu.

"If peradventure we fail, you can leave the country if you've the opportunity," said Brigadier Bachakar.

Retired Brigadier Mumtaz gave one final reminder as he pointed out to the officers that the time to kick start this operation is 2.30pm on the dot.

Brigadier Bachakar interjected and added his voice to the promptness of this operation and urged the officers not to be in a hurry, and it must be 2.30pm.

"Officers, this is meant to be a short meeting, may the Almighty Allah grant us a successful operation, thank you," said Rtd. Brigadier Mumtaz.

The military coup was scheduled to take off by exactly 2.30. pm. Brigadier Bachakar is assigned with the task of taking on the President, so he drove his car into the presidential palace at about 2.pm.

"Colonel, is the President in?" asked Brigadier Bachakar.

"Good afternoon sir, do you've an appointment with Mr. President?" asked Colonel Abdallah.

"No, but there are some matters concerning my battalion I'll like to discuss with him," said Brigadier Bachakar.

Colonel Abdallah courteously informed the Brigadier that the Chief of Army Staff is the appropriate person to discuss such matters with Mr. President, particularly when he doesn't have an appointment with the President.

Brigadier Bachakar pressed on, saying there's a personal favour he wanted from Mr President, he then urged Colonel Abdallah to call the President and inform him of his presence.

Colonel Abdallah reached for the phone and dialled Mr. President and told him the Brigadier wants to see him. After the phone conversation with the President, the Colonel turned to the Brigadier. "He said I should allow you in," said Colonel Abdallah.

"Good!" exclaimed Brigadier Bachakar.

Colonel Abdallah then asked the Brigadier to go through the usual security checks. The check ensures they aren't armed as they meet with the President.

Brigadier Bachakar was obliged to go through the checks before meeting with the President. During the checks, his service pistol was collected and kept for him to collect on his way out, but his inside man who's among the guards is waiting to hand him a pistol immediately he passes through the security checks.

After the checks, the Brigadier was told he's free to go in for his meeting with the President.

Brigadier Bachakar collected the pistol from his inside man and tucked it in his pocket and then went upstairs to see the President.

"Bachakar, how're you? I just left the mosque and wanted to rest my head when Abdallah said you're here," said President Ambo.

Brigadier Bachakar thanked the President for granting him audience, it's now 2.27pm. Unfortunately for the Brigadier, the handover of gun was spotted by another guard who alerted Colonel Abdallah.

While the Brigadier was waiting for the appointed 2.30pm as agreed before making his moves, Colonel Abdallah walked into the conversation, "Brigadier, please turn around and lift your hands up," said Colonel Abdallah.

Brigadier Bachakar immediately questioned the Colonel and asked what he meant by asking him to turn around. He dipped his hands in the Brigadier's pocket and brought out the pistol, the Brigadier was shocked to discover he has been surrounded by the presidential guards. Sadly, this well orchestrated plot has gone up in smoke even before it took off. President Ambo was quite in shock. "You mean, he's here to take me out?" asked President Ambo.

Colonel Abdallah said he supposed so, and informed the President that the Brigadier arranged with one of the guards who's his inside man.

"This must be a coup, call the TV and Radio stations right away and tell them to lock down immediately, then call intelligence, to be sure they haven't been compromised," said President Ambo. Sensing that this is more than a disgruntled Brigadier, and fearing that they may have been compromised, Colonel Abdallah rushed downstairs only to discover that the armoured tanks in the presidential palace has been immobilised. He then called for reinforcements from the armoury in the state capital only to discover it has been taken by the coup plotters.

"Abdallah, the broadcasting service has been taken over," said President Ambo. He quickly tuned the radio and asked the Colonel to listen in. "Hear this, they're already broadcasting," said President Ambo. Now that the presidential villa is now without a proper defence after the armoury is discovered to have been compromised. Colonel Abdallah had to shore up the defence of the presidential villa in whatever way he could, to keep the President secure.

"Oh my God, I'll get in touch with Brigadier Sale Mai, to know how to go about this," said Colonel Abdallah.

"How are we sure Sale Mai isn't a part of them, have you interrogated Bachakar?" asked President Ambo.

Colonel Abdallah urged President Ambo to allow him call Brigadier Sale Mai, and said he'll know if Brigadier Sale Mai is a part of the coup.

Brigadier Sale Mai, the country's head of military, was bringing reinforcements from Abidkitan the second largest city in the Republic of Kitan. "Colonel, can you hear me?" asked Brigadier Sale Mai. Funnily, the communication was breaking and after several failed attempts to get the Brigadier on phone. "Hello sir, Brigadier, is that you?" asked Colonel Abdallah.

"Yes, just hold the presidential villa, I'm coming with reinforcements," said Brigadier Sale Mai.

Colonel Abdallah asked the Brigadier of his whereabouts, and if he did hear the radio announcement by the coup plotters.

"Yes, I heard the speech, and I'm coming from Abidkitan because the armoury in Ansarouh has been put out of use," said Brigadier Sale Mai.

"Ok sir, I'll try to hold on, until you arrive," said Colonel Abdallah.

At about 6.45pm the government was able to regain control of the armoury in the state capital, as well as the Broadcasting services. There were few casualties, and the President made a broadcast to counter the broadcast of the coup plotters the moment calm was restored.

President Ambo: Today some disgruntled military officers staged a coup to destabilise our country, the Republic of Kitan. They want to take power through the back door, but by the grace of the Almighty Allah we're able to conquer them just as we've always done. I wish to emphasize my resolve to keep this country together and I'll not rest until all my enemies are no more. However, some of these military personnel have been arrested while the rest are on the run, but we'll catch them.

A week later, Colonel Abdallah was promoted by Mr President for his gallantry. Colonel Abdallah walked into the President's office. "Mr. President, you called me?" he asked.

President Ambo nodded in affirmation, he then handed the Colonel a letter and asked him to open it.

"Oh, promotion letter?" asked Colonel Abdallah.

"Colonel, you saved my life, you deserved much more than this," said President Ambo.

"Promoting me to the rank of a Brigadier means a lot to me, thank you sir," said Colonel Abdallah.

The President has been brooding over the failed coup, and the fact that he survived the coup by a whisker. He's now being plagued by the ease with which the armoury, the intelligence, and the entire military were compromised. Someone had to bear the responsibility for his inability to shore up his defences. A week after the failed coup, and while the President and his family were all seated in his living room. "Aasim, are you happy now?" asked President Ambo. Interestingly, President Ambo has it in for Aasim, and the fact that they don't see eye to eye on a lot of issues doesn't afford Aasim a passive response this time.

Aasim eyes were still glued to the TV, yet he asked his dad what's it, he's talking about.

President Ambo rephrased, and said he's talking about the coup.

"What about it, and what has my happiness got to do with it?" asked Aasim.

President Ambo went straight to remind his son that if he'd accepted the employment he offered him, he doesn't think his military intelligence unit and even the armoury would've been compromised and captured easily.

Aasim was passive in his response and was quite emotionally detached from the hysteria surrounding this subject. "I told you I need my travel documents because my fiancée is sick, you're talking of an offer that will never be," said Aasim.

"You mean you don't care if they'd kill me?" asked President Ambo.

"Dad, what do you want me to say? You wanted to kill me first and I still get flashes from that encounter in my memory," said Aasim.

"But I didn't kill you, and if I'd wanted to kill you nothing would've stopped me from doing it," said President Ambo.

Aasim continued to justify his position and said nothing will ever take away the picture of his dad pointing a gun at him from his memory. It didn't take long before Malik observed a change in his dad's countenance and sensed that things could get murky between Aasim and his dad, he then asked Aasim to stop, urging him show some respect. Aasim didn't go straight to let his dad know that he would've made himself a victim of his own vanity, but his hesitation to understand his dad's predicament, meant Aasim's actions is saying so, and it's deafening. Aasim grudgingly asked his brother the obvious. "Why don't you take the job as the head of the military intelligence unit?" asked Aasim.

Malik, who has been the poster boy of President Ambo's government, didn't hesitate to say he's understudying their dad, and he can't be in two places at the same time.

"I decided long ago never to walk in dad's shadow," said Aasim.

"Does that make you any different?" asked Malik.

"Of course yes, dad is Mr. President, while I'm a professional footballer, but you my friend are stuck in some crystal ball of dreams, of being the son of Mr. President," said Aasim. This pair is suddenly at each other's throats, and their bantering of each other could mean any unguarded utterance might attract their dad's wrath.

"Being the son of Mr. President is worth the while, isn't it?" asked Malik.

Aasim seemed bent on bantering Malik particularly now that the opportunity presents itself and reminded Malik that lurking in the shadows of a junta shouldn't be worth his while, and urged Malik to go out there and make a name for himself.

"What! Did I just hear you call your dad a junta?" asked Malik.

"You're understudying dad to be President, while my job will be to watch over the two of you as you go about killing people, isn't it?" asked Aasim.

Aisha interjected and asked them to stop the argument immediately. Sadly, President Ambo couldn't stomach any more of Aasim's indiscretion, and he was unwittingly fuming inside him because he begrudged having Aasim in his flat for refusing to work with him. President Ambo got pissed and turned to Aasim and said if Aasim can't protect him with the knowledge he acquired from the school fees he paid for sending him to school, then Aasim had better be dead. He then stood up and went into his room in a fit of rage.

Aisha saw her husband's disposition and understood what's about to happen, and quickly interjected. "Ambo, where are you going?" asked Aisha. The temperature in the house suddenly became fever pitched, and sadly her question didn't constrain her husband, so she quickly turned to Aasim in desperation. "Aasim, you've to leave here right now and go to your flat and stay," said Aisha. She then followed President Ambo to the bedroom.

President Ambo reached for his pistol. "Aisha, allow me to finish what I should've done long ago," said President Ambo.

"What's it with you and shooting people? For your information you're tearing your family apart," said Aisha.

President Ambo walked back to the living room, with his service pistol in hand, and trigger ready, he then turned to Malik. "Where's he?" asked President Ambo.

Aisha was quite glad she saved the day, yet she couldn't help but to point out to her husband that he seems to be on the verge of a hissy fit of rage at all times, and she hates this air of gloom that surrounds the room.

President Ambo isn't perturbed by Aisha's perception of the mood within the home, he turned to Aisha and insisted that gloom can remain for now until he's done with this boy.

"He has left," said Malik.

President Ambo has largely consigned civility to the bin as he unblinkingly confirmed to his wife that he would've killed Aasim if he'd met him. He continued pacing up and down in a fit of rage inside the living room, as Aisha stood in the way to prevent him from following Aasim to his flat. Aasim's comment got his dad hopping mad, and it's blindingly obvious that his dad can't stomach such direct rebuke from his son whom he hasn't taken a liking to of late. Point-blank rebuke makes his stomach churn, and Aisha seems to sense that Aasim has provoked the beast in the President and the only way to contain this beast is for Aasim to cower to safety.

"Why're you always feisty? I don't get this bubbling up because our whole life is more of a bumpy ride now," said Aisha. President Ambo wasn't keen for any further tiffs with Aisha after their last kerfuffle over Sadeq, he looked at her and said he doesn't care if they all end up in a rollercoaster of that bumpy ride Aisha just predicted because of a son that lacks adulation for his dad. Aisha quickly turned to Malik to give him a dressing down for initiating the brouhaha.

"Malik, do you know you're a part of the problem in this house? Let me remind you as you so much enjoy seeing your dad kill people, one day your dad will kill you and nobody will weep for you," said Aisha.

Malik lifted his hands up and showing his palms to his mum to indicate his hands are clean, as he insists he has done nothing wrong. He then suggested to his mum that Aasim should learn to give their dad some space, so as not to get caught-up in the crosshairs of their dad's temper.

"You're the eldest but most times you act as the least of your brothers," said Aisha.

"I didn't start this argument, so what do you expect I do?" asked Malik.

"You're a rabble rouser, who throws tantrums to ignite an argument between your brother and your dad," said Aisha.

"On the contrary, mum, Aasim's sarcasm puts him in the dilemma he finds himself," said Malik.

Malik seems to have had enough of the nagging, yet decided not to take all the blame for all that's happening. For a fact, Aisha hasn't fully forgiven Malik for taking side with his dad over the death of Sadeq, at this point anything Malik touches, she marks bad. She pressed on Malik and reminded him it's his responsibility to encourage his dad to eschew impunity, if he wants the people to accept him as their President when the time comes.

A month after the failed coup, a swift and secret military trial was conducted in which all the participants of the coup were sentenced to death, by hanging. The week following, the death sentences were hurriedly carried out to the surprise of the citizens of the Republic of Kitan.

Nawal returns from school a week later, and by evening of same day, she went to check on Aasim, but as she stood by the door and knocked the door. "Hello, anybody home?" asked Nawal.

"Nawal, when did you return from school?" asked Aasim.

Aasim then opened the door for her to come inside his flat, she walked in and made herself comfortable.

Nawal calmly informed Aasim she came in about an hour ago, and their mum told her about the altercation between him and their dad.

"Oh, you said mum told you about it?" he asked.

"Yes, isn't it true?" she asked.

"Yeah, it's true, that's why I've decided to stay away from his living room and anything that concerns him," said Aasim.

Nawal wasn't quite pleased to be kept in the dark over the latest incident between her brother and her dad, and sadly this family operates like the clannish club. While Malik and Umar act alike, Aasim and Nawal are miles away. "This is the second time dad is pointing a gun at you, what sort of joke is that?" asked Nawal.

Aasim smiled as he reminded Nawal, that their dad isn't joking about killing him and he knew for sure he's still looking for an opportunity to do it.

"Your comment of dad being serious about killing you just gave me goose pimples, and it sounds creepy and eerie, ooh, it makes my skin crawl," said Nawal.

Aasim seemed to have taken the focus away from his die hard stance against his dad, and accused Malik for trying to create an opportunity for their dad to kill him.

"You mean dad's temper is now untameable, and that he does all these because no one can stop him?" asked Nawal.

"Yeah," said Aasim.

Nawal went quiet for a moment and then sighed before she muttered under breath saying enough of dad and his wickedness. She then stood up and walked towards the refrigerator, asking what he has in his refrigerator.

"There is lots of stuff in there, just take what you like," said Aasim.

Nawal opened the refrigerator and said she can see that Aasim has her favourites. She stretched out her hand and reached for a can of fruit drink and two slices of cake.

"Will that be enough for you?" asked Aasim.

Nawal was quite hungry and said this is just an appetizer she proceeded to say she doesn't think it's also proper for Aasim to limit himself to his flat.

Aasim felt it's best to keep a safe distance from his dad by restricting himself to his flat because he thinks his dad's intimidation and obsession with power has spiralled out of control, and it's best to keep him at bay.

Nawal felt a comparison of her dad's government with other Arab nations isn't misplaced, saying they are peaceful, and their citizens are happy, and they maintain good relationship with the West, yet asked why her dad is different.

Aasim supported Nawal's assertion by stating the obvious, that even the Arab nations are beginning to cut ties with their dad, because despite all their help to make him do things differently for good, dad hasn't changed.

"I'm proud of all these Arab nations and I wish my dad can be like their leaders," said Nawal.

CHAPTER

SEVEN

The Uprising

The mysterious deaths of the presidential aspirants coupled with the recent deaths of the military chiefs summarily executed over their involvement in the failed coup caused a lot of ill feelings against the President and his family. Consequently, Ismailia who is a citizen of Kitan based in Tunisia and was among those who led the revolution in Tunisia during the Arab Spring has returned home to lead a protest against President Ambo Hussein.

In one of the evenings, Ismaila had to sit with some of his co-organisers of the protest in his late father's house, as they set out the road map of using their protest to send President Ambo Hussein's government parking. "My brothers, it's time for the Republic of Kitan to say goodbye to President Ambo Hussein and his family," said Ismaila.

Jabir who had little insight into inner workings of President Ambo's government thought Ismaila was having a laugh, and quickly asked Ismaila if he thinks a mere protest will make President Ambo to leave power. Ismaila has done this before in Tunisia and doing same in his hometown is something he holds so dear to his chest.

"Why not, our protests will attract the attention of the whole world, we did it in Tunisia and it succeeded, so why won't it succeed here in Kitan?" asked Ismaila.

Jabir insists that more is needed to send President Ambo packing, saying their President isn't like the former President of Tunisia who fled as a result of the uprising. He insists that President Ambo is an evil stooge who can't be taken down easily.

"How do we start the protest?" asked Mukhtar.

As far as Ismaila is concerned, there's no perfect way of starting a protest, insisting that all that's needed is a public who want their leader gone for good.

"But we'll need funds to finance the protest, won't we?" asked Zidane.

Ismaila urged his friends not to make a big deal out of the protest and said all that's needed for a successful protest is their mouth to do the talking. He however thinks they'll need to print a few hand bills which he'll finance. Jabir turned to Ismaila and asked what about the friends he talked about.

"Which ones?" asked Ismaila.

"The ones coming from Tunisia," said Jabir.

"They'll be here by next week, and they will assist us with funds," said Ismaila.

"Which means we're starting our protest the day after tomorrow," said Mukhtar.

Ismaila nodded his head in affirmation and urged all his friends to go home and pray to the Almighty Allah to bless their protest.

The next day Aasim and Ismaila met at the football field.

Aasim was surprised to see Ismaila, he then smiled and shook hands with him as they exchanged pleasantries. "How are you? It's been long we trained together," said Aasim.

"You're right, but I thought you've gone back to Germany," said Ismaila.

Aasim spent some time chatting and catching up with Ismaila and joked saying it's a good thing they train one more time together, he then engaged Ismaila in banter. "You know I enjoy the privilege of making jest of you with my soccer skills," he said.

"Your humility is one thing I like about you, compared to your brothers," said Ismaila.

"My brothers are nice people when you get to know them better," said Ismaila.

Ismaila knew too well that Aasim likes people talking about his brothers in good light, but Ismaila isn't one to be deceived, and he didn't hesitate to let Aasim know he knew his brothers as much as he knows him. "Though, I heard what your dad did to Sadeq," said Ismaila.

"Which Sadeq are you talking about?" asked Aasim.

"Your stepbrother of course! We knew each other in Tunisia where he worked as a mechanical engineer," said Ismaila.

"How much did you know him?" asked Aasim.

"We knew each other as people from the same place and that drew us closer, he had a very good heart like yours," said Ismaila.

"My heart isn't better than yours?" said Aasim.

Ismaila tried letting Aasim know he isn't out to flatter him unnecessarily and reminded Aasim he's quite aware of what he has done for most of the guys around here, and even in Abidkitan. Ismaila hailed Aasim, describing him as God sent to many of them. Aasim had to cut to the bottom line as he asked Ismaila if he would do the same if he were in his shoes.

"Yes, I would," said Ismaila.

"Then don't see what I've done as special," said Aasim.

Ismaila thought it wise to do the honourable thing, and said to Aasim that now that they've stumbled into each other, it will be a betrayal if he doesn't let him know there will be a protest the next day. Aasim understand too well that every protest in the land is most likely against is dad, and asked what it was they're protesting for or against.

"We want sincere democracy," said Ismaila.

Aasim was quite passive with the news as he smiled before asking Ismaila if he intends to replicate what they did in Tunisia. Ismaila was keen to know what Aasim was getting at, because he never discussed his actions in Tunisia with Aasim. "How do you mean what we did in Tunisia?" asked Ismaila.

Aasim had to let the cat out of the bag, as he subtly told Ismaila he saw him in the television leading the protest in Tunisia, he then jokingly asked Ismaila. "Is there any place I'll see my friend and not recognise him?" asked Aasim.

"In case you see me leading a protest in my own country just know it's for the good of Kitan," said Aasim.

Aasim stood on the fence on the matter, and his response was passive as before, yet appealed to Ismaila to show restraint in case the protest snowballs into something big. "Just know that I'm not stopping you guys from protesting, but remember my kindness as a reason why you should deal graciously with my family," said Aasim.

Ismaila smiled yet reminded Aasim that he told him about the protest not because Aasim can stop the protest from going ahead, but as a friend, he deserve to be respected.

"Ok, whatever you say," said Aasim.

They trained together for about two hours and Aasim returned home. The next morning, the protest kicked off with thousands of protesters carrying placards with various messages. Ismaila stood on a makeshift stage holding a mega phone.

Ismaila: People of the Republic of Kitan, it's time you stand up and take your destiny into your own hands. It was done in Egypt, Tunisia, Libya, and now it's our turn to do what's right for our children and for our unborn children.

Immediately after addressing the crowd, Ismaila gave way, and Mukhtar climbed the stage carrying a placard that reads "Ambo Hussein, time up."

Mukhtar: Arab nations are saying no to dictatorship, it's time for every citizen of Kitan to come out and live on the streets until we get a true democracy.

Jabir climbed on the stage carrying a placard that reads 'Ambo Hussein and his family will pay for all their crimes.'

Jabir: The crowd we see here is a reflection of the mood of the people, and this is an expression of how our people feel about Ambo Hussein.

Ismaila returned to the stage after Jabir finished addressing the crowd. "Let's send a message to Ambo Hussein," he said. The crowd began chanting "Ambo Hussein leave, leave, leave." The chanting continued unabated.

While the protest was going on, passersby encouraged by the courage of the protesters joined the protests. The police tried to break the protest but failed because of the resolve of the protesters. This prompted the Chief of Army Staff, Brigadier Sale Mai to call Colonel Hammad who's in charge of the 2nd Brigade battalion in Abidkitan where the protest was going on.

"Hello Colonel, are you aware of the protest taking place in Abidkitan, right under your nose?" asked Brigadier Sale Mai.

"Yes Brigadier, I've been observing the protest and I just finished speaking with the police chief, and he said the protesters have refused to disperse despite applying minimal force," said Colonel Hammad.

Brigadier Sale Mai in his usual audacious tone informed Colonel Hammad that the President wants that protest dispersed immediately, and that's an order. Colonel Hammad had to ask the Chief of Amy Staff the difficult but obvious question, and particularly after trying other means and the protesters refused to leave, he then asked if he should use live rounds.

Brigadier Sale Mai didn't hesitate to order Colonel Hammad to do whatever it takes to disperse the crowd, if it warrants a few people dying then he should do it.

"Ok sir, we'll move in immediately," said Colonel Hammad.

Brigadier Sale Mai left a note of caution for the Colonel as he reminded him to remember that the President is watching the protest with keen interest.

"Yes sir," said Colonel Hammad. President Ambo is small in stature but compensates this deficiency by being a bully, and sadly, this man is suffering from the Napoleonic complex which makes him someone to dread.

The Colonel went in with his men to disperse the crowd, and shot live ammunition killing six people, and that sent the protesters scampering for safety. This resulted in widespread anger against the President and even the military.

That night the organisers of the protests met in their secret meeting point to assess the success of the first day of the protest. The deaths were meant to scare people from coming out and Jabir was the first to voice his concern, as he turned to Ismaila. "Are you sure we're not making a mistake by embarking on this protest against Ambo Hussein?" he asked.

"No, we aren't making a mistake; we're doing what's right before the Almighty Allah and even before men," said Ismaila.

"What about all those people that died?" asked Mukhtar.

Ismaila maintained his cool, though devastated by the loss of life of some of the protesters, yet insisted that what matters is whether these deaths count for something. Ismaila turned to them and said it now behoves on them to make these deaths count for something.

"What do you mean by that?" asked Jabir.

"It means we've to continue until Ambo Hussein leaves," said Ismaila.

Mukhtar became terrified after hearing Ismaila insists the protest must go on, and he then asked, what if they kill more people. Ismaila owned up and said, definitely President Ambo will kill more people, but if they don't kill their resolve then President Ambo won't win.

Mukhtar looked glum because he sees nothing good coming out of this but a bleak future for himself and his friends and asks what if the police and the army are looking for them.

"Of course, we'll be targeted from now on, so we should learn to live in hiding," said Ismaila.

The day, the President and his military chiefs assess the aftermath of clearing the protest. President Ambo started by asking how many people died yesterday.

Brigadier Sale Mai informed the President that six people died the day before, four young men, a teenage girl and a little boy below the age of ten. He proceeded to ask the President about what action to take if the protesters choose to come out again despite the casualties suffered a day before.

"Ok, the number of deaths is relatively small and at least they will learn to stay in their homes," said President Ambo.

"We'll take our time to look for the organisers of the protest," said Brigadier Sale Mai.

President Ambo thinks the iron fist approach always does the trick, he laughed and said the death of these six people will scare them from coming out. Brigadier Sale Mai insists on knowing what action to take in case the protesters come out again, he subtly asked the President Ambo what if they come out again.

"Then we'll kill more people," said President Ambo.

Later that day, the death of the six protesters the previous day resulted in widespread protests in various cities which included Dwara, Baadi, Akuwat and Nabi with so many protests organisers springing up.

Malik learnt of the protest and quickly rushed to see his dad in his office. "Dad, you're here," said Malik.

"Yes Malik, anything?" asked President Ambo.

Malik looked anxious as he informed his dad there are protests going on. President Ambo didn't hesitate to say that's not possible because he crushed the protest yesterday.

"Which means the protest wasn't crushed, and it was rather fuelled than crushed." said Malik.

"What do you mean by that?" asked President Ambo.

Malik quickly turned on the television for his dad to see, as he told his dad that there are heavy protests going on in five cities right now in the Republic of Kitan.

President Ambo's ears tingled at the news of a widespread protest he quickly glued his eyes to the television, while at the same time asking Malik which of the cities he's talking about.

"We're talking about the cities of Dwara, Baadi, Akuwat, Nabi and Abidkitan," said Malik.

"What's going on? Yesterday it was only Abidkitan, and today it's four more cities," said President Ambo.

Sadly, President Ambo's penchant for quelling dissent and keeping them permanently quiet seemed not to have worked this time. Funnily, this President doesn't wear his heart on his sleeve, not because he has a heart and just doesn't use it, he doesn't even have one. Nothing riles President Ambo like when foreign news feasts on calls for him to leave office.

"Turn your TV to TWRR news, they are showing the protests," said Malik.

"The West has been looking for something negative to report about me, they've now gotten what they wanted," said President Ambo.

Malik hinted his dad that the protesters are filming the protests and uploading it on YouTube on real time. The world now has every bit and pieces of the actions on their phones and insists this is bigger than anything they have ever seen.

President Ambo spent a few minutes watching the protest on television and said from what he can see it's obvious that some of the protesters are friends to Aasim.

"Dad, you're right, Ismaila is a good friend to Aasim," said Malik.

President Ambo then suggested that Aasim should help bring Ismaila to him and maybe if he gives Ismaila some money he will help end the protest. Malik didn't hesitate to remind his dad that Aasim wouldn't want to get involved in this matter.

"Why? I'm his father," said President Ambo.

Malik had to remind his dad that since the day he went into his room to get his gun to kill Aasim for the second time, Aasim has never set foot inside his living room.

"What does that mean?" asked President Ambo.

"He does his own thing and limits himself to his flat since that incident took place, and he has cut off all ties with you, technically I suppose," said Malik.

"You're right, but I don't think I intend to shoot him," said President Ambo.

Malik had to hit the nail on the head and reminded his dad that from what he saw that day, if Aasim had stayed, his dad would've killed him. President Ambo then steered the conversation away from his rift with Aasim, and asked Malik to get Brigadier Sale Mai, because he needed to do something about the protests.

An hour later, President Ambo went to Aasim's flat to see if he could use Aasim's influence to quell the protests. He stood by the door, then knocked and waited for Aasim to open the door.

"Haven't you been watching the protests on TV?" asked President Ambo.

Aasim didn't hesitate to remind his dad that using the army to deal with the protesters instead of ameliorating the sufferings of the people to make them lay down their blades will make matters worst.

"My military isn't weak, and will never be when it comes to dealing with protests," said President Ambo.

Aasim looked away from his dad even as he insists it's spurious for anyone to think they can usurp the power of the people to decide how their nation is run.

"I'm the people and my wish must be theirs, but what do you think about the protests?" asked President Ambo.

"What has that got to do with me?" asked Aasim.

"You mean you're happy about the protests?" asked President Ambo.

Aasim knew too well that exchanges with his dad can quickly take a new twist, and he had rather stay on the fence, even as his dad probes his intentions concerning the protest. Aasim insists he isn't in a position to say whether he's happy about the protest or not.

This President does things only by force and makes his pursuit of peace suspicious because that's out of his character, and Aasim thinks there's no need for that because his dad's breathless and fawning words won't add a grain of rice in the plate of any citizen of the land.

"Do you know you're talking to your dad?" asked President Ambo.

"You walked into my flat, except your obsession with killing me has grown so much that you can't wait for me to fall into your trap," said Aasim.

"What obsession are you talking about, do you realise I'm your dad?" asked President Ambo.

"For your information, the most talked about topic in the digital void is the oppression of the citizens of the Republic of Kitan," said Aasim.

President Ambo interjected and urged Aasim not to worry that the protesters will soon return to their homes.

Aasim seems to think differently about this particular protest, he pointed out to his dad that shooting the people into submission doesn't produce a lasting result and keeping the people oppressed by the barrel of the gun, will not make him earn their respect.

President Ambo took all of his son's unsolicited advice on the chin because he has a bigger fish to fry, he then steered the conversation into the purpose of his visit. "I came here to ask you to bring your friend Ismaila, to me, and maybe I can talk him into helping me stop the protest," said President Ambo.

Aasim chuckled at his dad's request before subtly asking his dad if he's suspecting the plausibility of a seismic shift of political power.

"I'm just being upfront about this," said President Ambo.

Aasim advised his dad not to expect the protest to dissipate, when the imbalance hasn't been addressed. President Ambo dismissed Aasim's suggestion about pacifying the protesters, he then pressed on Aasim to bring Ismaila and his disgruntled cohorts to him.

"You mean I should bring him to you for him to be killed? That manoeuvre is something that won't get off the ground," said Aasim.

President Ambo pressed on Aasim saying he isn't killing anybody, and if he kills Ismaila what about the rest of the protesters.

"Ok, if you want me to talk to Ismaila then I'll want you to give me my travel documents," said Aasim.

President Ambo dipped his hand into his pocket and brought out Aasim's travel documents, and said he knew Aasim would ask for these, he then handed the travel documents to Aasim.

Aasim collected his travel document from his dad and urged his dad to give him some time, so he could bring Ismaila around.

"Ok, do that fast, and I want this done within the next two hours," said President Ambo.

Forty-five minutes later, Aasim put a phone call across to his mum, and said he's leaving.

"Leaving to where, Aasim?" asked Aisha.

Aasim replied his mum saying he's leaving for Germany and he's leaving now. "But your dad has your travel documents, so what are you travelling with?" asked Aisha.

"I just collected them from him, with the intention I'll help him stop the protest," said Aasim.

Aisha understands the protest is still going on, and she didn't hesitate to ask Aasim why he isn't stopping the protest if that's what he promised.

Aasim alluded to the fact that he only used stopping the protest as a ploy to get back his travel documents, and he knows for sure that his dad will kill Ismaila if he brings Ismaila to him.

"But your dad won't allow you to travel out of Kitan," said Aisha.

Aasim knows how to find his way with the roads, and said he's travelling by road to Qatar, and from there he'll take a flight to Germany.

Aisha understands that most of the protesters aren't overly fond of the President and his family members, and that raised her concerns then prompting her to suggest that travelling by road to Qatar might be risky. She then asked if he's sure he won't be attacked by the protesters.

Interestingly, Aasim has his way with people, so he had to assure his mum that the protesters won't hurt him, and said he won't be in any danger. He then urged her not worry about his safety, after all, he's the-go-to person, when it come to the common man in the street.

"Just be careful, Aasim, you never know people," said Aisha.

"Ok mum, I've heard you, goodbye for now," said Aasim.

Two hours later, after waiting for words from Aasim and getting none, President Ambo decided to look for Aasim whose flat was locked up. He then approached Colonel Abdallah to inquire of Aasim's whereabouts.

"Oh, Aasim? He left, carrying a travelling bag about an hour thirty minutes ago," said Colonel Abdallah.

President Ambo immediately smelt a rat and asked the Colonel where it was that Aasim headed with a travelling bag.

Colonel Abdallah immediately reached for the phone and put a phone call across to his men whose prying eyes gathers intelligence on his behalf. After the brief phone conversation, the Colonel who's now a Brigadier informed the President that he thinks Aasim was travelling.

"No, he can't travel, I gave him an assignment which he must carry out," said President Ambo.

Colonel Abdallah had to hit the nail on the head, and said words reaching him was that Aasim is on his way to Qatar.

"What! He isn't going anywhere, I'll call the airport to stop him," President Ambo retorted.

"Mr. President I don't think that will be possible, he travelled by road and must've crossed the border by now," said Colonel Abdallah.

President Ambo went bananas and the news that his son pulled the wool over his eyes in this insulting manner, got to him, and it was as if he was hit by a ton of bricks. "You mean, my own son messed with me in this manner, I'll deal with this boy," said President Ambo.

Colonel Abdallah was speechless and quickly interjected, saying if he'd known that the President is against Aasim's moves, he would've stopped him. This whole thing might get worse before it gets better.

"It's not your fault, Colonel, go and get me the Chief of Army Staff," said President Ambo.

It didn't take long before the Chief of Army staff arrived.

"Brigadier what is going on, and why did the protests increase?" asked President Ambo.

Brigadier Sale Mai looked like a man caught off guard by the protesters, and he's now on the back foot, as he quickly told the President that he learnt about the protests, but he doesn't understand why the deaths didn't scare them away.

President Ambo interjected and said the death of six people should be enough to create enough fear that's capable of stopping people from coming out for more protest.

Unfortunately, this isn't the case as Brigadier Sale Mai expressed his concerns with this particular protest and said yesterday the protest took place in only Abidkitan and today it has spread to five cities.

President Ambo thought he has all his ducks in a row in days past but was riled by the doggedness of the protesters and said he never experienced a situation where the citizens of the Republic of Kitan will stand their ground against him like this.

Brigadier Sale Mai had to hit the nail on the head, as he reminded the President that the protesters are emboldened by the trends in the Middle East, the Arab Spring.

"And they think, I'm the next to go?" asked President Ambo.

Brigadier Sale Mai had to ask the President if he should ask his men to move in, since the police haven't been successful in dispersing the protester. President Ambo had no choice but to give his blessing to the request by the Chief of Army Staff, but this time he increased the death tally by granting the military the permission to kill some protesters, but not more than twenty protesters in each city.

Brigadier Sale Mai exclaimed and said twenty protesters in each city will result in a hundred casualties. He then subtly informed the President that the casualty might be too much.

"No, I'll let these protesters know that my resolve to remain in power is more than their resolve to push me out of power," said President Ambo.

"Ok Mr. President, let me send my men in to clear the protests," said Brigadier Sale Mai.

President Ambo thanked the brigadier but urged him to be swift about it.

Brigadier Sale Mai ordered his men to clear the protests in line with the President's directives and also instructed his men to kill an average of twenty people from towns where the protest is taking place. Sadly, by the end of that day, there was outcry, there was wailing, and the street was nothing but blood and guts.

A total of a hundred and twenty five deaths were recorded and some of the protesters recorded the military crackdown on their phones and uploaded them to YouTube for the world to see.

A day after the military crackdown on protesters, Ismaila and his friends met to count their losses. Mukhtar felt very sober as he told his co-organisers of the protest that Zidane was killed yesterday. Mukhtar isn't sure anymore, as he seeks assurances that they wouldn't end up holding the hat because he feared the military will kill them all, and yet the essence of the protest won't be achieved.

Ismaila understands that fear has now taken hold, even as they swell in ranks. "Yes, Zidane is dead, and may the Almighty Allah grant his soul rest and accept his soul in paradise, I want you to know he didn't die for nothing," said Ismaila.

Mukhtar isn't convinced there's light at the end of the tunnel, particularly now that the bullets are beginning to pick them out one at a time. He remained quite teary and asked his compatriots if they think it's wise to continue this protest.

Ismaila had to convince Mukhtar and reminded him that if what they started wasn't right, he then asked why five more cities join the protest yesterday. The death of a hundred and twenty five protesters isn't something for Mukhtar to shrug off, it actually makes his skin crawl. He insisted that the deaths were too many, and said it hurts to see innocent citizens dying just like chickens. Ismaila's hope is on the international community, and he looked at Mukhtar before assuring him that the world is seeing the actions of Ambo Hussein.

"The world knew already, that was why they closed their embassies here and froze our government's assets," said Mukhtar. President Ambo Hussein's message of brute force got to Mukhtar, and it's quite intriguing how he inflicted fear in this young man.

Ismaila muttered under his breath, saying they knew before but now they know better. While they were still talking, Jabir walked into the house.

"Where have you been Jabir? You should understand we're being watched," said Mukhtar.

Jabir was out and about monitoring what's going on out there, and interestingly, two more cities have joined the protests.

"Mukhtar, I told you it's working in our favour, the Almighty Allah is on our side," said Ismaila.

Mukhtar turned to Jabir and asked what cities he said joined the protest. "The city of Shambihya and the city of Denrur," said Jabir.

"Are you sure about this?" asked Ismaila.

"Call your friends in those cities they'll tell you, and even go to YouTube they're posting the videos of the protests in real time," said Jabir.

Sadly, the actions of President Ambo has precipitated a knee jerk reaction, that has set the frontiers of the destiny of these protesters, and they either chicken out or take their destinies in their own hands.

Ismaila was quite pleased to hear that the ducks are lining up in their favour, he then worked it out in his head and said it means seven cities are protesting today, which means over half a million citizens of the Republic of Kitan will be on the streets. Jabir prefers to look backward before going forward he then interjected and asked about Zidane.

Ismaila suggested they go and see Zidane's parents to express their condolences and promise them they'll continue to fight for what Zidane died for.

Ismaila and his co-organisers walked into the home of Zidane's parents as they pay him a condolence visit.

Iffat received the protests leaders who have come to comfort him over the death of his son, Zidane.

"My children, you're all welcome, I told my son Zidane but he wouldn't listen, Ambo is evil and not a man to be toyed with," said Iffat.

"Baba, the death of Zidane is a big loss, but his death isn't a waste, it counts for something," said Ismaila.

"What did it count for? My son just died for nothing, Ambo is still there, do you think you guys can dethrone Ambo?" asked Iffat. Ismaila continued to persuade Iffat that Zidane's death is a big blow, but they'll hold Ambo to account for this.

Iffat got upset, with Ismaila's insistence that Ambo Hussein would be held to account.

"How can you children make Ambo pay for my son's death? Great men like Sheikh Suleiman Zurumi, Brigadier BachaKar, and even the President's own uncle Shiekh Abdul were all taken down, who held Ambo to account for these crimes?" asked Iffat. Sadly, Iffat is expressing the glaring truth, after the presidential aspirants, the military and even the international community have all largely failed to get Ambo Hussein out of power.

Ismaila remained unwavering as he reminded Iffat that he led the uprising in Tunisia and the President eventually fled even when the so called great men in Tunisia failed. He assured Iffat that one day with the help of the Almighty Allah, they'll chase Ambo away.

"Baba, please accept our condolences," said Jabir.

Iffat didn't mince his words when he urged Ismaila and his friends to return to their parents, he advised that the thought of taking Ambo Hussein down should remain only in their heads, because no parent should suffer the loss of a child.

"We can't go home, I see victory at the end of this, all we need is the courage to pull through," said Ismaila.

Iffat became quite upset. "Pull through what? With the death of a hundred and twenty-five people, go around town all you will hear is weeping, families weeping over their loss," said Iffat.

"Baba, I understand, I expect the same reaction from any parent who just lost a son, your reaction isn't misplaced," said Ismaila.

This condolence visit has turned into an admonishment, and as they set to leave, Iffat left a note of caution as he advised the young men to all return home to their parents and forget about making Ambo pay, he insisted that the monster is apocalyptic.

Iffat's words struck a nerve in Mukhtar which exacerbated his earlier concerns about the crackdown on protesters. As they leave Zidane's dad, Mukhtar asked Ismaila what think about the note of caution by Zidane's dad, and then said the old man seems to be making some sense.

"Yeah, just as any sensible parent, but this protest must continue until Ambo pays for his sins," said Ismaila. One thing Iffat and these protesters have in common is the fact that they could no longer put up with the howling winds of narcissism in their nation.

President Ambo heard the news that two more cities have joined the protest and the protest in each city has grown much bigger than the previous day. He became restless and despaired, and he then stood up and angrily walked into his living room where Malik and Aisha were already sitting and watching television.

"You mean the two of you're watching television, while the people are protesting against me?" asked President Ambo.

Malik turned to his dad and said they were also following the protest, and that's what his mum and him were discussing, just that a TV commercial was what he saw on screen. Yet, Malik said he thought his dad was able to disperse the protesters the day before.

"Shambihya and Denrur have joined the protest and the protest has gotten bigger," said President Ambo.

"Dad, maybe we should take a different approach in dealing with the protest," said Malik.

President Ambo exasperatingly asked how then he should handle this because he might kill them all. This man is single-minded, shrewd, and his character flaws lies in the only language he speaks, and that's brute force.

Aisha isn't the quiet one anymore, as she quickly asked President Ambo how he thinks killing his citizens will earn him the respect he's seeking.

"Aisha, I'm not ready to hear any of your negative talks," said President Ambo.

Malik had to remind his dad that he noticed that the protesters are posting the videos on You Tube. President Ambo retorted saying that's where all these foreign TV stations get the nonsense they're reporting about him. There's nothing the President finds needling than the fact that the digital void, the internet is now awash with videos and images of the citizens of the Republic of Kitan being brutalised by their leader. Among the things that riled this President the most is the media feeding frenzy.

Sadly, this isn't just about what was said about the despot, it was how it was said that got him kicking off and throwing his toys out of the pram.

Malik stepped in suggesting he could stem the flow of media posts, and said he'll speak to the director of telecommunications to start jamming the internet, maybe that will stop them from using the internet. President Ambo finds it quite difficult dislodging this last vestige of resistance, it was as if the light had just been grabbed away from top of his bushel. He then suggested speaking to his military chiefs on the next strategy.

Malik had no knowledge of Aasim's earlier betrayal of his dad and suggested to his dad to speak to Aasim to help him speak to some of his friends.

Aisha interjected and asked Malik to just leave Aasim out of this, accusing Malik of being a rabble rouser who's trying to set Aasim up against his father.

"But if Aasim had worked with dad, all these things wouldn't be happening," said Malik.

Aisha isn't ready to be shut out, and she refused to be alone to gather dust all the rest of her life. She gave Malik the dressing down as she reminded Malik that Aasim is the only disillusioned son she has, describing the rest of her children as mere puppets acting out their dad's puerile script. The President is in despair and needed words of hope and not banter from his begrudged wife, he then turned to Aisha and said he expects his family to be on his side in times like this when rebellion and political upheaval is the order of the day.

"Too much blood has already been spilled, and the blood of the innocent are crying for justice," said Aisha. She stood up and was about to leave the living room, and then stopped. "Wait a minute! Have you thought about the curse by those Christians' you persecuted?" asked Aisha.

After Aisha left, Malik turned to his dad, and asked what he thinks about what mum just said.

"Your mum just mentioned something very pertinent, I don't believe in curses but I'm beginning to think otherwise," said President Ambo.

Malik then retorted and said he worry more about the curse by those Ulamas his dad punished than whatever curse issued by those Christian infidels.

President Ambo muttered and said he's being faced with the brutal realities of governance, but dealing with curses adds a different twist to the mix.

"What do we do? It's like what those Christian worshipers said is coming true," said Malik.

President Ambo needed to deal with his troubles, but one at a time, and he had to deal with the curse first to get it out of the way. He immediately asked Malik to bring those behind the curse before him, and maybe he'll have a word with them to rescind the curse.

"But Aasim said they left for Egypt after that incident, If Aasim had been around maybe he would've been able to reach out to them," said Malik.

"It means your dad is paying the price for your overzealousness, and unfortunately your brother seems to distance himself from me in time as this," said President Ambo.

"I'm sorry, dad," said Malik.

President Ambo summoned courage as he puts up a brave face and asked Malik not to worry, saying if dialog doesn't work, then his military might will.

"I know your mum can press Aasim, but her disposition suggests otherwise," said President Ambo.

President Ambo subtly muttered under his breath and said his wife switched sides from being a wife to a rival, since the death of her son Sadeq.

"Dad, killing Sadeq was a step too far," said Malik.

"The deed is done, Malik, and I've to live with it," said President Ambo.

"Let's hope mum will come around," said Malik.

President Ambo said he doesn't think his wife will come back to seeing him as her knight in shining armour again, and said he thinks he has lost her. He then proceeded to confess to Malik that he now realised Sadeq means a lot more to his mum than he previously thought, and after a sombre moment, he stood up from his seat and left.

Sadly, the killing of Sadeq is a watershed moment for Aisha, and she will never remain the quiet submissive wife after that incident.

CHAPTER

EIGHT

The Troll Farmers

The protest against President Ambo Hussein persisted as the protesters remained on the streets insisting their protests would continue until their president pack up and go.

The protester seemed to get helping hands from citizens of other Arab nations joining in to make the protest louder and bigger, but this time, the involvement of troll farmers has added a new twist to the protest.

Brigadier Sale Mai walks into President Ambo's office, and requested his attention, saying he needs to see this.

President Ambo looked curious and asked the Brigadier what's it he wants him to see.

Brigadier Sale Mai quickly played a YouTube video for the President to see, and at the same time informed the President that the video has gone viral, and the international community are already reacting.

President Ambo was quite enraged after watching the video. "What! Isn't that Malik, why would Malik use a chainsaw to chop a person into two halves?" asked President Ambo.

"I was shocked by this video, the gruesomeness of this graphic video is beyond imagination," said Brigadier Sale Mai.

President Ambo was gutted by the content of the video insisting that Malik has taken this too far, and it's time for him to start curtailing his son's excesses.

Brigadier Sale Mai proceeded to inform the President that Amnesty international is already documenting this as part of the human rights abuses by the government of President Ambo Hussein.

President Ambo just kept muttering over and over, that he just can't get his head around why his son would use a chainsaw to chop a person into two, he then requested for Malik to see him immediately.

Minutes later, Malik walks into his dad's office. Dad you sent for me, and why're your faces looking like this, is anything the matter?" asked Malik.

"I must confess, I'm disappointed in you, when did you grow the heart of engaging in the horror of cutting a person into two halves," said Malik.

"Me! Chainsaw, do you think I could do a thing as ghastly as that?" asked Malik.

President Ambo quickly played the video for Malik to see for himself, he then asked his son if he's involved in a scheme of making people disappear without his knowledge.

Malik was in shock to see the video. "Oh my God, that isn't me, I didn't do anything like that," said Malik.

The grim realities of being known for blood and guts means you can be labelled as working side by side with the devil himself.

"What do you mean, isn't that your shirt? I know you with that shirt and wrist watch, every citizen of the Republic of Kitan know you with this shirt," President Ambo retorted.

Malik became furious that even his own dad is accusing him for a crime he didn't commit. "I said, that isn't me! Who's it that's setting me up?" asked Malik.

"You mean that isn't you?" asked President Ambo.

"Take a look at the shirt, mine has a button hole on the tip of the collar and this shirt doesn't have that. More so, there's no birth mark on this person's neck, at least you know I've a birth mark," said Malik.

Brigadier Sale Mai listened to Malik's defence and suddenly turned to President Ambo, and said he thinks he knows what's going on.

"What's going on, Brigadier?" asked President Ambo.

Brigadier Sale Mai informed the President that trolls have joined the rebellion, and that they post fake videos to increase negative reaction against the President.

President Ambo was riled to hear of this thick conspiracy to finish off his government and asked the Brigadier if he meant the protesters make someone up to look like his son, just to make his people hate him the more.

"Now the world thinks I actually used a chainsaw to cut a person in two," said Malik.

"This video has actually increased the sentiment of the people against your dad," said Brigadier Sale Mai.

President Ambo looked distressed after realising the crafty hands of the protesters are beginning to beat him to it. His efforts to inhibit the spontaneity of this protest has failed largely because the protesters seem one step ahead of him in the scheme of things and this makes him go cuckoo. He then ordered the Brigadier to find out where this troll factory is located, and fish out those behind this gross hypocrisy because he wants to them pay for this.

Malik was still reeling from the action of the troll farmers targeted at his person. By the evening of the next day, Malik walked into his dad's living room to inquire if his dad has heard from Brigadier Sale Mai, and said he tried calling the Brigadier earlier but the Brigadier said his men are still combing. Sadly, this civil disobedience has morphed into a multi-headed hydra. The President's focus before now was about dealing with the curse placed on his son, and now, it's about dealing with troll farmers that have come into the fray.

"I want them brought before me and when I do, I'll teach them how to use a chainsaw to chop a person into two," said President Ambo.

Malik's sabre rattling in the past seemed to make him the perfect candidate for the troll farmers. He continues to rile over his betrayal before the world, saying this is a carefully orchestrated act of betrayal, and the world now hates him even when they haven't met him.

Aisha seemed to remind Malik of the obvious truth and said the troll farmers posted videos of acts him and his dad are capable of committing, and urged Malik to stop talking about betrayal.

"Mum, so you're convinced I'm capable of cutting a person into two with a chainsaw?" asked Malik.

Aisha didn't mince her words in emphasizing the obvious as she turned to Malik and insisted that his dad is very capable of cutting a person into two halves with a chainsaw. She stressed that the horror her husband is capable of enacting is beyond conception.

President Ambo was touched by his wife perception of him, and he quickly turned to Aisha, and then asked if she's implying that he's capable of using a chainsaw to chop a person into two halves.

"I know you! And know perfectly well what you're capable of doing, killing my son right before my eyes as well as killing his father is the gravest of sins," said Aisha.

"Mum, but...," said Malik.

Aisha interjected and angrily hushed Malik and telling him to shut his mouth, before insisting her husband is apocalyptic and Malik's support for his dad after committing such gruesome acts means he's also capable of doing the same.

"When I lay my hands on those shenanigans, they would realise what a brute of a man I'm," said President Ambo.

Aisha laughed hysterically and reminded her husband that at least her assertions about him are right because he's flagitious and dark.

President Ambo seemed to have had enough and became furious at Aisha's hysterical laughter. He had to rebuke her, saying instead of showing empathy over Malik's betrayal all she did was paint her husband and son, as monsters.

Aisha seemed ready for trouble, as she continued to take the mickey out of her husband and said Malik put himself forward as a monster and his dad helped prop him up to be one. She then stood up to leave but turned to Malik. "Your dad just killed over a hundred protesters, who does that, if not a monster?" said Aisha.

"You're pushing me, Aisha," warned President Ambo. The President stood up in anger and left. The next day, President Ambo puts a phone call across to Brigadier Sale Mai to see if he has succeeded in tracking the troll farmers. Funnily, President Ambo can't wait to lay hands on those behind the deceitful video portraying his son as perpetuating horror.

President Ambo called the Brigadier and reminded him that it's been seventy-two hours since he gave an order to uncover the location of the troll factory that's painting his son as a monster of horror.

"Mr. President, I was to call you before your calls came in, I just discovered the troll factory," said Brigadier Sale Mai.

"Good, round them up, I'll skin them alive," President Ambo retorted.

Brigadier Sale Mai quickly apologised to the President for not being able to make his wish of skinning the perpetrators of this video alive come true. He went on to inform the President the place is deserted, and the entire building is empty.

President Ambo yelled, asking the Brigadier what he meant by the building being deserted and asked to know who the perpetrators are.

"Intelligence gathered shows those behind this video came from abroad, they crossed the border three nights ago," Brigadier Sale Mai.

President Ambo was quite pissed to learn that hired hands are now crossing the border into his country to mess with his reputation. He then asked if the border crossing was into the country or out of the country.

"They left the country three nights ago," said Brigadier Sale Mai.

"Meaning, foreigners are fuelling the rebellion of my people against me," said President Ambo.

Brigadier Sale Mai had to dispel every misconception and advised the President that there's every possibility the perpetrators are citizens of the Republic of Kitan based abroad.

"Who are their family members? I need to punish anyone related to these traitors," asked President Ambo.

Brigadier Sale Mai subtly informed the enraged President Ambo that they aren't able to identify those particularly responsible, but those who heard them speak confirmed they are natives.

President Ambo then ordered that the building used to perpetrate this crime must be demolished and the owner of the building punished.

Brigadier Sale Mai had to relay another disappointing information to the President as he informed him that the building used for this act belong to the foreigners he ordered out of the country.

He went on to say that the building has been abandoned and they were left open without locks.

President Ambo was sick to his stomach that he's unable to punish someone for this act. Sadly, he's unable to squeeze the necks of these perpetrators until they chock to death as he has planned, he has been beaten again by the protesters, and all he could do was to order Brigadier Sale Mai to be on the lookout.

"Thank you, Mr. President," said Brigadier Sale Mai.

CHAPTER

NINE

The Chlorine gas

Nafisat Khan is the daughter of the Governor of Shambihya, Nafisat and Nawal's friendship has been going on forever, and more so, they're course mates in the university they both attend in Turkey.

Nafisat was on phone with Nawal. "Hello Nawal, what's up?" asked Nafisat.

"I'm fine Nafi and are you still in Turkey?" asked Nawal.

Nafisat laughed and asked Nawal to check her phone, to see the number that she's calling her with.

Nawal quickly looked to see the phone number Nafisat was calling with and exclaimed. "Oh, you're in Kitan," said Nawal.

"Yes, of course, that was why I asked you to check your phone," said Nafisat.

"Most times all I do is check the name of the caller and I always forget I've two of your phone numbers; one is Turkish and the other Kitan," said Nawal.

"By the way, Nawal, what's up with the night clubs?" asked Nafisat.

Nawal muttered her frustration as she reminded Nafisat that she's in Shambihya and while she's stuck at home with her dad in Ansarouh, and distance doesn't give them the luxury of enjoying the night clubs together.

Nafisat cheekily reminded Nawal that it's still possible for them to meet, after all, she can either come over to Shambihya and they go to her house after clubbing or she'll come to Ansarouh, and they go to Nawal's house after clubbing.

"The way you're sounding so enthusiastic about going clubbing, have you forgotten that I'm the daughter of President Ambo Hussein, and my dad is a conservative Muslim?" asked Nawal.

"You and I knew your dad is a conservative Muslim right from time zero, but you do know how to have your fun," said Nafisat.

"I do have my fun, but I don't rub it on his face in a manner that will irk him," said Nawal.

Nafisat remembered her dad's subtle caution urging her to be watchful of her actions and utterances whenever she visits Nawal in the Presidents' villa. She quickly reminded Nawal that her dad is a stern looking man and it makes her fret, which is why she avoids coming over to the presidential villa most times.

"Let me see if I can work something out," said Nawal.

Nafisat urged Nawal to let her know immediately she's able to work things out with her dad, because she really needs to have some fun before going back to school.

Nawal laughed and cheekily scolded Nafisat, telling her to stop sounding as if all she does in Turkey isn't about having fun. The social interplay between these girls is sort of cheeky but comforting, and Nawal's Laissez-faire attitude means she kills this friend of hers with kindness, and that keeps her attached to Nawal.

Aasim is now in Germany cosying up with his fiancée and leaving behind the troubles in his father's house. In one of the evenings Aasim had to spend some time out with his friend, Maman.

"Maman, sorry I'm late, and how long have you been waiting?" asked Aasim.

Maman jocularly reminded Aasim they agreed 5.pm but it's 6.pm now, yet stretched out his hand for a handshake and said it's good to have him back in Germany.

Aasim apologised to Maman saying they would've arrived earlier than they did but Nicole didn't dress up on time. After his handshake with Aasim, Maman then turned to Nicole and laughed. He then bantered with her saying she looks alright, and does it mean the sickness disappeared the moment Aasim arrived.

Nicole burst into laughter and was quite jocular. "Tell that to the birds," she said.

Aasim passed his hand around Nicole, as he cheekily said Nicole has been lovesick and she's right to feel abandoned by her husband to be. Nicole went with the banter as she turned to Aasim and urged Maman to ask Aasim how he felt when he saw her after long while.

"Aasim, you've got a question to answer, what did you do to her?" asked Maman.

"Nothing, we only took stock, that's all," said Aasim.

Maman laughed and said if not for Nicole's experience in the hands of Aasim's dad, nothing should've stopped her coming over to Kitan if it becomes difficult for him to leave.

Nicole replied saying she has got no problem with Aasim's mum and brothers, but his dad is just something else.

"I'm going to work on that, and with time my dad will learn to accept her," said Aasim.

"Guys, let's go if you're ready," said Aasim.

Nicole asked Aasim where in particular he's taking her and Maman, because she seems keen for a sneak peek of where the days' outing will be.

"Just a place where we'll have a nice time, just don't ask me where until you get there," said Aasim.

After her conversation with Nafisat, Nawal summoned courage to request time out with her friend from her dad. She then left her side of the flat the next day, and walked into her dad's living room.

"Dad, I'm going to Shambihya to see Nafisat," said Nawal.

President Ambo yelled in quite a squawky tone, because this isn't the kind of talk he wants to engage in. "Nawal, Shambihya is forty-five kilometres from Ansarouh, why now?" he asked.

"Dad, I don't understand the harsh reaction, I'm bored, and I want to go out to see my friend," said Nawal.

President Ambo reminded Nawal he left an instruction that no member of his household should leave the presidential villa. This domestic quarantine didn't go down very well with this party animal. Nawal then chuckled and said she's aware but that was last week and she believes that by now the instruction must've been reversed. President Ambo insists the instruction is still in place, and gave Nawal the alternative of asking her friend to come over to the presidential villa.

Nawal might have to spook her dad by telling him what her friends think of him, as she subtly informed her dad that her friends don't like coming over because he's always stern looking and never friendly.

"You're telling your dad to his face he's an unfriendly man, isn't it?" asked President Ambo.

"No, that's what people say about you," said Nawal.

While Nawal continued pressing on her dad to have her way, Malik walked into the conversation and reminded Nawal she's already twenty four years old. He then asked when she'll learn to listen to and obey simple instructions.

"Why do we have to be locked up in the house, have you asked yourself, if we brought this on ourselves?" asked Nawal.

President Ambo shunned Nawal, saying enough of this nonsense. "If you must know, the protest is still on and I can't take the risk of letting you fall into the hands of my enemies," said President Ambo.

Nawal was quite misty-eyed as she begged her dad as if her life depends on it, and promised him she wouldn't go in the direction of the protesters, she then drew closer to her dad and said she'll be back in three hours time. Interestingly, she turned on the charm of the last child on her dad, and before you know it, President Ambo's heart softens up.

"You and your brother, Aasim, are my biggest headaches. I'm using up my energy trying to stop you from walking into danger, and instead of your brother helping me stop this protest, he ran off to Germany because of a woman," said President Ambo.

Nawal tried to keep Aasim out of the conversation and said Aasim's fiancée was sick that was why he had to go.

"What's she sick of? Tell me, except she's lovesick," said President Ambo.

"Dad, please I'll be back in a few hours time, I'm bored and just need to go out," said Nawal.

President Ambo caved in as he feared that Nawal could nag him to death on this subject but insisted that Nawal won't be going with her car and rather Colonel Abdallah and some guards will accompany her.

"I don't mind, thank you dad," said Nawal.

Now that Nawal has succeeded with her dad, she quickly decided to get back to Nafisat on the outcome of her conversation with her dad.

"Babe, guess what?" asked Nawal.

"We're going clubbing tonight," said Nafisat.

"No, you missed it," said Nawal.

"Please cut to the chase, what's the outcome of your conversation with your dad?" asked Nafisat.

Nawal whispered to Nafisat that she'll be with her in an hour time but there won't be clubbing.

Nafisat was quite disappointed that the clubbing thing won't be a possibility and asked why Nawal didn't tell her dad she will be passing the night in her place.

Nawal was even grateful for the latitude of spending three hours away from home and reminded Nafisat that the three hours permission she got was the consequence of a heated conversation amid tears.

"Though, these three hours is better than nothing," said Nafisat.

"See you soon," said Nawal.

"I can't wait," said Nafisat.

President Ambo called Sheikh Labaran Kahn the Governor of Shambihya.

"Hello Mr. President," said Labaran Kahn.

"Labaran, how're you?" asked President Ambo.

"I'm fine Mr. President, and are you calling about the protests in Shambihya?" asked Labaran Kahn.

President Ambo have bigger fish to fry, his reply to Labaran Kahn was that he knew the protest is still on and they'll talk about that later, but for now he's calling him to discuss Nawal's visit.

"What about her?" asked Labaran Kahn.

President Ambo went on inform Labaran Kahn that his daughter is coming over to his place to see Nafisat. Labaran Kahn exclaimed, saying his daughter never even bothered to talk about it.

"These kids like playing with the intelligence of the elderly, I want you to keep an eye on her, so she doesn't put herself in any danger," said President Ambo.

Labaran Kahn had to put an emergency security meeting on how to deal with these protests on hold until Nawal arrives and leaves. President Ambo smiled and said that's a good idea and urged Labaran Kahn to do that for him.

An hour later, Nawal arrived at Governor Labaran Kahn's residence, accompanied by Colonel Abdallah and other security details.

Nafisat came out of the house to receive them as the convoy drove into the Governors' compound.

"Oh babe, good to see you, and what's up?" asked Nafisat.

"I'm fine, Nafisat, just that I've been bored because my dad doesn't let us out of his sight," said Nawal.

These girls are quite secular, and their lifestyle away from the prying eyes of their parents is quite in contrast with that of their conservative Muslim parents.

They walked into the house. "At least, I've succeeded in taking you out of his sight even for three hours," said Nafisat. Labaran Kahn was sitting in his living room as they walked through. "Nawal, how're you?" he asked.

"Governor Kahn, I'm fine," said Nawal.

Labaran Kahn engaged Nawal in a brief conversation, telling her Nafisat never told him Nawal is coming.

"But dad, you knew she was coming, by your actions I can tell you were aware she would be here," said Nafisat.

"My dad must've called him," said Nawal.

"It's a good thing I know because you girls could be careless, considering the security situation of the country," said Labaran Kahn.

"Ok dad, I'm taking her to my room," said Nafisat.

"Ok, you're free," said Labaran Kahn.

Nawal turned to Colonel Abdallah. "Colonel, you and your men should relax in the living room, while Nafisat gets you some refreshment," said Nawal.

Nafisat took Nawal to her bedroom where they continued with their girly, girly conversation. Interestingly, before Nawal made herself comfortable she asked Nafisat if she has something to drink in her house.

"Why're you asking? I thought you came with at least a bottle of wine," asked Nafisat.

Nawal admonished Nafisat, reminding her she should know that her dad forbids them from taking alcohol and Nafisat's place is the only place she can secretly drink a little alcohol whenever she's in the Republic of Kitan.

"You know I just came in last night, and I don't have any at home, unless we have to go and buy some," said Nafisat.

Nawal understands what it cost her dad to let her out of his sight for a short period of three hours, and she's also certain of her dad's instruction to Governor Khan to keep a watchful eye over her. She had to remind Nafisat that Governor Khan won't let them out of the house, but Nafisat enjoys the privilege of being the only child because she always has her way with her dad. She winked her eyes at Nawal and told her not to worry about her dad, and said she'll tell him they're buying non alcoholic wine. These girls aren't just as modest and religious as they pretend to be, they're actually rascals by their predisposition, but pretend to be as innocent as though they can't kill a fly when they are around their parents.

Nawal had to let Nafisat know they are barking up against the wrong tree as she reminded her that shops in the Republic of Kitan don't sell alcoholic drink, because it's against the law.

Nafisat whispered into Nawal's ear and told her not to worry because there's a secret spot where she buys it from. It's a secret and her dad who's the governor has no knowledge of this.

"Ok let's go then," said Nawal. They left the room and walked downstairs to the living room.

Nafisat stopped in front of her dad and said they're coming.

"Where are you girls going?" asked Labaran Kahn.

Nafisat subtly informed her dad she wants to get wine for Nawal because she doesn't have any in her room.

Labaran Kahn needed to keep these girls in a tight leash and had to deny them the latitude of straying around. He told his daughter he has some bottles of wine in the house and asked her to take one. Nafisat was upfront as she craftily told her dad that his choice of wine isn't their brand.

"Then what's your brand, and I hope you aren't talking about alcoholic wine?" asked Labaran Kahn.

"No dad, we don't drink alcohol, Colonel Abdallah should go with us for security reasons," said Nawal.

"That's good," said Labaran Kahn.

They left the house accompanied by Colonel Abdallah and his guards. Sadly, these guards had no knowledge these girls are out to buy alcohol and unfortunately, the guards are there to keep them secure, but they aren't policing their moral code either.

They left the house and went to a remote part of Shambihya, where alcoholic wine is secretly sold, close to where Amira whose sister Halima was killed during the crackdown on protesters days back.

"Sadiqat, see," said Amira.

Sadiqat was lost as to what Amira was talking about, she then asked Amira what it was she's asking her to see.

Amira advised Sadiqat to turn around quietly and urged her to do so slowly without creating any suspicion.

Sadiqat turned around slowly, then muttered and said, that's Nafisat and Nawal, the Governor and the President's daughters, she then proceeded to ask what's it was they're doing here.

"They come to buy alcohol; the governor's daughter comes here to buy alcohol but not often," said Amira.

"You mean these little kids drink alcohol?" asked Sadiqat.

"That's not my concern, Sadiqat," said Amira.

"Then what's it, that's your concern?" asked Sadiqat.

Amira quietly whispered into Sadiqat's ears and said she has prayed to the Almighty Allah and the Almighty Allah has just brought an opportunity to her for her to have her revenge. It's obvious that Amira's loss left her devastated, and she remained quite unforgiving because she hasn't relinquished her right to vengeance to the International Community and even to the Almighty Allah.

"What revenge are you talking about?" asked Sadiqat.

"I now have the opportunity to kill Ambo Hussein's daughter," said Amira.

"Stop talking trash, don't you see the bodyguards around her? They'll kill you from a distance," said Sadiqat.

"Provided I get my revenge, and it doesn't matter if they kill me," said Amira.

Sadiqat understands quite well the ramifications of her friends' audacious move. She then tried as hard as she could to stop Amira, begging her to please not do this, she begged her in the name of God not to follow through with this madness, but this girl is keen on taking her pound of flesh from President Ambo Hussein without a dint of fear.

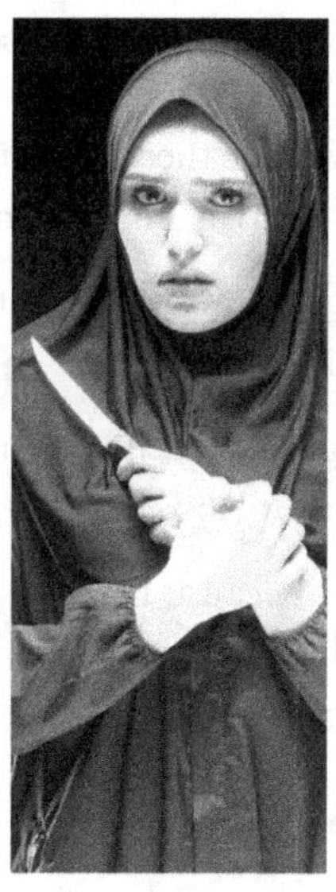

Amira stood up and went into the house and took a sharp table knife and hid it inside her clothes and walked to the shop as if she wanted to buy something from the shop while Nawal was still inside.

Colonel Abdallah saw Amira walking into the shop and hushed her to stop in quite a harsh tone. "Where are you going, young lady?" asked Colonel Abdallah.

"I want to buy something.

"You've to wait for us finish, and then you can go in," said Colonel Abdallah.

Amira quickly put up a show, displaying the teary disposition of a weakling, as she pointed to a can of spice from outside the shop. "I just want to pick that spice, my soup is on the fire and could get spoilt by the time I finish waiting for you," she said.

"Ok, just do that quickly and leave," said Colonel Abdallah.

Oops, this Colonel that was newly promoted to the position of a Brigadier for his attention to details has just made a fatal mistake. "Ok, thank you," she said. Amira picked the spice and inched closer and closer to Nawal, she then thrust the knife through Nawal's heart and the guards fired at Amira immediately and she died.

Colonel Abdallah screamed. "Call the ambulance, please call the ambulance now," he said.

"Sir, the ambulance might take time, let's rush her to the hospital with the car," said Sergeant Abba.

Colonel Abdallah wept because he couldn't help himself as he watched Nawal's life slipping away, and she mustn't die before she's rushed to the hospital.

Nafisat screamed. "No Nawal, please don't do this to me, come back," she cried.

Colonel Abdallah put a call through to the President and was panting as he said hello to Mr. President.

"Colonel, why're you breathing so high, are you on your way back?" asked President Ambo.

Colonel Abdallah didn't hesitate to inform President Ambo that an incident has occurred. President Ambo was quick to ask what incident it was that he's talking about.

Colonel Abdallah was in great despair even as his voice cracked as he informed the President that Nawal has been stabbed, and they've just arrived at the hospital.

President Ambo growled and exclaimed. "I kept my daughter in your care and you're telling me she was stabbed, were you sleeping, and how's she?" he asked.

"She has been stabbed in the heart," said Colonel Abdallah.

President Ambo screamed. "No, not my daughter! Colonel, my daughter mustn't die, and if she dies, you die," said President Ambo.

Aisha heard her husband's scream and came from the bedroom to the living room. "What's it! Why're you screaming?" asked Aisha.

President Ambo turned to Aisha, and said Nawal has been stabbed and it's serious.

Aisha screamed. "What! How did it happen?" asked Aisha.

President Ambo turned to Aisha and said he'd no idea of how it happened. "Let's just get a convoy ready and leave immediately," he said. Minutes later President Ambo and Aisha left for Shambihya.

While on their way to Shambihya Aisha dialled Colonel Abdallah's phone to inquire of Nawal's condition. "How's she and I hope she's ok?" asked Aisha.

"No, she isn't, the doctor tried to save her, but he just confirmed her dead," said Colonel Abdallah.

"What! No, no that can't be true," Aisha cried. She then grabbed President Ambo by his shirt, and accused him of killing her daughter, she then let go of her husband, and cried the more.

"No, no, this Colonel has killed her," he screamed.

On arrival at the hospital in Shambihya, Colonel Abdallah took President Ambo to the bed where Nawal's corpse was.

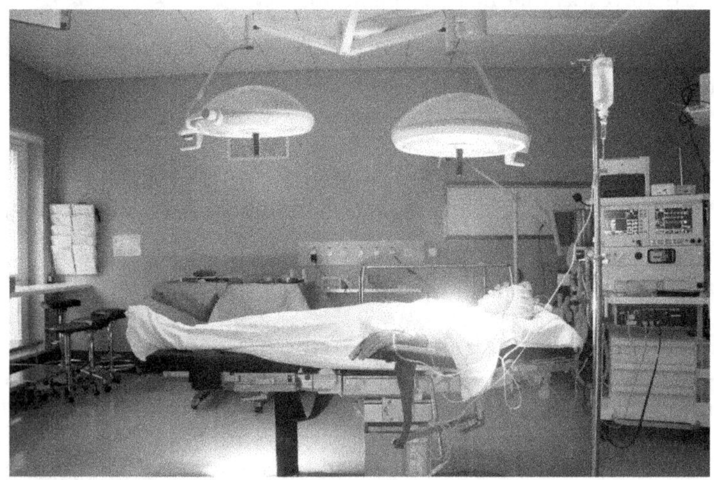

President Ambo was quite broken to see his daughter's lifeless body, he held his head in despair. He then turned to the Colonel. "I gave my daughter to you and asked you to watch over her and now you're showing me her corpse?" he asked.

Colonel Abdallah apologised to President Ambo, saying he's sorry, and went on to say they killed the girl responsible, but it all happened so fast. Unfortunately, Abdallah hadn't the faintest idea of what's coming.

"How fast did it happen, aren't you supposed to be vigilant?" asked President Ambo. The President was quite shaken with the sight before him and in his grief-stricken state, he then stretched his hand and pulled Sergeant Abba's Pistol from the holster.

"Mr. President I'm sorry, I tried keeping her in a tight leash, but they said they wanted to buy something from the shop," said Colonel Abdallah. Aisha held Nawal's lifeless body and wept in a remarkable display of emotional outburst. "What's going on with my family? Oh, Ambo you caused this," said Aisha.

President Ambo then raised the gun he took off Abba, and pointed it at the Colonel, and reminded Colonel Abdallah of his earlier promise that the Colonel will die if Nawal dies.

Colonel Abdallah apologised unreservedly to the President, and begged him not to do this, reminding him he has served him faithfully.

Aisha interjected urging her husband to drop his hand. "Ambo you don't have to do this, killing the Colonel won't bring Nawal back," said Aisha.

President Ambo seemed keen to follow through with his promise to the Colonel and said since he can't keep his daughter safe then he has outlived his usefulness. He fired three shots at the Colonel, and he died right there inside the hospital and he pointed the gun at Nafisat who has been crying.

"Mr. President, what are you doing?" asked Nafisat.

President Ambo was quite stern looking, as he reminded Nafisat that he told her father to look after Nawal, and he didn't. "Now Nawal is dead and, you're alive," President Ambo Muttered.

Aisha had to stop her husband who's on killing spree and she had to ask him what he will achieve by killing a twenty two years old girl. She then reminded him this is a hospital and there are sick people here and urged him to stop making people scamper for safety with his gun shots. She rushed and removed the gun from his hand.

President Ambo went on to grab his daughter's lifeless body and began to weep. "Why didn't I see this coming? I shouldn't have let her out of my sight," cried President Ambo.

Aisha turned to Sergeant Abba and asked her to take Nafisat to her dad right now. She understands that her husband's hands were a shudder but that doesn't stop his killing spree, and it's possible he could revisit killing Nafisat if she hangs around.

Thirty minutes later, the President puts a phone call across to Nafisat's dad, Governor Labaran Khan.

"Labaran, I asked you to watch over my daughter, and now she is dead," said President Ambo.

"Mr. President, I tried to stop her from going out, but she insisted she wanted to drink wine, and I asked her to take one of the ones in my home just to stop her from going out but she said she has a different brand," said Labaran Khan.

"Why did you do this to me?" asked President Ambo.

Labaran Kahn was mum for a while, and was quite shaken, because it's obvious that he's now in the crosshairs of the President. His daughter already told him President Ambo wanted to kill her as well if not for Aisha's intervention. "I was shocked when my daughter told me about it, and I wanted to come over immediately but was afraid you might kill me, so I decided to wait until you're calmer," said Labaran Khan.

"I just want you to know I'm not happy with you," said President Ambo.

"I'm sorry Mr. President, I didn't see this coming, and even my daughter is broken by this incident," said Labaran Khan.

"Don't tell me about your daughter, at least she's still alive and mine is dead, as I said before, I'm not happy with you," said President Ambo.

While in the hospital, Aisha called Aasim who was in Germany, and sadly, of all her children Aasim is the only sane shoulder she thinks she could cry on.

Aasim was rustling on some snacks, with Nicole seated by his side as they watched a movie when his mum's phone call came in. He then walked to the balcony to pick the call, and funnily, he could sense distress in his mum's voice. "Mum, what's it, and how are you doing?" asked Aasim.

"I'm not doing fine, Aasim, they've killed Nawal," cried Aisha.

"Oh, not now," he cried. "Who did this and how did it happen? He asked.

"From what we learnt, the girl's sister was among those killed by the army during last week's protest, she saw Nawal and decided to take her revenge," said Aisha.

Aasim's world has just been torn apart as he sobbed uncontrollably with the phone held close to his ear. He then asked his mum where and how this incident happened, and asked if there were no guards with her.

"There were guards with her, but they said it happened so fast and that they weren't able to stop her," said Aisha.

Aasim interjected and said if Colonel Abdallah was with Nawal he doesn't think this sad incident would've happened. Sadly, Aasim seemed to have overrated the Colonel as they always call him, even though he has been promoted to the rank of Brigadier.

"Colonel Abdallah was with her when it all happened, and your dad has just shot him for his carelessness," said Aisha.

"You mean, he's dead already?" asked Aasim.

"Yes, your dad just killed him," said Aisha.

"Ooh, killings, that's dad's signature," said Aasim.

"He doesn't even look like a person who has just taken a life," said Aisha.

Ambo Hussein was looking washed out, but that doesn't stop his knack for taking life.

"Dad's evil is beginning to catch up with us, and I don't know if there will be an escape from this," said Aasim.

Aisha muttered, saying her worry is that her children shouldn't pay the price for the actions of their parents.

Aasim realised his mum would need him now, much more than ever before, he then promised he'll be on his way home the next day.

"That will be good, I'll love to have a sane person around me and not your deluded brothers," said Aisha.

After his phone call with his mum, Aasim became sober and was quite teary when he walked back to the living room to join Nicole. She immediately sensed something has gone wrong back home, because her man was quite warm and jocular before the phone call and has now suddenly become teary. She asked what it was, saying Aasim's facial expression looked like he has just seen a ghost.

"My sister has just been stabbed," said Aasim.

"What, you mean Nawal?" asked Nicole.

"Yeah," said Aasim and tears rolled down his cheeks.

"Baby, why are you crying and is it that serious?" asked Nicole.

"Yes, she's dead," said Aasim.

"Oh my God, oh, my God," she cried.

Leaving behind the troubles in his father's house is now a tall order for Aasim, particularly now that his sister has been caught up by his dad's karma.

Aasim arrives in Kitan two days after Nawal's death.

He walked into his father's living room for the first time since the last altercation between them. His mum was seated in one end of the room, while his brothers were also seated but there was absolute quiet in the living room, he then looked for a spot not too far from his mum and sat down. "Mum, how're you doing?" he spoke in quite a low tone.

Aisha nodded, and said she isn't fine but told Aasim it's good he's here. He then turned to his brother.

"Umar, how're you?" asked Aasim.

"I'm fine, how was your trip?" asked Umar.

"Not too bad, just broken by this incident, which other guard was with Abdallah when this happened?" asked Aasim.

"They said Abba was with Colonel Abdallah," said Umar.

"Why should he be this careless?" asked Aasim.

"Dad killed him right in the hospital," said Umar.

"So I heard, he has met his doom as well," said Aasim.

Malik and Aasim didn't exchange pleasantries, but only nodded at each other in a gesture of salutation, and after thirty minutes of Aasim presence in the house, Malik turned to him and asked if he has asked about their dad since he arrived, or possibly gone to greet him.

Aasim pretended not to hear Malik, but instead decided to ask Umar about the training he went for in Qatar.

"It went well," said Umar.

"Mum, where was Nawal buried?" asked Aasim.

Aisha replied Aasim, saying she was buried at the cemetery, but urged all of them to please be calm and stop talking because she needed some quiet time. Sadly, this family has lost one of their own, and the loss is one that kept them reeling from inside.

Fear, they said, makes the wolf to be bigger, Amira has just dismissed her fears, and by her actions, she has diminished the fear for this untouchable President. Days after the death and burial of Nawal, and while this family mourns their loss, the daily protests continued unabated, President Ambo summoned the chief of Army Staff.

"Mr. President you sent for me?" asked Brigadier Sale Mai.

"Yes I did, come in Brigadier," said President Ambo.

Brigadier Sale Mai walked in, but he was quite careful, he understood too well that the President is pained, and his eyes were red. He thanked the President, as he walked into the President's office.

President Ambo didn't mince his words when he opened up to the Brigadier that these protesters have hurt his family, by killing his only daughter and he must teach them a lesson. It's quite obvious that the President have something showy in mind, one that will leave scars in the hearts of many, and make the ears of many to tingle. The wind now blowing throughout this nation isn't just any wind, it's a wind of genocide, a gust, sort of. While many watch with a bated breath, it's now arguably obvious that stopping this rollercoaster of events precipitated by these twists and turns might be a tall order, and it's only a matter of time for all to know who will come out of this unscathed.

"What do we do Mr. President?" asked Brigadier Sale Mai.

President Ambo's revenge is nothing but blood and guts, and funnily, he just descended into the deep end of barbarism in his quest to send a strong message to those who intends to get dirty and murky with him. He looked the Brigadier in the eyes and without mincing words, said he wants something that will kill these protesters in large numbers, so they'll know he's evil as well.

Brigadier Sale Mai then suggested to the President if he should order his men to kill at least thirty protesters from each city, and that will give between a hundred fifty and two hundred deaths. His understanding of killing in large numbers meant something more than the previous twenty people per city.

Sadly, the President isn't selling sensation, and stoicism isn't his thing and not his cup of tea either. This is because he has something more than ugly in mind, he has set is sight on committing horror and a blood bath, one in which the international community will open their mouth but will find it difficult to shut. "Can you bomb them?" asked President Ambo.

Brigadier Sale Mai cringed at the utterances of the President, he now understands that President Ambo's heart was filled with utter darkness and nothing could make him back down at this point. Yet, the Brigadier made it clear that bombing unarmed protesters might be too pronounced and he doesn't think it's appropriate under the circumstance.

President Ambo steered the conversation into something more apocalyptic. He subtly asked the Brigadier if there's anything worst than bombs, because these protesters had made him look like a loser before world. He then insists on taking his revenge on the people.

Brigadier Sale Mai gave a suggestion he might later regret, because he suggested that gassing the protesters should be worst than bombing them, but he strongly advised against it because it's not a good idea.

"Oh good, gassing them should be the best and Brigadier allow me to worry about whether it's a good idea or not," said President Ambo.

Brigadier Sale Mai recoiled immediately as he reminded the President that he's referring to the international community, the United Nations and others.

President Ambo didn't hesitate to remind the Brigadier that he has already cut ties with the international community, and has no need keeping anyone happy, he then ordered that chlorine gas be deployed later that day.

"Ok, Mr. President," said Brigadier Sale Mai. The army chief then left the president's office.

By the evening of that day Chlorine gas was used to disperse the protesters, though not in all the cities where protest was going on but only in Shambihya, the city where Nawal was killed. Shambihya killed Nawal, so Shambihya should bear the brunt.

That evening three hundred and twenty two protesters died in Shambihya alone. This prompted the United Nation Security Council to hold an emergency session after which a resolution condemning the gas attacks on civilians in the city of Shambihya was announced against the Republic of Kitan.

However, the United States went a step further to draft a motion for a military response to the reckless and barbaric gas attack on innocent civilians in the Republic of Kitan.

The next day Nassib called his elder brother, Maman, and funnily he's calling with quite a different phone number "Hello Maman, it's Nassib," he said.

"Nassib what's up with your voice? You're sounding so emotional," said Maman.

"Haven't you been watching the TV?" asked Nassib.

Maman didn't follow the happenings in his home nation, his club went on away match and that kept him away from the news from back home. "I've been watching the protest in Kitan, just that I haven't had chance yesterday and today," said Maman.

Nassib had to bring his brother up to speed on the atrocities of President Ambo Hussein, as he informed him there was a gas attack on the protesters a day before and three hundred and twenty two people died, though they are still counting.

"Ambo Hussein is becoming apocalyptically evil and deserves to be thought a lesson, and I hope you guys are safe?" asked Maman.

Nassib sobbed as he broke the news to his brother that their sister, Hadiza, was among the dead. Maman spoke in general terms as he expresses his concern about the horror enacted by President

Ambo, unbeknownst to him his sister was among the casualties, and he will soon start speaking in specific terms, as opposed to speaking in general terms.

"What! No, tell me it's not true," cried Maman.

"It's true, we just buried her this morning," said Nassib.

This news was too much for Maman to take in, it was quite a chilling reminder of the horror at home.

"I'm coming home, Ambo Hussein has done enough," said Maman.

Nassib interjected and reminded his big brother that his coming home to grieve over their sister's death makes sense, but if it is about coming to challenge Ambo Hussein, then his visit will be quite unnecessary. "What can you do to him when you and his son, Aasim, are friends?" asked Nassib.

Maman was quite enraged, and he has chosen not to be on the back foot any longer as he insists he isn't coming home for Aasim, rather he's coming for his dad. Maman was quite determined this time as he reminded his brother that Aasim can't stop him this time that the President has just killed his sister.

"But what about your football matches?" asked Nassib.

"I'll take compassionate leave, and I can't be here while my family members are dying, how then can I concentrate?" asked Maman.

CHAPTER

TEN

Meet the Martyrs

Maman whose sister was among the dead following the chlorine gas attack, came home from Germany to take part in the protest days after the gas attack.

On arrival, Maman had to start with pressing the right buttons, and that's building alliances and his first phone call is to Ismaila the leader of the 'Ambo Hussein must go protests.' "Hello Ismaila, this is Maman," he said.

"No, I must be dreaming, and you should be in Germany, Maman," said Ismaila.

Maman smiled and said he'd to return home because his sister was among the dead in the gas attack that took place in Shambihya.

Ismaila reinforced his message about their narcissistic President. Sadly, these two has one thing in common, and that's shared misery. Ismaila had to remind Maman that the atrocities of Ambo Hussein have become more despicable and sickening that a civilised society like theirs can't stomach any longer. The pain inflicted by this President has gone suffuse, and Maman didn't need to be the man on back foot this time. He's quite upfront, as he said he's has come to join in the protest but he'll want them to do things differently, maybe it will help them get a better result. Interestingly, Ismaila is a free spirit and has no trouble doing things differently provided the ranks are swelling for good. "Oh, it's good to hear this, our ranks are swelling," said Ismaila.

They chatted over the phone for a while, lucky for them, big brother wasn't listening to their conversation, and Maman had to save the intimate details of their conversation for later, as they agreed to meeting in the evening. He then urged Ismaila to please invite the protest leaders in each city, so they could all meet at once.

"When should I be expecting you?" asked Ismaila. "I'll be coming from Shambihya to Abidkitan, so let's make it 7.pm," said Maman. Sadly, even though Maman didn't witness his sister being murdered he seems to have a visual picture of his sister's trauma in her last minute.

"Ok, that'll be good, and at least we can meet without the prying eyes of saboteurs because it will be getting dark," said Ismaila.

"Thank you," said Maman.

"Lest I forget, three of my friends are coming, two from Egypt and one from Tunisia, they want to sacrifice themselves for this struggle," said Ismaila.

"You mean they want to become Martyrs?" asked Maman.

"Yes, and I wouldn't want to spoil their sacrifices," said Ismaila.

"Ok, we'll talk about that in the evening," said Maman.

Involving martyrs implies blood and guts, and that's grim. It's obvious these protest leaders had other plans up their sleeve unbeknownst to the protesters in the street.

Maman called his friend, at least to save face and peradventure they bump into each other.

"Hello Aasim," said Maman.

Aasim recognised the voice immediately he heard the 'hello' on the other side of the phone, he then asked Maman, if that's him.

"Yes, it's me," said Maman.

Aasim wasn't expecting this phone call from his friend, because he had no idea he's in town, and neither did Maman inform him he's coming home. Aasim jocularly reminded Maman that he should be in Germany, and this isn't his German phone number.

"I'm in Kitan," said Maman.

"You must be joking! When did you come without letting your friend know you're coming into town?" asked Aasim.

"I came in two days back," said Maman.

"Will you check me out later in the day?" asked Aasim.

These smiles and laughter between this pair might be short lived, and their friendship might soon go sour, when all cards are on the table.

"Hmm no, I've a lot to sort out today; maybe we should make it tomorrow," said Maman.

Aasim interjected and asked Maman how he knew he's currently in the Republic of Kitan because they were together last week in Germany.

"I knew you lost Nawal, Nassib told me about it just yesterday," said Maman.

"And you never bothered to talk about it, or even tell me sorry about my sister's death?" asked Aasim. Unfortunately, Aasim seems to be playing the victim's card, not knowing everyone is in one way or the other a victim of his dad's brutishness.

"Do you know why I came home?" asked Maman.

"I don't, but as a friend, words of condolence from you to me, isn't what I should've to ask for," said Aasim.

Funnily, Aasim's entitlement for a condolence seems to be misplaced because he had no idea Maman was grieving just he was. They have both lost their younger sisters, and they had no idea that the destiny of their friendship is now on a collision course.

Maman hesitated for a while but then went on to ask Aasim. "Do you know my sister, Hadiza, was among those killed by your dad with the Chlorine gas three days ago?"

"What! You mean Hadiza is dead?" asked Aasim.

"Now you get it, Hadiza wasn't among the protesters, she was at home and your dad killed her," said Maman. Maman's comments were quite punchy, and it immediately left an indelible mark in Aasim's heart. Aasim had no knowledge that his friend has been taken over by resentment over his dad's brutal crackdown on protesters.

Aasim was left reeling over the news of his dads' fatalities, and said this whole thing has become more complicated, and then apologised to Maman for his loss over his sister.

"Don't worry, Aasim; we'll see possibly tomorrow, this won't spoil our friendship.

In this case Maman has chosen not to forget and move on, particularly now that the memory of his sister's death is fresh. It's now time for Maman to attend the meeting of the organisers of this protest, but his brother wants him to be careful because of the prying eyes of the big brother.

"Maman, where are you going? Remember, there are soldiers and policemen everywhere in the city," said Nassib.

"I've a meeting in Abidkitan," said Maman.

Nassib quickly reminded Maman that a drive from Shambihya to Abidkitan is about an hour and might be risky because there are soldiers on the way. More so, Abidkitan is the second largest city as well as the commercial hub of the Republic of Kitan, and this means more soldiers on the way.

Maman had to inform his brother of his whereabouts, and in case he disappears suddenly, Nassib will know where to look because the days are evil. He told him he's having a meeting with his friend Ismaila, the one that travelled from Tunisia to lead the protest.

"Don't you think it's dangerous, because the government is secretly eliminating people who they consider a security risk," said Nassib.

Maman understands that his brother is taken over by defeatism but urged Nassib not to worry and promised to be careful, yet insists on making the trip because the government of Ambo Hussein must be taken down.

"What about Aasim?" asked Nassib.

Aasim is the reason behind the good life Maman is enjoying in Germany, his reply to Nassib was that he has no choice but to walk a tight rope between protecting his friendship with Aasim while also leading this revolution against Aasim's dad.

"Ok, just be careful," said Nassib. Maman then left Shambihya to Abidkitan. The meeting was titled, the meeting of the concerned citizens of Kitan.

"You're all welcome, and guys meet my friend, Maman, he came in from Germany two days back. His sister was also killed in the gas attack, and sadly, we all carry the scars from Ambo Hussein's brutality in one way or the other," said Ismaila.

Maman thanked the guys for coming, he turned to the corner and saw Jabir. "You're here?" said Maman.

"Yes I'm here, a broken man. Welcome Maman, and how was your trip?" asked Jabir.

Ismaila introduced his men to Maman. "This is Mukhtar, Zahed, Ahmed, Sharara, and Jabir whom you know already," said Ismaila.

"Maman, what's the plan?" asked Jabir.

Maman is just getting involved for the first time yet he's diving straight into the deep end of this revolution. Maman informed the attendees that from his findings there use to be a change of guards by 8.am daily at the presidential villa. During this period the guards will be on parade without any opportunity to take cover from sudden surprises.

"Ok, that's a good information, what surprises are you talking about?" asked Ismaila.

Maman continued and said the three suicide attacks will take place consecutively throwing the villa into confusion, and then they'll go in immediately and finish up the operation.

"Before the suicide bombers get there, they'll be spotted and shot," said Jabir.

Maman explained further that each of the martyrs will drive a car loaded with explosive, and even if the Presidential guards shoots at the driver, the car will still ram into the building and explode.

"Do we have the finance to buy three cars?" asked Ismaila.

"I'll buy three cars, though, they might not be new ones, but they'll be good enough for this assignment," said Maman.

Ismaila exclaimed and said this is a perfect plan, he then turned to the other guys in attendance and asked if they have any question.

Jabir felt it will be unwise engaging the military, because they could play directly into President's Ambo's hands. He then suggested that instead of getting their own hands dirty, they leave the United Nations, whose resolution includes discussions for a military response to deal with Ambo Hussein's barbaric acts. He then proposed they wait and use the military attack against President Ambo to their advantage.

Time is now of the essence and Maman can't wait because he thinks every minute spent to dither and delay will impact on their chances of success. He then advised they allow the United Nation to do their thing, but President Ambo must've been out of office by the time the military strikes will take place.

"When do we intend to execute this operation?" asked Mukhtar.

"At most three days from now, and right now, our brothers are coming from Egypt and Tunisia. I'll take Ismaila to get the cars by tomorrow, before their arrival," said Ismaila.

Ahmed is keen to know why Maman is in so much hurry about this operation, he interjected and asked if there's anything they needed to know about the date.

Maman had to address the elephant in the room, so he doesn't look like he has come to steal the show and lord himself over those that started this revolution. He then said they need to be fast, because since the death of Colonel Abdallah, the head of the President's guard, a replacement hasn't been appointed, and as a result, security at the presidential villa will be porous.

"Guys, we have got a perfect plan, so let's work with it," said Ismaila.

The martyrs arrived the Republic of Kitan the next day.

Ismaila had to formally reconvene a meeting so he could introduced them to Maman, and said this is Al-Wahhish, Khafiz, and that's Abu. Maman then asked if these are the friends coming from Egypt and Tunisia.

"Yes, Al-Wahhish and Khafiz are from Egypt, while Abu is from Tunisia, they have come to sacrifice themselves for our nation," said Ismaila.

"Brothers, you're welcome, do you've any wishes that you want us to remember you with?" asked Maman.

"Brothers, I just want you to pray to the Almighty Allah to accept our sacrifices," said Al-Wahhish.

"Brothers if this revolution succeeds, please I want you to assist my mum, I've an aged mother," said Abu.

Ismaila turned to Khafiz and asked him what wish he wants them to observe on his behalf, Khafiz had same request as Al-Wahhish, as he urged them to pray to the Almighty Allah to accept their sacrifices. This revolution has moved away from mere street protest, it's now taken to a whole new level because the protesters have decided to play the President's own game with him. They've now decided to take blood and guts to his doorstep.

Maman brought out a piece of paper and a pen and handed it to Abu, he then asked him to write an account number they can pay money into for Abu's mum upkeep.

Abu thanked Maman for being up front in making his request happen. He wrote the account number of his younger sister in Tunisia, as well as her contact details. Maman then muttered under his breath, saying Ambo Hussein is now a menace that requires powerful heroes like these three men to take him down. Having surrendered themselves to be martyred, these three heroes are now speaking the language of blood and gut, which is the one language President Ambo Hussein understand as they take violence to the President's doorstep.

"Ok guys, we now know everything is set for tomorrow morning's operation," said Ismaila.

Maman then advised that they all pass the night in Ansarouh, the state capital, so that as early as possible they can start their operation. This whole process is moving with startlingly rapid progress, and they're hoping on catching the president on the back foot, particularly now that Colonel Abdallah is out of the equation and the villa's prying eyes is diminished.

Ismaila asked the guys if they have any questions, to be sure they're all on the same page. Ahmed asked about the arms, and inquired if the arms are ready.

"Of course, the arms are ready, and Ismaila kept them somewhere. The explosives and the cars for the suicide mission are ready as well," said Maman.

"Ok, that's good," said Osama.

"Before I forget, do we all know how to shoot a gun, I mean handle a gun?" asked Maman.

"Yes of course, all the guys here can shoot, and I took my time to make this selection," said Ismaila.

Maman then proceeded to ask how many foot soldiers they have at their disposal.

Ismaila replied and said he has about a hundred committed foot soldiers that will complete the job after the martyrs' sacrifices.

Maman has only been privilege to meet with the key organisers of the protests, but their hench men were left out in these meetings but will be there to finish the job.

CHAPTER
ELEVEN
Friends in the battlefield

The attack on the presidential villa took place at exactly 8. am as planned when the parade was going on. An explosive-laden truck rammed through the fence of the presidential villa throwing the entire place into confusion; in the middle of that confusion another truck rammed into the building and exploded and so did the third truck killing a good number of the presidential guards. Though the driver of the first explosive-laden truck was shot dead as he approached but the truck rammed into the building anyway. "Guys let's move in," said Maman.

The guys moved in, throwing military grade smoke canisters, which added to the presidential guards' confusion because they weren't prepared for this.

Ismaila used his hand to give directions, and asked some of the guys to go the other way while some should follow him this way.

There was a gun fight and most presidential guards left after the blast, were taken down, and while this gunfight was going on President Ambo peeped through his bullet-proof window and realised his villa has been taken. During the fire fight, all Ambo Hussein's sons rushed into their fathers' secured living room as they scampered for safety.

Everything is happening so fast, Aisha rushed and peeped through the window, and all she could do is to scream, saying they're under attack, and asking what's happening.

President Ambo didn't see this coming, all he did was to mutter under his breath as he said the end has come, and why didn't he see this coming.

Aasim's attention was on his mum, and asked if she's ok.

"How can I be ok, when I know in the next few minutes our heads will be on display to the amusement of the world?" asked Aisha.

"Dad, what do we do?" asked Malik.

President Ambo was confused, and he suddenly froze on his feet, it was as if he was waiting for the bogey-man crawling out of the dark allay to get to him. This whole thing caught him of guard, and he suddenly found himself on the back foot, presumably, this proud and egoistic man has just lost is mojo. Aasim quickly asked Umar to stay close and urged him not to go outside.

Malik had to take charge of keeping everyone safe, he quickly asked his dad to make the family's secret tunnel available. There was occasional exchange of gun fire that slowed the pace of the approaching assailant which gave President Ambo and his family some time to make their way to the tunnel before the protesters are able to break into the house.

President Ambo then asked Malik to tell his mum and his brothers to come, while he opened the tunnel and closed it once they got in. Malik rushed to the living room. "Mum, Umar, Aasim, let's go into the tunnel now, they have just broken into the house and are already coming upstairs." he said.

"This whole thing is happening so fast, who are those behind this?" asked Aasim. Unfortunately, for Aasim, standing in the fence meant accepting the vulnerability of being caught on the back foot.

"The protesters of course, who else?" asked Malik.

Umar turned to his dad and asked if he should get his dad's gun because they might need it for self defence. Sadly, going to get the gun might cost a minute or two, and that delay might be fatal for this family.

"No, there's no time, just come let's go," said President Ambo. They all rushed into the tunnel to escape the death that's lurking.

In the midst of that confusion, President Ambo, his wife Aisha, and his three sons, Malik, Aasim and Umar went into the tunnel and escaped. By the time the armed protesters got to the living room they were gone.

After combing the property, the protesters didn't find anyone, Sharara then shouted out to Ismaila that they've escaped, and there isn't anyone in the flat. Maman was quite disappointed that there's no one to be punished for his sister's death, he then urged them to check the entire building. Ahmed confirmed they've combed the entire building already, and then insists he doesn't think there's anyone in the building because it's all clear.

Maman insists this family can't just disappear into thin air, and presumably they must be hiding somewhere because he saw Ambo Hussein looking through the windows during the fire fight, so he was in this house minutes ago.

"There use to be a rumour of a tunnel from this building bursting out by the riverbank," said Ismaila.

"You're right, just that I don't know how true that rumour was," said Maman.

Ismaila quickly suggested that they should all head to the riverbank peradventure they are escaping through that route. Military reinforcement wasn't quick enough to come to the President's rescue, and it was as if providence wasn't on his side. These guys needed to catch this President as soon as possible and deliver him to the people before military reinforcement comes in to quell this revolution.

"Ok, let about twenty of us move immediately to the riverbank, while the rest remain here, but try to catch Ambo Hussein alive so he can face trial," said Maman. They made their way to the riverbank looking for a possible exit route for a tunnel.

On a second thought, they got some cars within the villa and drove quickly to the riverbank.

Thirty minutes later, Ambo Hussein and his family came out from a tunnel near where Ahmed was standing. "Guys, look at them running away, they are here," screamed Ahmed. It's arguably obvious that Ahmed isn't letting this despot and his family make a break for it, he went after them and pointing his gun at this cowering family.

"Stop, stop, don't shoot, don't," said Aasim. Ahmed continued pointing the gun at the President and his family. Aasim inched closer to Ahmed, and raised his hands up in surrender and while Ahmed pointed the gun at them still trying to pull the trigger, Aasim disarmed Ahmed using his military skills and shot Ahmed.

President Ambo Hussein, Aisha, Malik and Umar are all hiding behind Aasim with their hands up in total surrender. Maman and the rest of the pack hurried down to where Aasim was, while he still had Ahmed's gun in his hand. "Aasim, drop that gun," said Maman.

Aasim was quite in shock to realise that the friend he shared a table with ten days ago in Germany is behind his debacle. "What! Maman, you're behind this, you, my friend?" said Aasim.

Maman was weak and taken over by emotions, the moment he came face to face with Aasim. The first thing Maman did was to apologise unreservedly to Aasim, but said if he'd told Aasim about this, then Aasim would've stopped him and give his dad the opportunity to slaughter more people, which is something he can never acquiescence.

"Aasim, I'm sorry it has got to this, just put the gun down, so we don't take on each other," said Ismaila.

Aasim still had the gun he took off Ahmed pointed at his friends, he then asked them what's it they want.

"First put the gun down, Aasim, I know you're physically stronger than any of us here, and you've got good military skills, but you can't defeat the whole of us," said Maman. They had their guns pointed at Aasim, Ismaila pressed on Aasim to put the gun down, and reminded Aasim they aren't out for him, he then urge him again to please put the gun down, reminding him he can't defeat all of them.

"We'll spare you, but your dad and your brother will face the music," said Maman.

Aasim had no choice but to start talking, maybe he can talk his way out of this. "I know my dad put us in this situation, but my brothers and my mum have no hand in this," said Aasim.

"Your brother is worst than your dad, and I suppose you're aware of how badly he has hurt people in this land," said Maman.

Aasim is now boxed in the corner, and sadly his friends are now the ones deciding if he lives or dies today, yet he pressed on as he said it's obvious his brothers were misled by their dad who made them think they were acting aright.

Maman dismissed Aasim's excuses. "You'll leave us to decide that, please just shift so we can finish this right now," said Maman. After realising that he's in for surprise, and his fate is now in the hands of those he once called his friends, Aasim handed his gun over to them. After handing the gun over, Aasim insists they have to kill him if they must kill his family. Aasim knew these guys have a soft spot for him, but they hate his dad and his brothers like the plague, so he has to play into their emotions to keep his dad and brothers from harms way.

Ismaila now had the once dreaded President Ambo Hussein at his mercy, he suddenly became jocular, and said look at your dad and brothers hiding behind you like rats hiding from an eagle.

"Aasim, you've given us a difficult choice," said Maman.

"For the sake of our friendship, and if there's any time you can pay me back for whatever good I've done to you, it's now," said Aasim.

Sharara couldn't stomach the fact that Aasim is standing in the way, he quickly pointed his gun at Aasim. "Since you said we've to pass through you, then you've to die because I must kill your dad, your mum and your brothers right now," he said.

Ismaila urged Sharara not to shoot. "Wait, stop, don't shoot Aasim because he's not in our to-do list," said Ismaila.

Sharara isn't in the mood for further dawdling, and he isn't making friends either, he then turned to Ismaila and said Aasim is standing in their way, so he has no choice but to add him to their list. Just as Sharara was just about to pull the trigger Maman became quite infuriated with Sharara's insistence on going through Aasim, he then shot Sharara immediately, to stop him from pulling the trigger on Aasim. "Nobody here should hurt Aasim, not even a finger should scratch him," said Maman.

"Maman, please just let us escape, take the country, take the presidency, but let us go, and at least your revolution is a success since the President has fled," said Aasim.

Maman thinks Aasim's request is quite a tall order, because his reason for joining the revolution was to have his own pound of flesh from President Ambo Hussein for killing his sister. "What about my sister Hadiza, who will pay the price for her death?" asked Maman.

Aasim continued to plead for his family, and begged the guys, reminding them that if there's any time he needed help from them that time is now, he then urged Ismaila to please help him.

"I need my pound of flesh from your dad, and the guys out there need theirs from your brother," said Maman.

Aasim is now at the mercy of these guys, he then said he knew they deserve their pounds of flesh but urged them to do things differently.

Maman looked at Aasim with so much love, and reminded him his request is a big ask but his failure to grant this one request would mean he has just bitten the finger that fed him, or rather, he has betrayed the guy that showed him to the world. "Aasim, I'll hate myself forever if I turn down this one request you've ever asked of me and I'll equally hate myself forever for letting your dad go, but for your sake, we'll let your dad go," said Maman. Ismaila gave Maman the look of 'what are you doing' but Maman gave a nod as a gesture of apology. Ismaila had to finish this struggle conclusively and needed a proof to show to the hundreds of thousands of protester sprawled across the various cities of the Republic of Kitan. Ismaila quickly brought out his android phone, and said. "Wait a minute, before we let your dad go, your dad should announce his resignation from office, let's have it on tape," said Ismaila.

"Dad, you'll have to announce your resignation," said Aasim. This President was glad to still have his head on top of his neck, he just escaped death by a whisker, and he's quite shaken but had to fulfil the demands of the impatient protesters. The situation quickly took a new twist because just as President Ambo was about to start making his resignation speech, a military reinforcement arrived for his rescue, and President Ambo heaved a sigh of relief, and stopped. At least his dawdling has paid off, and these guys won't steal the Presidency from him. Ismaila and Maman suddenly realised they are facing a military onslaught, they pointed their guns on President Ambo, and asked the military to back off, hence they will shoot. Sadly, the commander that led this rescue mission, has an axe to grind with this distressed President, the commander is a cousin of late Brigadier Bachakar whom President Ambo Hussein executed for his role in the failed coup. He subtly asked his men to back down and allow the protesters finish what they started. President Ambo Hussein was disappointed and in utter dismay, as the military commander who was meant to rescue him, stood by and watched, and did nothing but allow the protesters kick him out of office. It was quite an eerie scene, and even Aladin's genies won't help at this point. The only hope he had was the military, and they have just failed him, he had no choice but to comply and announce his resignation.

President Ambo: I Ambo Hussein, the President of the Republic of Kitan, do wish to inform the citizens of this republic that their calls for me to leave office have been accepted. Consequently, I'm resigning from the office of the President of the Republic of Kitan with effect, from today 5th March.

News of the attack on the presidential villa has gone out, and some of the protesters are already heading for the presidential villa and this could leave President Ambo and his family at the mercy of large number of protesters, and make things get ugly.

Aasim wants his family to get moving, so they could make their way out of sight and out of reach, immediately. He then pointed to their family yacht. "Mum, let's take the yacht, and cross to the other side of the sea," said Aasim.

Ismaila interjected. "Aasim, leave the yacht. That's the property of the people of Kitan, take a boat," he said.

"Guys, the speed boat may not be safe enough to take us across the sea," said Aasim.

Maman tapped Ismaila on the shoulder, signalling he wants to have a word, Ismaila stepped aside and communed with Maman and after a moment of conversation. "Aasim, you can go with the yacht," said Maman.

"Thank you, guys," said Aasim. Ambo Hussein stood statue-still in shock as he lost everything.

They entered the Yacht in Panic, ride it across the sea towards Turkey as they escaped from the Republic of Kitan.

While on their way, and out of harm's way, Malik had to lay the blame for this shameful experience on Aasim. "If you've assisted dad all this while, we shouldn't have been in this mess," said Malik.

"How, in what way?" asked Aasim.

Malik felt Aasim didn't put his jujitsu skill to use, and he didn't use his military skill either. "You've got the skills to disarm these guys, but you didn't put them to use, cowering in shame was in contrast to your size," said Malik.

Aisha interjected and shunned Malik as she asked him to zip it, before reminding him of all the people he encouraged his dad to kill, and then proceeded to ask if these people are animals.

Though, taken over by the surprise attack on the President's villa, Aasim went on to say Nawal would've been alive today if their dad had acted with restraint, and too many innocent lives have been lost.

"Aasim, you tried to warn us about a day like this, considering the revolution that was going on in the Middle East," said Umar.

Aisha thanked Aasim for saving their lives today, and she then turned to her husband. "Ambo, have you thanked your son?" she asked. "Mum, leave dad alone, you can see he's still in shock and quite shaken," said Malik.

Malik was still trying to come to terms with the sudden loss of all the privileges he had enjoyed all his life, and he has this deep-seated grudge against his brother for not working with their dad to avert this doom that just befell them.

Umar interjected and reminded Aasim that his love for the people hasn't paid off after all. "Aasim, you called Maman your friend, but he betrayed you." he said.

"No, he didn't, and we'll continue to be friends. Do you know the gas attack in Shambihya killed Maman's sister, Hadiza, even when she wasn't among the protesters," said Aasim.

"You mean Hadiza is dead?" asked Umar.

"The truth remains that whatever five of us will go through will be nothing compared with three hundred and twenty two people killed in one day by dad. Can we imagine what those families are going through?" asked Aasim.

"The way your dad and Malik were going, I knew we'll end in shame, but I actually didn't know how," said Aisha.

Just as the yacht ferried them to the other side of the sea, a flicker of recollection momentarily flashes through Aasim's mind as he remembered the words of the Grand Imam of Ansarouh urging him to stay close to his dad because he will be needed someday.

Ambo Hussein remained mum all along as his children talked about how they find themselves in their present state. Sadly, this once-proud-man whose words causes jitters in people is now looking as lost as a child denied of his pack of candy. He brought out his phone, trying to find a contact in his phone but the whole incident made him shudder.

Malik's attention has been focused on his dad, and he watched as his dad kept fiddling with the phone in search of a contact in his shaky state. He then asked his dad what it was he was looking for.

"I'm looking for a contact," said Ambo Hussein.

Malik collected the phone from his dad and asked. "What contact are you looking for? Let me help you," said Malik.

"I need Mistura's phone number," said Ambo Hussein.

"Mistura, the Central Bank Governor?" asked Malik. He scrolled through the contacts and a minute later, "This is it, dad," said Malik. It was quite a burden of suffering for Malik to see his dad in such a vulnerable state, the first time his dad was powerless before his eyes.

Ambo Hussein then asked Malik to dial the number because he wants to make a quick transfer of funds before the Central Bank Governor becomes aware of his departure from office. Malik dialled Mistura's number, "Its ringing dad, take it," said Malik. Ambo Hussein then collected the phone from Malik, the moment Mistura picked the phone call.

"Hello Mr President, where are you? I heard there's gun battle in your Villa," asked Mistura.

"I'm right in my villa and yes, you're right, but I want you to transfer fifty million dollars to my account in Qatar right now," said Ambo Hussein.

The news of the gun fight in the presidential villa has filtered into town, but his departure from office just happened minutes ago, and the news of his departure might take some time to get out because Aasim called Maman aside and asked him to delay the broadcast of his dad's departure until they cross to the other side, and out of harm's way.

Mr. President, that won't be possible, the maximum I can transfer right now is twenty million dollars," said Mistura.

"Why can't you transfer the whole fifty million dollars?" asked Ambo Hussein.

"That's the amount available for immediate transfer right now," said Mistura.

"Ok, transfers the twenty million dollars immediately," said Ambo Hussein.

"Ok, Mr. President, I'll do that right away," said Mistura. Minutes later, the money was already in Ambo Hussein's account in Qatar, and within the hour Mistura realised the President has been chased out of office.

Ambo Hussein and his wife travelled to Turkey where they already had a lot of properties, they were granted political asylum and they live in Turkey to date.

Malik and Umar also live in Turkey to date.

Aasim returned to his fiancée in Germany and married her a month later, Aasim's wife went to court and made a case for the release of her husband's assets which was frozen by the German government and all assets in Aasim's name were released to him.

Maman returned to Germany a month later, he's still friends with Aasim who remained grateful to Maman for allowing his family escape despite all their wickedness.

The Republic of Kitan celebrated the departure of Ambo Hussein, the Pariah. The United States and its European Allies, with the support of the Arabs helped to install the governor of Ansarouh as the interim President to prevent the country descending into anarchy.

Every asset belonging to the Republic of Kitan was released by the United States and its European Allies to enable the rebuilding of the country.

And finally, Maman continued sending money to Abu's mum for her upkeep as he has promised.